WE, THE
WILDFLOWERS

WE, THE WILDFLOWERS

L.B. SIMMONS

SPENCER
HILL
PRESS

We, the Wildflowers
Copyright © 2020 by L.B. Simmons
First Edition

Library of Congress Cataloging-in-Publication Data available upon request

Published in the United States by Spencer Hill Press, New York, New York
www.SpencerHillPress.com

Distributed by Midpoint Trade Books
A division of Independent Publishers Group
www.midpointtrade.com
www.ipgbook.com

This edition ISBN:
9781633921115 paperback
9781633921122 ebook

Printed in the United States of America

Flower Illustrations by: Sofia Pirrello
Cover by: Hang Le
Design by: Mark Karis

In honor of my mother, the original Wildflower.

I hope this story is everything you knew it could be.

I miss you every single day.

Their strength and ferocity stem from below the surface where their roots are tangled, interwoven in such a way that for the remainder of time they bloom together, and when winter finally prevails, they perish as one. But even in death they remain connected, thriving within the comfort only they can provide each other, until spring brings them to life once again.

—GENESIS MONROE, WILDFLOWER NUMBER ONE

WINTER

PROLOGUE

The hallway around me is…*spinning*.

And spinning.

And spinning.

And spinning.

I try to feel nothing, yet now I feel everything as I'm forced to acknowledge the consequence of a poorly made decision. All because I wanted to experience something… anything but feeling alone.

Abandoned.

Insignificant.

You did this to yourself.

You only have yourself to blame.

Much like the walls around me, the words circle around and around and around…unforgiving accusations and blame. I slam my hands against the sides of my head and cover my ears, trying to make them stop, but it doesn't work. Out of frustration, I thread my fingers into my hair and yank as hard as I can.

Shut up.

Shut up.

Where do you think you're going anyway?

They don't want you.

Shut up!

They won't even look at you.

I choke back a sob and shake my head, refusing to hear them. To believe them.

Several minutes pass before the harsh murmurs finally lower to faint white noise in my head. I peel my eyes from the marbled floor, and only then do I realize I'm standing in front of my parents' bedroom door.

That's when I feel it. A tiny glimmer of hope. My heart begins to race as it flickers to life inside me.

I need you.

I reach desperately for the words, fumble for them as I try to grab hold, but they are out of reach. Always out of reach. Uncontrollable tears stream down my cheeks as my mind splits in two and begins its battle.

You stupid girl.

They want nothing to do with you.

I need you.

I need you.

I inhale deeply, trying to gather my strength. I have to win this war. I will not let them ruin me. I *cannot* let them win. I refuse.

Just as I lift my arm to knock, raised voices drown out the ones in my head, leaving my closed fist hanging in the air.

"So you're leaving again? With your whore of the month?"

"*Diane.*"

I swallow deeply in response to his calculated tone. Although the door separates us, I can picture my father's expression perfectly. Cold, callous eyes narrowing in my mother's direction. Jaw ticking wildly in frustration. Yet, when he speaks, his voice remains unaffected. As though he's merely swatting words like flies, when in actuality, he's pounding them with a mallet.

He sighs deeply. "It's business. You know that."

"Right," my mother scoffs. "It's always business, Tristan. Never any twenty-something *extracurriculars*, right?"

Her words are slurred—as usual. I can picture her, too. Cheeks reddened by the alcohol, pouty mouth curved to the floor—stress carving lines into her skin that will be erased come Monday—wavy blonde hair that refuses to cooperate, and her light brown eyes? Puffy from tears and so very sad.

I am her mirror image in every way.

My father's bored tone turns glacial. "A twenty-something extracurricular as you once were?"

The slamming of a suitcase jars my entire body, and I place my hand flat against the door to steady myself.

"We've been over this a thousand times, Diane. I didn't ask to be saddled with a wife who mistakenly believes the world revolves around her and no one else. Nor did I ask to be burdened by the responsibility of life with a kid. All I asked was for you to be at my side when required, for you to service my needs whenever necessary, and to stay on birth control while doing it. Which you purposefully *did not* do."

My mother's soft sobs become desperate wails the more he speaks.

"You trapped me in this marriage, Diane. We both know that. And because of that, you are nothing to me. You don't deserve to know what I choose to do with my time."

The suitcase hits the floor. "I do, however, take satisfaction in knowing you have a sixteen-year-old reminder that the old adage is true: money can't buy happiness, no matter how many millions it may be. Your child is nothing more than the result of a night I wish had never happened."

His words are like a punch to the gut, forcing every breath of air from my body upon impact. And with it, all hope inside me is extinguished. I begin to tremble with its loss, and suddenly, I'm so cold. My chest throbs and aches, as though there's a black hole where my heart should be.

I feel it spreading throughout my body…devouring the will to live.

I'm so tired.

Tired of trying.

Tired of fighting.

Tired of hoping.

I no longer hear the desperate cry of *I need you* because there is no longer need.

There is only truth.

You are a burden.

They wish you had never happened.

You are nothing.

The voices beat me into submission, forcing me to recognize what I really am.

Nothing...

There are no more tears when I turn my back on my parents.

My body is numb, impossibly light even, as I seem to float toward my father's office.

With frigid fingers, I push open his private bathroom door.

I hear nothing when I open the drawer and pull out the straight razor he's used for years.

When I lift it in front of the mirror, my eyes are unseeing as I inspect its reflection.

And though fear and hesitation lurk in the distance, I give the voices free rein, allowing them this victory so they may provide armor against such useless emotions. Because the voices are right.

I am nothing.

Although my throat is clamped shut, I somehow manage to murmur, "Ashes to ashes. Dust to dust."

A sense of relief washes over me as I begin to fade from consciousness, and a lazy smile crosses my face when the darkness finally swallows me whole.

* * *

Murmurs fill the air, but I don't dare open my eyes. I don't need them to know that gauze is wrapped around both of my arms from wrist to elbow. And I definitely don't want to be on the receiving end of looks of pity from the nurses, or familiar glares of disapproval from my parents, if they're even here.

So I remain still, listening to the beeping and wondering what the hell I'm going to do now. I'm glad for whatever drugs I'm on because they seem to have muted the voices for a while at least.

A light knock sounds, startling me. Then, a soft, feminine voice. "Mr. and Mrs. Campbell?"

I hear shuffling, most likely my father standing, then the clicking of heels as someone enters the room.

So, they're here…Surprising.

"Yes, I'm Tristan Campbell, and this is my wife, Diane. May we help you?"

"Actually," the woman clears her throat, "I'm Claudia, from Sacred Heart. We spoke on the phone."

"Right. Yes. Do you have any updates?"

"I do." The door shuts softly, and I wait patiently while they take their seats. "I have a lovely woman who is willing to take Chloe into her home. She runs an offshoot of Sacred Heart only a couple of hours from here, a very small home that typically houses three to four residents, all from different backgrounds. As you have requested expedited processing, I have prepared the paperwork to have Chloe discharged to our care, then I can take her to the home from here."

Her voice lowers in volume. "Thank you for your donation, by the way."

"Of course." His tone remains composed. "Always glad to help those in need."

Bullshit. Where were you when I needed you?

I wish I had the courage to shout my thoughts. But I don't. I'm too tired to do anything but lie here.

So, I do. I hide behind my eyelids and listen. I listen as they discuss the home, as my father demands I remain in high school—though his disapproval is clear when it's explained it will be public schooling and not private—as he boasts about money he'll give me that I'll never touch—because I will refuse to take his money—and finally the sounds of a pen scratching paper as they sign my life away.

They say nothing as they leave me alone in the room.

No "I'm sorry."

No "goodbye."

No "I love you."

I would say it hurts, but I don't think I can hurt anymore. There is nothing left of me that can be hurt.

And as I listen to the machines around me, all I can think is that while their beeping would suggest my heart still beats, each sound they make is a lie.

I'm no more alive than they are.

ONE YEAR LATER...

SPRING

1

A subzero draft rushes my face, signaling the high school's air conditioning has clicked on, but I don't hear it. Nor do I hear Mr. Alexander's monotone history lecture about East and West Germany. While I'm completely aware it's important information, my mind has wandered. *Again.*

I've grown a lot over the past year. Learned a lot about life and myself in general. And though there have been many lessons, some definitely harder than others, the most important of them is this.

Sometimes rock-bottom has a hidden safety net. You don't see it, but when you land, when you've reached the lowest of lows, somehow you don't hit the ground. You strike that net, and then you're thrown so high, you fly. Sure, it's scary.

But sometimes, it's necessary.

The thought lingers, and subconsciously I tug my finger-less gloves into the crook of my elbow. The texture of the knit is comforting as I mentally trace the scars that will forever line the pale skin of my forearms. Permanent reminders of the night I almost lost my life, but was miraculously saved to live another one.

You see, Sacred Heart was—no, *is*—my safety net.

My parents sending me to live there was the best thing, the only good thing, they have ever done for me, because within its walls, I've found more of a home than I've ever experienced. I've found a place where I'm seen. Where I'm acknowledged. Where I'm loved and accepted.

I've finally found…a family.

Gently tapping my pencil against the grain of my desk, I swallow my urge to grin and glance at the person next to me. The first person I met when entering the Sacred Heart home, and one of my best friends.

Genesis Monroe.

Light-green eyes crossed, she presses two fingers firmly against her temple and pulls a mock trigger, clearly as enthused with world history as I am at the moment. Pink hair conceals her face as she falls limp in her seat, and I shake my head and roll my eyes, chuckling softly to myself.

That is, until I see the person right behind her, hanging himself with an imaginary noose. He's the second person I met and immediately adored, Adam McNamara, and he's seemingly accepted his feigned death with honor. Neck angled and tongue lolling from his mouth, his blue eyes brighten with humor before he tosses me a gratuitous wink. Breathy laughter bubbles through my nose, and the more I try to keep it at bay, the more it refuses to cooperate. Tears prick my eyes as a giggle desperately seeks escape.

"Chloe Campbell. Would you like to contribute something to this discussion other than amusement at your friends' incredibly disrespectful behavior?"

Damn it. Busted.

Genny miraculously springs back to life, the legs of her desk screeching across the floor as she bolts upright. Adam and I snort in unison. We're totally *not* helping my situation.

I close my eyes, inhale deeply, then twist to face the front of the room. Mr. Alexander's pinched expression invites more laughter, but thankfully I maintain my composure.

"I'm sorry," I respond, clearing my throat. "What was the question?"

"To fill the gaps in your unfortunate attention span, we've been discussing the fall of the Berlin Wall today, at length." His bushy brows lift. "So, what do you feel was the impact of its fall on the Cold War as a whole?"

My stare is blank, and I blink. Repeatedly.

Mr. Alexander frowns, then angles his head. "This is not a difficult question, Miss Campbell."

The answer he seeks is well beyond me, but luckily the soothing, deep baritone of a familiar voice captures everyone's attention with three tersely spoken words.

"It ended it."

I don't have to look at him—I know exactly what my

eyes would find. Black hair haphazardly spiked in all directions. Green eyes a shade darker than Genny's, locked on the floor even when he speaks. Long legs kicked out in front of his desk, booted feet crossed at the ankle, and an unmistakable expression of boredom carved into the most handsome face I've ever seen.

Lukas White.

As of a couple months ago, Lukas became the final Sacred Heart inhabitant, and therefore the fourth member in our crew.

"That's right, Mr. White. Concise as always, but nonetheless, your participation is much appreciated." After sending a pointed stare my way, Mr. Alexander turns around, effectively communicating his disappointment before dismissing me fully.

And with *that* wonderful accomplishment under my belt, my mind once again drifts, consumed with thoughts of Lukas White.

We don't know much about him really. Nothing more than the rumors running rampant throughout the school. We've *heard* he did some time in juvie, but for what, we're not sure.

What we *do* know is that he rarely says much. But when he does speak, people listen. There's just something about him that demands respect. His voice is strong, his words direct. He doesn't waste them on meaningless discussion, but chooses to use them only when necessary.

Otherwise, he rarely speaks. Except to us.

And he doesn't make eye contact. Except with us.

I see it. I know Genny and Adam do, too. The reasons why remain unspoken, but we understand it. Hell, we lived it. There's an undeniable sense of camaraderie between those who survive their own personal hell, and because of that, we give him the room he needs to just be, without questions.

I think that's why he's somewhat comfortable with us.

No, actually, I *know* that's why.

And it's also why he's one of us. Like knows like. We're been bonded by pain, but together, we're rooted in resilience.

We are four.

We are the Wildflowers.

2

I amble across the courtyard with my lunch tray, glancing from my usual—cheeseburger, no onions, with a side of curly fries—to our table. Or rather, to Genny seated atop our table, scowling. Her tank top is light pink, lending an almost feminine quality to the rest of her outfit: camo-green Dickies and black Doc Martens. With her hot-pink hair, light dusting of freckles, and luminous green eyes, she looks like a very pissed-off version of Strawberry Shortcake right now.

Beside her, Adam threads his fingers through his chin-length, light blond hair as it's tousled by the wind, pinning it to his head so he can better see. From his huge grin, I'd gather that Genny's giving the familiar menace standing in front of them a piece of her mind. I slip into their conversation and silently set my tray on the table.

"Like I said, you can't sit here." Genny shrugs,

unrepentant, brows raised.

Eric Warner has clearly made the wrong decision by trying to confiscate our table, again. He shows absolutely no fear as he slams his tray down next to mine.

"This is not your table, you emo bitch."

My head jerks back in shock, and Adam's expression hardens. Genesis grins. Slowly, she leans forward, brazenly meeting Eric's angry stare. And when she finally speaks, her voice is low and her tone controlled. "Let me explain it to you. First of all, *I*"—she gestures to herself—"am not emo. I'm punk. Check the internet before your next attempt to conjure an insult, Needle Dick."

Eric glares, spurring Genny's widening grin as she gestures to the surface below her. "And second, this is our table. Do you have a name of biblical origin? Because if you don't, you can't sit at the Jesus Table. I mean, it would be heresy if you did. Jesus said so. In the Bible." She shrugs again. "Somewhere."

I laugh. Adam laughs.

Eric does not.

His expression solidifies into one of unmistakable hatred, then he braces his weight, splaying both hands on either side of his tray. Slowly, he creeps into Genny's space, his eyes sinister, his tone laced with loathing. "That's golden." He lowers his stare to the several track marks dotting her arms, her open display of the scars demonstrating just one of the many differences between her and me. "If anyone knows about needles, it's you."

I suck in a breath and narrow my eyes, boring holes into Eric's pockmarked cheek. Adam, however, smiles shamelessly as he looks over my shoulder. At the exact same time, the sun above us is eclipsed, and I say a silent prayer that God isn't too pissed we pulled His Son into our territorial dispute.

"Back off, Warner."

Lukas. He towers above all of us. I squint with one eye shut while looking up at him, and my lips curl inward to hide my smile.

Genesis relaxes, shifting her weight on to her hands and easing back. Both brows arched, she silently dares Eric to say anything else.

He doesn't. Not at first.

After this rather uncomfortable standoff, Eric finally grabs his tray, then pivots in Lukas's direction. "One day, all of you assholes will pay. Mark my words. You're all a drain on society, and the world would be better off without you."

He aims a furious glare at each of us before finally turning away in search of another poor, unsuspecting table to infect.

Lukas remains standing, watching Eric over his shoulder. Eventually, Eric settles himself three tables away, right next to Leah Allen, head cheerleader extraordinaire. He mutters something under his breath, and in turn her ebony ponytail whips to the side as she looks in our direction. Eric turns as well, but it's only Leah I notice. Her expression is glacial, bitter with disgust.

Why the hell does she hate me so much?

Lukas sets his tray next to mine, saving me from the throes of Leah's diabolical, yet oddly hypnotizing glare. Slowly he shakes his head, his mouth lifting minutely at the corners. "Jesus would not approve."

Genny gives him an encouraging nod. "Not *my* Jesus. Because while *my* Jesus excuses certain indiscretions, he can't overlook *someone being a complete prick!*"

Eric scowls at us and Genny narrows her eyes menacingly in his direction, pausing before she adds, "Which is exactly why *he's* not allowed at the Jesus Table. However, you assholes are welcome any time."

Our collective laughter fills the air, and I slide onto the bench while Lukas does the same. Genny remains seated on her throne, chomping her carrot while eyeing the back of Eric's head, and Adam takes his seat across from us. Once we're all settled, I take a bite of my burger, chewing thoughtfully in an attempt to ignore the way Lukas's presence seems to affect me.

How it *always* affects me.

Like the way goosebumps rise along my arm when his brushes against it.

Or how his scent is burned into my brain, you know, just for safekeeping. Or torture.

Or the way every single cell of my thigh tingles as his leg settles against mine.

All things I regularly dismiss, because there are certain lines not to be crossed within the Wildflowers.

I swallow my food while reinforcing my denial, but I

feel myself blush anyway. As its warmth spreads across my face, Adam glances up from his BLT and locks eyes with me. He quirks a brow, sets his sandwich down, and grins.

I scowl back.

His smile widens, unapologetic. Not always one for the rules, this guy.

After inhaling a Zen-like breath, I scoot approximately five inches—the maximum distance allowed before any distancing becomes noticeable—then set my half-eaten burger back on my tray and finally break the silence.

"So...the Bible and our names. That's new, and a bit overwhelming. Just gonna toss that out there."

Genny turns her attention from Eric to me. Her expression morphs from anger to unconcealed excitement, the past few minutes clearly forgotten thanks to this new topic of conversation.

"Dude." She twists on the cement tabletop, facing us completely before continuing. "It's a sign. I know it. You know I've been on this name kick lately? Well, I was researching the meanings of our names, when it hit me. All of our names have biblical origins. Add in their actual meanings, and I mean, seriously, it's a sign. We were meant to find each other."

She points toward the sky and nods reverently.

I frown and shake my head. "There's no 'Chloe' in the Bible."

"First Corinthians 1:11. Check it, bitch." Genny doesn't miss a beat.

I laugh, noting privately that the mention of a name in a Bible is in no way the same as "biblical origin," but to make her happy I simply agree. "Okay, well, I'll take your word for it. That being said, I seriously doubt that God, in all His infinite wisdom, sat down one day and said, 'Hey, I'm gonna make sure these four random kids have biblical names just so they can eat at the self-proclaimed Jesus Table.'"

Genny grins and swallows a mouthful of salad. "Oh, ye of little faith."

"What? Now we're the Jesus Freaks? I thought we were the Wildflowers, as ordained by you," Adam says, finally releasing me from his stare as it's redirected to Genny.

"We are. But our names cement the fact that we were brought together for a specific purpose. I just know it."

"I still don't understand this 'wildflowers' thing," Lukas says. "And by the way, my name isn't biblical, so that kind of shoots your theory to shit."

"Eh, close enough." Genny forks another piece of lettuce, then continues. "'Lukas' is a derivative of 'Luke.' An apostle of Jesus, who just so happens to be in the Bible. Hello?"

She looks at me, then adds, "And you'll meet our wild-flowers soon enough. Then you'll understand." She winks, and I smile.

Lukas opens his mouth, but is silenced by Genny's raised hand. "And the meaning of our names is ridiculously on point. Like, totally meant to be." She begins to count on her fingers.

"Genesis. I am 'the Beginning.' The founder of this

group. So, inherently, I'm Wildflower Number One."

She looks at Adam. "Clearly, 'Genesis' and 'Adam' go together. Consequently, 'Adam' means 'Son of the Earth.' Seeing as I met you first, my vision for this group found root in your existence. You, my dear, are The Second Wildflower."

"Chloe"—she points at me—"your name means 'green shoot' and 'fresh bloom.' You are just beginning to blossom. And as you find root, bloom beautifully you shall. That makes you Wildflower Number Three."

She then turns to Lukas. "And you. Well, the biblical meaning of 'Luke,' or 'Lukas,' is 'light giving.' You are our light, our sustenance so to speak. And that's why you have been named The Fourth, and Final, Wildflower."

Lukas pauses mid-chew, eyes Genesis warily, then swallows. "I've been called a lot of shit. 'Light,' however, has never been mentioned."

Our smiles become frowns. I grit my teeth and clamp my jaw shut, but the truth frees itself, clawing its way up my throat before launching off my tongue. "That's because you've never really been seen."

The words come out in a rush, and I watch Lukas's dark brows form two perfect arches in response. Warmth begins to seep into my cheeks, *again,* and I look skyward, avoiding further eye contact. When a lucid image forms in my mind, I say, "Right now, you're a storm. You thunder and strike to frighten those who don't understand you, but *we* do, and you don't scare us. So, we give you the time you need, because one day your clouds will break, and eventually, you will shine."

I have no idea if Genesis and Adam see what I see, but I blunder on. "So, yeah, I think Genny is spot on with the meaning of your name. Because with the right people, those who truly understand you, a light as strong as yours is felt long before it's seen." With every single cell in my body, I know she's right. He is our sustenance, our light. Something tells me a smile from Lukas White would be enough to sustain a thousand broken souls. Mine included.

As soon as the words are freed, everything shifts. Lukas looks at me with a slight tilt of his head, eyes narrowed. Adam swallows the last of his sandwich while nodding in understanding. And Genny, well, she's Genny. She responds with a vibrant, "Exactly. What she said." Her thumb flies in my direction. "Now, we just need the ceremony."

"Ceremony?" Lukas inquires, brows raised.

"But not until he's ready," she adds ominously.

I nudge him gently with my shoulder, swallowing my heart. "It's mandatory. And it's harmless." I grin while rising, tray in hand. "For the most part."

As I make my way to the trashcan, Genny falls in next to me, muttering under her breath, "*Totally* making him a headdress full of flowers. Just because I can."

I laugh while she disappears into her own mind, most likely thinking up said floral headdress, which will undoubtedly serve no purpose other than embarrassing the shit out of Lukas White.

"You're such a bitch," I remark, shaking my head and dumping my trash into the bin.

"That I am, my friend."

I giggle, knowing the ceremony, while harmless in nature, is a life-changing event. Three hundred and eighty days ago, I was a shell. Alone. Consumed by darkness. But Genny found me. Took *me* in…with my scars, and my darkness, and my hopelessness. She and Adam brought me into the Wildflowers, truly welcomed me, and gave me a sense of…acceptance. I'm not fully healed. Hell, who knows if I ever will be? But their welcome was a simple yet significant accomplishment. They saw I was more than nothing. Just like now we see more in Lukas.

And now…it's *his* time.

3

Hefting my backpack onto my shoulder, I shuffle through the usual crowd, ignoring the snickers and guffaws clearly directed my way while walking to the bus. I'll never understand the need for people to ridicule others. People who deem lives other than their own unworthy.

Lives like ours.

As much as I try to exercise my inner strength, to be like Genesis with her zero fucks to give about, well, pretty much anything, I cannot get over my own need for approval. And I have no idea why.

Well, actually, I do. We've covered it in therapy at Sacred Heart a million times. Yet as much as I understand it, I can't seem to gather the courage necessary to stand up for myself. Every day on this campus I'm a witness to my own goddamn failure.

An eerie sensation washes over me all of a sudden, and I feel the hairs on my neck begin to rise. *Shit.*

I look up just in time to see the "W" of the "West High School" insignia and realize I've unknowingly landed myself smack-dab in the middle of an angry hornet's nest.

Like, *literally.*

Our mascot is the hornet. And these girls, with their thigh-high pleated skirts lined in black and yellow, are our cheerleaders.

I try to block out their buzzing, but the cruel murmurs always get through. Sweat beads along my upper lip, and as always, I keep my focus fixed on the ground, redirecting an instant surge of nervous energy to my legs to walk faster.

"Oh my God," Leah Allen gasps theatrically.

Breathe in deeply, stay calm. Breathe in—

"Is that…my shirt?"

The shame chokes me, making it impossible to breathe. My throat clamps shut and the blood previously driving my legs seems to suddenly flood my face, stalling my forward movement.

As laughter begins to echo around me, I feel exposed. Vulnerable.

Breathe.

"It totally *is*. I remember that blouse. I threw it out last year when I donated it to 'those less fortunate,' as my mother phrased it. Looks like it landed in exactly the right hands." More cackling from the group. "How ironic, rejected trash wearing someone else's rejected trash. It's kind of sad, actually."

And to think I actually felt pretty when I put it on this morning. Now, I want nothing more than to rip the floral tunic from my body. Instead, I'm stuck where I stand, my only movement the rapid rise and fall of my chest. The wind takes pity on me, lifting the ends of my dark blonde hair and whipping it across my face, obscuring tears as they brim in my light brown eyes.

I refuse to look up, knowing I'll see the mocking stares of those watching, and their fake grins, and their fake pity. My eyes stay locked on the gravel beneath my sandals.

"Are you fucking kidding me?" Genny's sarcastic tone fills the air, and the crushing weight on me lessens. I inhale my first decent breath. "The only sad thing about this situation is *you*, Leah. Your toxic presence is infecting the precious air entering our lungs. Quite possibly with some undiscovered strain of airborne STD."

Genny shudders theatrically beside me. "It's gross. *You're* gross." She shoos Leah and her cheer posse with her hands. "You can go away now."

I finally find the courage to lift my gaze. Leah's mouth is open, her eyes wide with shock. Seconds tick by, then her perfectly glossed lips pucker as she begins to speak. Genesis just gives her a stern shake of her head and puts her hand up. "Just don't. We both know I'll run you into the ground in front of your precious entourage. I'm feeling rather benevolent today, so I'd hate to ruin that by announcing to the world that you're fucking Cody Manton. As in the boyfriend of Amy here." Genesis jerks her head in Amy's direction before concluding, "I mean, that would be in really poor taste, but I'll do it if I have to."

Leah pales.

Genny shrugs, open palms lifting skyward along with her shoulders.

And Amy?

Well, Amy gasps and whirls, taking off in the opposite direction.

The rest of them might as well be watching a tennis match, their ponytails whipping back and forth between where Leah stands gawking at Genny and where Amy is racing off to, clearly distraught.

After a long pause, Leah regains her faculties. Although she remains silent, her eyes narrow on Genesis, and she wordlessly resumes her leadership role, turning to follow Amy and taking the herd with her.

After releasing a long breath, Genny mutters, "Fucking sheep."

"Seriously," I remark, taking a heavy breath.

Genny's hands curl around my shoulders, and she turns me to face her. Her stare is hard, but her voice is gentle. "This has *got* to stop, Chloe. None of those girls are better than you, yet you give them the power to make you feel otherwise. You're beautiful, both inside and out, while they are neither. They mask their ugliness with labels, with brands, to filter out those they deem to be less. They know nothing other than the precious, coddled life they've been given."

Her hands tighten, as does her gaze. "And what pisses *me* off is, you *know* this. You're not oblivious, yet you refuse to accept what you already know. You want to get out from underneath them, accept *yourself.* Embrace what you have to offer to those around you, both good and bad. And if people don't get it, if they don't understand, fuck them. *They're* not worthy."

A wide, knowing grin spreads across her face. "Somewhere deep within you lies your very own bitch mode—I feel it as sure as I breathe. I will find it. I will expose it. I will nurture it. But it will be *you* who finally unleashes it. And what a marvelous sight *that* will be."

I cover her hands with my own, allowing her words to give me strength as I conjure up an insult. "Screw them."

Genesis angles an ear in my direction and prods me with a finger. "I'm sorry. I can't hear with all the judgment being cast our way. Could you maybe say that a little louder?"

Tears leak from my eyes, not from fear, but from relief. I nod, then shout, "Screw them! And their ridiculously short skirts!"

With her hands still firm on my shoulders, Genesis blinks twice, then bends toward the ground, overcome with laughter. I struggle to remain upright while she releases a heinous snort, and offers apologetic smiles to onlookers as they pass by. When she finally rises, Genesis inhales deeply then shakes her head, still grinning. "So as of right now, your bitch mode seems to be set on Kitten." She winks. "But don't worry, I'm *all over* this shit. With my help, we'll move that setting right past Sublimation-of-Anger straight onto the feared Who-Gives-a-Shit." Tapping the end of my nose with her finger, she adds, "My little lioness-in-training."

We hold each other's gazes until her eyes narrow, signaling her refusal to disengage until I accept her words. Eventually, I relent with a curt nod, and her mouth breaks into a satisfied grin. Genny offers me the crook of her arm, and together we make our way through the onslaught of students with looks of "what the hell just happened" on their faces.

Surprisingly, I feel none of their stares. There is nothing in this moment other than me feeling safe and drawing on Genny's strength.

Her belief in me. In my capabilities.

She sees me.

I grin, shaking my head in awe as we walk. When we make it onto the bus, I smile at our driver, Mr. Porter, as we pass him, head straight to the rear, and plop down in our usual seats. Five minutes later, the boys take their usual place in front of us, and I pretend not to notice Lukas by lowering my head and nonchalantly digging through my backpack.

Still bent forward, my eyes meet Adam's as his head hangs over the back of the seat, watching me with a shrewd stare. I glare back at him, willing him not to speak. His smile broadens.

He quickly glances at Lukas, then gives me a lengthy look and says, "Wow, Chloe. At the risk of sounding"—he pauses, his laughing eyes wide as he mouths the word "gay" into his cupped hands—"you look positively gorgeous today."

Unable to find anything in my bag, I relent, chuckling as I ease back into my seat. Adam's sexuality is no secret. Not anymore. In fact, it was the very reason he was sent to Sacred Heart. I can't imagine the pain he endured, having a family that adored him, that *loved* him, only to reject him because of their refusal to accept something so natural. I'm sad for him.

I guess I'm also sad for his family, because their beliefs have ensured they're missing out on one of the most wonderful people who ever graced this earth. That because of their restrictions, their need to conform to the demands of a religion *translated* by *man*, they'll never truly know Adam. Nor will they understand the positive impact he has on those around him.

When I look at him, I don't see his sexuality. I see *Adam*, and I'll never understand people who see anything else.

That being said, he's not any less of a pain in my ass.

With his playful stare still trained in my direction, Adam nudges Lukas with his elbow. "Doesn't Chloe look gorgeous in that shirt? It brings out the gold flecks in her eyes."

Lukas faces forward, unmoved. "Yeah. Sure."

I suck in a breath at his dismissive and harsh tone.

Yeah. Sure.

His words are sharp. They sting.

Genesis speaks from beside me, redirecting my attention. "Actually, Chloe…that shirt looks like shit on you.

We should burn it, it's *that* awful."

Adam's face falls, contorted in confusion, but I smile gently.

My eyes lock with Genny's, and I remember what she said. *Embrace what you have to offer to those around you, both good and bad. And if people don't get it, if they don't understand, fuck them.*

As the true meaning of her words washes through me, I'm fueled by a courage I've never allowed myself to feel before. A wide grin crosses my face before I answer. "We totally should."

Twenty minutes later, after tossing our backpacks in the entryway of our home and heading outside, the shirt is ablaze within the safety of the acreage behind Sacred Heart. Genny and I laugh, giddy as we watch the flames. The other two Wildflowers have very different reactions. One watches the fire in silence, jaw tensed, his eyes fixed on the glowing embers. The other watches us warily, as though we've lost our minds.

But my mind has never been clearer.

I've never felt stronger.

I refuse to remain a kitten any longer.

4

"Do I even want to know what you four were up to out there?"

The tiny body of Mrs. Mary Rodriguez blocks the back door of Sacred Heart, her weight braced by her upper arm against the jamb. A plastic spatula dangles from her fingers. Her amused expression is undeniable as the loose, gray tendrils of hair framing her face flutter in the breeze. But as soon as her tawny-colored eyes find mine, her amusement falters.

"Chloe, what happened to your shirt? You looked so pretty wearing it."

My eyes drift downward, taking in the plain white tank I had layered underneath. Tugging at the gloves still covering my arms, I grin then shrug, looking back at her. Instead of feeling insulted like most girls my age would, my heart warms. *She notices. She notices me.* That a small change in my wardrobe flagged Mrs. Rodriguez's attention, well...it means more than she'll ever know.

From beside me, Genesis opens her mouth to speak, but I take command and silence her with my words. "I didn't like the way it made me feel. So, we burned it."

The honesty of my statement hangs in the air, and I'm grateful to the others for giving me this small victory. Mrs. Rodriguez's looks between us, her eyes narrowed in keen observation. Behind us, the undeniable squeak of Adam's Vans breaks the silence, but when his warm hand lands on my shoulder and squeezes, I feel the pride and solidarity relayed through his touch.

Mrs. Rodriguez's expression melts with the gesture, and she envelops me in a hug. Before releasing me, she whispers in my ear, "Then burn it we shall." She gives me a squeeze and steps away, her tone masterfully switching from compassionate to unrelenting. "Dinner at seven. Group at eight."

Genny looks up to the ceiling and groans. "Fuck me. Seriously?"

There is a faint swish, and Mrs. Rodriguez's black spatula is suddenly pointed in Genny's direction. "*Ugly* people resort to *ugly* language, Genesis. Choose your words wisely."

"Christ, I just did. I chose colorful, expressive words, Mrs. Rodriguez."

Genny's expression matches her tone—mock innocence. I snort back laughter. Mrs. Rodriguez tries to hide her grin. After blessing herself as a preventative measure and shaking her head, she becomes serious again.

"Be mindful, young lady. Your color bleeds to those around you." Her response is stern, but not uncaring.

Surprisingly, the silence between them remains unbroken by whatever clever retort we've come to expect from Genny. It's there. I recognize it in her expression. But somehow she manages to trap it behind puckered lips while considering Mrs. Rodriguez's words. Once her decision is made, Genesis gives a relenting grin and a slight dip of her head in acknowledgment.

Mrs. Rodriguez's expression warms, and she whips around. "To your rooms for homework, then if you're done, meal prep in the kitchen begins at five."

Our response is immediate.

"Carrots!" Genny shouts.

Somehow my voice is next. "Green beans!"

"Salad!"

Eyes wide, Genny and I turn, facing the boys behind us and in particular, the loser now responsible for peeling the onions.

"Oh my *God*." My tone is shrill with victory. I always get stuck with the stupid onions. "I totally win at life today!" I point at the loser while dancing some ridiculous jig that I refuse to describe.

Lukas stares back at me, lips curved in the barest hint of a smile, the closest to amused I think he's ever seemed. Then, in his deep voice, he admits defeat.

"Onions."

Exhilarated, I continue dancing. I know I should probably stop but I can't, because I totally *won* today.

But as our eyes lock, my movements begin to slow until finally my entire body stills. I can no longer move, because I can feel the significance of this moment. Not for me.

But for Lukas.

His green eyes are lit with curiosity, and a nervous flush heats my cheeks. I bite my bottom lip and tuck a section of hair behind my ear.

Next to me, Genny clears her throat, but it's Adam who speaks.

"While I love an impromptu bonfire, I'm going to need an explanation of what the hell just happened out there."

Genny scoffs. Swiping a piece of burnt grass off her Dickies, she says, "Leah Allen happened. Bitch."

"Genesis!" Mrs. Rodriguez yells from across the house.

A satisfied grin crosses Genny's face as she links her arm with Adam's, heading toward the stairs. "I'll tell you on the way to our rooms." Her pink hair swishes over her shoulder when she turns back in my direction. "See you there?"

Still silent, I nod. Her eyes dance between Lukas and me before she dips her head. The corner of Adam's mouth lifts as he, too, assesses us. Then he tosses me a wink, gives Lukas a respectful chin lift, and grins shamelessly in my direction before going upstairs with Genesis.

Their murmurs trail after them, and only when they can no longer be heard do I dare look at Lukas. His gaze has dropped, now aimed at his boots, brows tightly drawn. He rakes his hand through his disheveled hair.

Confused at his sudden change in demeanor, I watch him closely, waiting for something, anything, that will offer some clue as to what he's feeling. The silence between us stretches painfully into awkwardness, and I decide it's time for me to leave.

As soon as the ball of my foot hits the hardwood floor, it creaks loudly in protest, and a string of curses runs through my mind that would make Mrs. Rodriguez's ears bleed. Lukas jolts to attention, his eyes launching from the floor to meet mine. Panicked, I freeze.

And for some random reason, the *Mission Impossible* theme song begins playing in my head.

Dun dun dun da dada…dun dun dun da dada…

I force a placating smile onto my face and begin to slowly wheel in the other direction, but my movement is stalled by Lukas's hand on my arm.

De da doo…de da doo…

I twist to face him, and he silences the music in my head with two simple words. "Thank you."

Stunned, my head jerks backward. "For what?"

His grip tightens, not painfully, but in a way that tells me he needs time. Needs to be heard. And as I finally brave a glimpse of his face, the need to flee escapes me. I relax, lost in the calm eyes staring back at me. They're so different from the usual storm I find there.

Lukas's expression is…vulnerable, something I've never seen. "I just…I uh, I…"

"Yes?"

He shakes his head and looks at the floor before again meeting my eyes. His jaw is clenched so tightly, I'm surprised he can speak. "Until today, there's nothing I've been thankful for in my life. Ever."

I'm sad, but I give him the time he needs to collect his thoughts. I refuse to let him go unseen. I see his storm already brewing and ready to whisk him away, but I won't let him go until he's ready. I will remain in this moment with him as long as he lets me.

"But I have to thank you, Chloe, for seeing something other than my darkness." He breaks his stare, and as he steps away he shrugs, seemingly uncertain of his own words. "You give me…hope."

He shakes his head, but says nothing else. He turns briskly, takes a few steps toward the stairs, then stops. With his back to me, his voice is soft, barely audible.

"You did look pretty today, Chloe. I'm sorry…" His arm lifts, and he scrubs his head with his hand again, a gesture I'm quickly learning is a sign of his discomfort. "I'm sorry I didn't, I couldn't, say that earlier. I saw what happened, and…" He runs his fingers through his inky hair, and his tone turns cold. "I'm glad you burned that fucking shirt."

Clearly finished, he quickly turns and follows Genny and Adam upstairs, leaving me alone with the sound of his heavy footfalls.

I should be excited, but instead, I only feel guilt. While a part of me is thrilled that Lukas notices my appearance, and actually approves, the guilt is for something else.

But I have to thank you, Chloe, for seeing something other than my darkness.

In the wake of those words, I'm left with the devastating realization of how many people I've neglected to see because of my own blinding anger at never being seen myself.

I've blamed so many people over the years for not seeing me, but the awful truth is...I'm just as guilty as they are.

5

Unfortunately, "Vulnerable Lukas" disappeared as soon as he left that afternoon. His storms resurfaced, transporting him to whatever dark place in his mind he tends to retreat to. He was generally indifferent and, once again, barely spoke to me. But he wasn't mean. He was never mean.

Four weeks have passed, and I miss that moment of light. I want to see his smile. The day is warm, the sun is shining, and as usual I'm shuffling my way to the Jesus Table—head down, tray in hand, backpack in tow. Today I'm wearing a simple lavender maxi dress that flows in the breeze as I walk, with a lightweight plum cardigan to cover my arms. The silver gleam of my sandaled foot catches my eye, barely peeking out from under the hem of my dress.

I smile.

I love these sandals.

Mrs. Rodriguez gave them to me last week, and I don't think I've taken them off since they were removed from the box.

My hair is down, the blonde tendrils brushing my back with each stride. After hearing Adam whine for twenty minutes this morning about "displaying my natural waves for all to see"—cue the eye-roll—I reluctantly relented.

Well, actually, he hid our blow dryer, but you know, *whatever*.

It's honestly been nice having my hair down, not that I'll tell Adam—

Smack.

A surprised squeak escapes me—my tray is flipped up against my chest. I feel a burst of chocolate milk ice cold against my skin as it sinks into the fabric of my dress.

"Bitch!" Leah exclaims.

'Cause my eyes were glued to my feet, I'd missed the mean-girl train in front of me, Leah Allen of course leading the way. *What the hell?*

I look up in shock, and Amy Martindale stumbles into Leah from behind, beginning what can only be described as an extremely unrehearsed slapstick routine of a mean-girl pileup. And as this plays out in front of me, as I take in each of their ridiculous expressions upon impact, I just can't help myself.

I laugh.

And just like that, my happy, happy day is back on track.

At the sound of my laughter, Leah homes in on me, her narrowed dark-brown eyes bordering on black as fury fills them. In this moment, this calm before the inevitable storm, I can see how pretty she'd be if she wasn't—and I'm quoting Genny here—such a bitch all the time.

Minus the dollop of mustard sliding down her cheek, of course.

Oddly mesmerized, I watch it descend in what seems like slow motion until some greater power hits the play button and real time resumes.

Then I hear Genny's boots against the pavement, and Leah lunges in my direction, fingers outstretched and curved. Without thinking, I grip my tray in my hands and slam it into Leah's overpriced Ralph Lauren blouse. She flies backward, and I swear to God above, whoever hit the play button decided to change it up by pressing rewind, because it's the pileup all over again, but in reverse.

Then, just when I thought the situation couldn't possibly get any more hilarious, they all tip over like a row of dominoes.

And as each one collapses, I laugh.

And laugh.

And laugh.

Tears rise and blur my vision, but I don't need to see what's happening to know it's absurd. The curses, the shrieks of horror, the wails…the entire scene is playing in high definition in my mind.

Oh God. Leah's face. The food in her hair and her purse. This couldn't get any better—I will remember this moment forever.

I wipe the tears from my eyes just in time to see Leah jump to her feet and throw her head back. She's eerily silent at first, then what begins as barely a guttural growl crescendos into an ear-splitting battle cry.

Once it's released, she slowly, ominously, lowers her stare.

Suddenly this situation isn't so funny anymore.

My adrenaline spikes as I watch her reach into her purse, but I breathe a sigh of relief when she pulls out a portion of decimated hamburger instead of a handgun. Mustard and grease trickle onto the side of her bag, and a tomato plummets to the ground when she thrusts the patty in my direction.

She stares at the damaged leather, then sniffs, chin trembling. A tear falls, landing smack dab next to the tomato as she meets my eyes.

"You have no idea what you've done. What this will cost me."

Genny, who has been surprisingly quiet through this exchange, decides to take this time to offer her two cents. "This is not Chloe's fault. *You* ran into *her*. Not the other way around. So maybe, *just maybe*, you can figure out how to share the fucking sidewalk instead of taking your half out of the middle like an entitled bitch."

Adam, clearly more observant than She of the Imminent Implosion less than three feet away from me, gently warns, "Genny."

I look over at him. He's alert, ready for anything. Thankfully, because not even a second later a greasy hamburger patty is launched through the air and smacks against Genny's favorite Sex Pistols T-shirt.

Oh shit.

Adam shakes his head in defeat.

Genny's eyes narrow in the direction of the offender. Leah scowls back, ready to pounce.

Where the hell is Lukas?

Just as I watch Genny fly in Leah's direction, two strong arms circle my waist, lift me from the ground, and pull me out of the danger zone.

Infuriated that I'm missing the beatdown of a lifetime, I whip around to face Lukas, but am struck silent by the anger in his expression.

"Look up."

My face pinches in confusion. "I am. Like, right now. You have at least a foot on me."

His eyebrows slam together, so I add, "Height wise."

He shuts his eyes and inhales deeply before opening them again. "When you walk, *look up.*"

"What?" I feel as though we're having two separate conversations.

Lukas balls his fists, one at each side. I fight the urge to laugh because seriously, I have no clue, and clearly it's ticking him off.

My amusement is short-lived, however. I sober immediately when he leans into me, so closely I can smell the clean scent of his soap. His eyes narrow. "You want people to see you, but they can't see what isn't there. You make yourself invisible by keeping your head down and avoiding eye contact. All that does is make you look weak. It makes you an easy target."

A shriek sounds in the distance. Lukas tilts his head. "Case in point."

I bristle at his harsh tone. "Well, even with *your* obvious lack of eye contact, *I* still see *you.*"

His response is a slew of sentences I never thought him capable of stringing together.

"I didn't ask to be seen. I don't *need* to be seen. But for whatever reason, *you* do. I don't understand it, and I don't have to, because that's *your* Goliath. Not mine. And it's something you can easily overcome. I refuse to watch you cower anymore. So, when you walk, *look up*. Give them no other choice but to see you."

Then, as though he hasn't said enough, he adds, "Your victim card has officially expired."

What. The. Hell?

He's so wrong. I don't carry a victim card.

But when I open my mouth, I've got nothing to say.

You make yourself invisible by keeping your head down and avoiding eye contact. All that does is make you look weak. It makes you an easy target.

Is that what I do?

Is that what people see? An easy target?

God, he's right.

Lukas says nothing but reaches forward, surprising me when he grips my trembling chin. With a gentle nudge, he forces me to meet his eyes, and I'm relieved to see my friend staring back at me. No anger. Just…Lukas.

His perfect jaw is tense. But when he speaks, his voice is gentle. "I'm sorry. I'm not so good with…people. I don't mean to come across angry or annoyed. It's just…"

His black brows press closer together. "You see so much in everyone around you, yet you see nothing in yourself. It's fucking frustrating."

My first thought is to apologize, but I know an apology now will only make things worse. I bite my bottom lip to keep from interrupting him.

"Someone as extraordinary as you should walk with your head held high. Only then will you recognize the effect you have on those around you. Because in the end, it's not about what others see, but how you see yourself."

My eyebrows lift in surprise and I can do nothing but stare at him, mind-blown.

The silence must fluster him, because he lets go of my chin to rake his hand through his hair. And then, he's gone.

I stand there, unsure of what the hell just happened, until a familiar voice says, "Disney screwed things up for every impressionable adolescent."

I turn to find Adam, hands jammed in his pockets while taking slow, deliberate steps in my direction.

"What?" I ask.

He grins at my confusion. "I mean, anyone can whip up some magical love story by romanticizing what they want to see. That's easy. But in all honesty, love isn't always sunshine and rainbows. True love is when you're faced with truths you don't want to hear, with words difficult to accept, but they're spoken to better you as a person, without fear of consequence."

Dreading exactly how much he heard, I gesture in the space previously occupied by Lukas. "It's not…we're not…"

Adam shakes his head, dismissing my stammering. "I'm just saying, fuck Disney. That's all."

I make no comment on his random observation and steer the conversation into safer, much saner territory. "So… where's Genny?"

He chuckles, then throws an arm over my shoulder and tucks me into his tall frame. "Well, there was a lot of screaming and a few failed attempts at drawing blood, then Mr. Wyatt showed up and everyone took off. Genny wanted me to tell you she has your backpack and to meet her in the bathroom beside the cafeteria."

I glance at my ruined dress, feeling defeated. *Crap.* "She's going to dress me, isn't she?"

Adam gives me a sympathetic look, and I frown in return.

He laughs softly as he guides me toward the cafeteria. I lean into him and nestle my head in the crook of his neck. A warm breeze stirs around us as we walk, its soft gust launching several tiny blades of freshly cut grass into the air.

Adam inhales deeply. "You smell that?"

I breathe in. "The grass?"

"No." He shakes his head, then gives my shoulder a tender squeeze. "The winds of change."

6

The winds of change begin within the next ten minutes.

Literally.

Instead of my pretty lavender dress and shiny silver sandals, I find myself in a pair of worn-out Docs (two sizes too big), ripped fishnet stockings, a plaid pleated skirt, and a black, oversized crop top with a skull on it.

Let me repeat that.

With. A. Skull. On. It.

After searching for, and thankfully finding, an extra pair of fingerless gloves in my backpack—I mean, any normal girl can never have too many pairs, am I right?—I slide them up my arms and finally exit the stall, only to scowl at my reflection. I grit my teeth while yanking on the hem of the shirt, but it's a lost cause. The cotton quickly retracts to its original length, leaving a tiny sliver of skin exposed along my midriff.

I swear I hear the skull laughing.

Wait, no. I stand corrected.

That would be Genny.

Her eyes full of mirth, she approaches me from behind, meeting my horrified gaze in the mirror. Her pink hair is pulled into a high ponytail, the shorter strands falling free along the nape of her neck, covering the collar of her Sex Pistols T-shirt. The same shirt she was wearing earlier, the imprint of the hamburger patty still greased into the fabric right above her left boob.

"I am *not* wearing this in public," I announce, pulling again at the bottom of the crop top.

Her expression hardens. "*I* wear this in public."

I sigh. "Yes. And you look great in it, Genny, because it's *you*, not *me*."

Genny scoffs, shaking her head. "My dear Chloe." She curls her fingers over the tops of my shoulders, centering my reflection in the mirror. "You have no idea who you are."

Her expression morphs from amusement to sincerity as she begins to explain. "I'm punk. I'm all about rebelling against those who preach conformity and speaking my mind however I choose. I express myself through what I wear, the music I listen to, and the way I conduct myself in general, because I refuse to bend to archaic rules that make no exception for variation. Differences stoke change, and change is inevitable. But it's the inability to accept those differences that hinders our movement forward as a society."

And here I thought I'd met my speech-that-blows-

Chloe's-mind quota for the day.

Genny continues, ignoring my wide-eyed expression. "That's who I am, unapologetically. I will continue to fight for what I believe in until the day I die. Yet the question still remains: who are you? And I'm sorry, I do not accept that you're the pretty, pretty princess you try so hard to be. That's your attempt to be what they want you to be, sure, but it's not who you are. Your biggest challenge lies in"—she tightens her hold on my shoulders—"no longer denying your past, but facing it. And as you accept your reality, your hardships and triumphs, each of these defining moments become tools for embracing difference and creating change, not only for yourself, but for those around you."

Her shoulders lift and she smiles gently. "Life goes on, Chloe, with or without you. It's what you leave behind for others to carry forward that should define you, not what you wore to school last Thursday." She chuckles. "Or for the remainder of today. You look hot, by the way. Not in a 'defining' way, though. Do not mistake what I'm saying."

My head feels like it just exploded. "You're exhausting."

"I've heard much worse."

With Lukas's speech still fresh in my mind, I find courage to lower the walls guarding my innermost fears. My voice trembles as I ask, "How do you do it? How do you just not care about what other people think and say?"

I glance at the spots on her shirt, shining like a badge of honor across her chest. Slowly, my gaze drifts to her arms, the scars lining them, the courage she demonstrates in their open display…the true source of my question.

Her curious gaze follows mine, and for a moment, I panic in anticipation of her response. But when she lifts her eyes, they're full of compassion and understanding. "Silence the voices, you mean?" She taps her temple. "In here?"

I swallow hard and nod once, her question rocking me. I've never discussed the voices with anyone. But with that acknowledgement, I realize I might not be the only one who's fought against them. Or who's given in to their taunts.

A sad smile curves her lips. "I tried unsuccessfully for a long time." She gestures at her marred arm. "The drugs didn't work, though—they only softened them to a dull roar. It wasn't until my mind was clear, and my body clean, that I was finally able to grasp the truth: the voices were *my* hateful voice sounding *my* fears. I was projecting my anxieties onto others, and giving them the power to dictate how I felt about myself. When I was finally able to grasp that, to understand that it was me running my own soul into the ground, I took control of the voices. I silenced them. No, I *owned* them. After that, no one could make me see, or hear, or feel anything about me that wasn't my own true perception of myself. And let's be honest"—she grins widely—"we both know I think I'm pretty fucking awesome."

A burst of laughter bubbles up in me and I can't help but snort. "You make it sound so easy."

"Well, it's definitely not easy, but it is possible."

After a lengthy look, she drops her hands, and I watch as she leans in to retrieve my stained clothes and shove them into her backpack. After slinging hers over her shoulder, she hands me mine and opens the bathroom door. I turn, successfully avoiding my reflection, and my eyes narrow on her backpack. "No books today?"

Genny's face pinches, her expression horrified. "No books ever. How else would I be able to make room for my expressive attire?"

"Right, because one punk outfit a day clearly isn't enough."

Her brow arches and she angles her head. "Clearly."

I roll my eyes, sulking theatrically as I pass her.

She laughs, then bumps my hip with hers as she falls into step with me. The boots she gave me are heavier than I expected. I feel as though they're going to fly off my feet with each stride I take. And with the luck I've been having today, I wouldn't be surprised.

"Dude!" Genny exclaims when we're almost to class, causing my heart to seize. I frown in her direction, but the effort is wasted because she doesn't bother looking at me. "I was going to tell you this at lunch, but we all know how that ended."

I scowl.

She beams back, taking in my new ensemble. "Too soon?"

I remain silent.

She continues, unfazed. "Our wildflowers are in full bloom, my friend. I know this because I ditched third period today and visited to the pond instead. Honestly, who cares about covalent bonds?" She jerks two thumbs toward her chest. "Not this girl."

"Genny, point?" I urge, half laughing, half groaning.

Her eyes flash. "Wildflower ceremony, tomorrow."

I stumble, but luckily, I stay upright. Not that it matters much. These stockings are ripped to shit anyway. "Really? You think Lukas is ready?"

Genny nods. "I do. And with the wildflowers now in full bloom, I believe it with absolute certainty. They're telling us it's time."

Highly doubtful, but I decide to forgo the nature lesson for the time being, only to feel Genny grip my arm, bringing us both to a stop. Seems I was once again off balance and about to fall over my own feet. I'm seriously contemplating a self-inflicted face-plant just to get it over with.

"He's right, you know. You do need to look up when you walk. If nothing else, it may help with your tragic inability to get from point A to point B without catastrophe striking."

My face heats. "You heard that, huh?"

"Duh."

"Adam?"

She nods. "Don't you see? Lukas is changing, Chloe. And I can't think of a better time to give him a reason to continue doing so. He's one of us, and we take care of our own. So tomorrow, we share our stories with him, and whether or not he chooses to shed light on his own, we use the ceremony as a way to help him understand he's not alone."

I grin—her belief in the Wildflowers is extremely contagious. "So, like last year, when you and Adam took me in."

"Exactly." Her expression turns whimsical. "Except this year, s'mores."

I crinkle my nose, confused.

"What? I'm hungry. I didn't get to eat lunch."

I glare at her.

"Don't you want some s'mores?" she inquires innocently.

My stomach grumbles, because of course it has to right at that moment, and Genny barks a triumphant laugh.

"Sounds like we're in agreement—s'mores it is!"

7

Looking up from the ground proved to be an exercise of will I just didn't have the energy to attempt today. After Genny and I parted, I kept my head down, eyes locked on my borrowed combat boots. I didn't need to see the people around me to know they were gaping at my appearance. Their snickers clued me in to that right away. So, I did what I do best. I counted the tiles as I walked the hallways attempting to block out their murmurs.

When that didn't work, I hummed various theme songs in my head. It started with *Star Wars* and *Superman*, but when I briefly glanced upward to see Leah and her herd of followers on the opposite side of the hallway, it quickly changed to *Jaws*. And as I imagined a great white launching from the crowd, its mouth wide open right above them, I managed a smile, successfully sidestepping them without being seen.

Now, it's last period, and I'm exhausted. Mentally. Physically. Emotionally.

Slouched over my desk, I scribble various geometric shapes on a piece of notebook paper, successfully tuning out the physics lecture about circuits.

Seriously? When the hell am I ever going to use mega ohms in real life?

Try never.

So I doodle, because doodling will maintain my basic brain function during this mind-numbing class, said basic brain functions being essential to life.

Unlike circuits.

I'm finishing up what could be the world's most perfect octagon, when out of the blue, Genny's words echo in my mind.

"It's what you leave behind for others to carry forward that should define you…"

My pencil stops, and I contemplate the harsh truth behind her statement. What's the point of our existence if we leave nothing behind to signify we were here in the first place?

I mean, it all seems kind of pointless otherwise. Which leads me to wonder, is there a specific reason for our existence? Is every life granted for a reason? Or are we meant to be nothing more than insignificant pieces of a never-ending puzzle?

I nibble on the end of my pencil, shredding the eraser between my teeth.

If we are all pieces of an endless puzzle, do we have to be insignificant? Do we even have a say in whether we are a defining part, distinct in our edges? Or is our existence chosen for us, and if so, does that mean I'm destined to be nothing more than some filler piece?

Rapid-fire questions come one after another, creating a whirlwind of thoughts that cloud my mind. With each new thought, the truth of my meaningless existence looms. And *my* truth, as it becomes clear to me, is more wretched than I could've imagined. Because by my own volition, I have cast myself as a spectator of my own life.

A slow burn begins to churn in my stomach, and my entire body thrums with a sudden influx of energy. That's when it happens.

I clench my teeth, overcome by an emotional surge I haven't felt in years.

Anger.

My head shakes back and forth in silent rejection.

I am not a filler piece. I do not accept that.

Right on cue, I hear Lukas in my mind.

"Because in the end, it's not about what others see, but how you see yourself."

As I take root in those words, my soul is stirred, unfurling as though waking from a long sleep. It stretches languidly, and as it does, I revel in the unfamiliar warmth seeping through my body, energizing my heart and soul. I know this now, without a shadow of a doubt: I've been *existing*, not *living*.

Only I possess the power to free my soul.

The laughter and joy I've experienced within the last year has been necessary and sustaining, but when it comes to actually living, well…that decision couldn't and can't be made for me. For years, I've allowed others to dictate how I see myself. I've accepted their opinions. *I've* been suffocating *my* soul.

But I'm tenacious.

And today I take my stand.

I will live.

"Because in the end, it's not about what others see, but how you see yourself."

My eyes flit to my torn leggings and pleated skirt, and I lift my foot, examining my Docs.

Who am I?

Well, while I do know I shouldn't be defined by what I wear, I have to admit, I feel a little…badass right now.

Am I a badass?

I lift my head, finding enough courage to glance at the kids around me. No one is paying attention to me during my epic realization, so I take time to really look at them.

Eric Warner is staring at Leah, who is next to him. He clearly likes her, and he's hoping she notices him.

I frown. I may have a bit of badassness in me, but I've done enough vying for others' attention to sympathize. Even if he is an asshole.

So, I'm part badass, part caring. *Good combination.*

I openly assess everyone in class. There are kids

studiously taking notes, others laughing with friends while passing notes, and some who give me curious looks when I happen to meet their eyes.

And with each stolen glance, I smile as I peek a little into their souls.

They're all just kids. People.

They're not all-powerful beings.

They're like me.

No, they *are* me.

Every person in this room hides their own insecurities, their need to overcompensate for the secrets they hide from everyone else, and I think they do it by creating façades so others can't see their weaknesses.

But *I* can, and I beam with the realization.

It seems I do, in fact, possess my own superhuman ability.

Because every single part I've played in my life resides in this room, and I can read them all.

Is this my edge?

Empathy?

It seems so much less significant than actual super-powers like invisibility or teleportation. But it also seems like it could make a real difference in the world around me instead of just making it infinitely easier for me to run away.

The bell rings, drawing my attention to the front of the classroom. I watch the door as it swings open. Students file slowly toward the hallway, and I stand along with them, shouldering my backpack. As we shuffle out of class, I feel strengthened by my newfound ability, no longer looking at the floor, but at the faces surrounding me. To those that meet my eyes, I give a small smile, and I'm shocked when they actually (usually) smile back.

My gaze remains level as I trek through the hallway to my locker, and even when I'm outside.

The sun is bright and the fresh fragrance of spring fills my nostrils. Inhaling sweet scents of floral blossoms and cut grass, I smile to myself, excitement growing within me.

I meet the eyes of everyone willing to look at me, and grin even wider as they assess my appearance. There's a surprising mix of shock, approval, and indifference in their returned glances.

But even more astonishing is the awareness that I feel absolutely nothing about others' reactions to my clothing or to me. I keep my head held high and walk with pride, my contented smile possibly looking borderline drug-induced to those who don't know me.

Speaking of which…

I eagerly glance around the parking lot, trying to find the other Wildflowers while approaching the bus, but it seems like they aren't here just yet.

My eyes drift over several groups of people, until they finally lock on Leah Allen making her way to a brand new white BMW. I track her through the crowd, astonished when I see her head tipping in a familiar, submissive angle…down, toward her feet. The brand new purse she's proudly displayed for the last couple of days, the same one that soaked up some of my hamburger at lunch, dangles from her wrist.

An older man opens the driver's side door and steps out onto the pavement. Her father, no doubt. He's impeccably dressed in a three-piece suit that's most likely tailored, but it's not his clothing that captures my attention.

It's his harsh, exasperated expression. Anger so eerily familiar, so close to my heart, I can't look away. He stalks to the passenger side of the car like a predator eyeing its prey. As though sensing blood in the water, he homes in on the purse, yanking it from her arm and waving it in front of her face. Leah offers no explanation when he begins to shout. She simply folds into herself while maintaining her lowered stare, flinching every now and then as he wildly gestures.

Oh my God.

When he finally stops yelling, his entire face is crimson, and the veins lining his throat bulge as if they'll pop. He forces the purse back into her chest, then grips her upper arm with one of his hands while using the other to fling the car door open. He shoves her into the seat, and when she's settled he leans down to whisper something in her ear. Although she manages to keep her head upright, her normally stoic expression crumbles.

Fear and foreboding seal my throat shut, making it almost impossible to breathe. Right now, our dreadful history is irrelevant. Without thinking, I take a step toward the car, driven by an overwhelming need to protect her from whatever he will do next.

As if she knows, her head swings in my direction. We

lock eyes and just as I take another step, she offers me a stern shake of her head. I stop, but as though connected by some thread of understanding, we don't look away. And in this brief instance of kinship, Leah drops her mask, allowing me to see the pain she's so expertly hidden beneath the guise of "bitch." Pain I recognize as no different than my own.

"You have no idea what you've done. What this will cost me."

My brows draw together as I recall her words, and she offers me a sad, defeated smile in acknowledgment. My initial perception of her begins to change, splintering my heart from the inside as unexpected solidarity takes hold between the two of us.

Betrayed by those who are supposed to love us, to protect us from the very hurt they inflict, we find some commonality. Connection, no matter how fleeting.

Just as quickly as her mask was lowered, it slides right back into place. Leah's expression steels, all signs of vulnerability gone, and she looks forward, away from me, once again.

I would like to believe for that millisecond, Leah gave me a tiny glimpse of her weakness. Her secret. I don't think I'll ever know for sure.

A strong gust kicks up around me, whipping my hair over my shoulder. With my hand, I secure the frenzied strands at the nape of my neck, watching the white BMW as it pulls out of the parking lot.

Winds of change, indeed.

I inhale deeply and look skyward, attempting to understand the emotions rolling through me.

Frustration.

Anger.

Disappointment.

But most of all...guilt.

The first day I dig deep and find the courage to look up, I find myself seeing into the eyes of someone so much like me. Yet so different in how we handle our pain.

When the walls we've put up are taken out of play, in a way, we're really the same person. We're both innocent children, seeking nothing more than the love and acceptance of shitty parents, but coming up with absolutely nothing to hold on to.

I take in the people surrounding me. Some laugh and joke with their friends. Others read silently, on the curb or under a tree, successfully avoiding the masses of people surrounding them. I frown when I see a girl crying while talking on the phone. I wonder how many others I've willingly ignored while blinded by my own insecurity. I shake my head, and make a vow to myself.

Never again.

This is my purpose. My defining edge. My mark to be left on the world.

And from this day forward, I will find focus not on the ground beneath my feet, but the souls in front of me, silently screaming with the need to be seen.

From now on, I will see them.

8

Leave it to me to have my grand epiphany at 3:30 on a Friday afternoon, giving me no time to really exercise my newfound ability on my peers. It was kind of...anticlimactic.

It's been twenty-four hours, and I have left absolutely no mark on the world yet. So, with a new excitement coursing through me, I decide to try my hand at making an impact in group tonight.

The chairs are arranged in an arc. I lift my head, making unwavering eye contact with the person seated in front of us. Sally Gillespie, our counselor, quietly returns my gaze. Her eyes are intelligent, her blonde hair is gathered in an unassuming ponytail, and she's clad in her usual counseling attire: black yoga pants and a T-shirt with some funny phrase that only a psychologist would appreciate printed across the chest. Tonight, however, I actually understand the joke, and snort when I read it: *Pavlov? That name rings a bell.*

She's beautiful. Sweet. Soft-spoken. But best of all, she's open-minded as we divulge our innermost thoughts and fears, knowing there will never be any pressure to speak before we're ready.

Our instincts have been honed by hardship, so we've all developed an extremely protective nature when it comes to baring our souls. Sally has never once questioned us about it—she just gives us the time we need open up and talk to her. And when she counsels us, it's always with respect and patience.

So, yeah, she's good people.

Sally shifts in her chair, and I stubbornly maintain eye contact. While my natural instinct screams for me to look away first, I don't. I refuse to break our connection. I'm sure my expression is borderline feral, but I will no longer give in to my own weakness.

She eyes me suspiciously, head angled, brows furrowed, for no more than half a second. Then she grins knowingly before clearing her throat and redirecting her attention to the other Wildflowers.

"So, I'm getting an interesting vibe tonight. Anything you'd like to discuss before heading into familiar territory?"

My hand shoots upward, and three heads swivel in my direction. Sally chuckles, leaning to the side to lift the ever-present Speaking Stick from the floor. It's quite possibly the most horrendous thing I've ever laid eyes on.

It's crowned with worn, wilted feathers in an eclectic

array of colors. I take hold, and the bell dangling from the bottom jingles with the exchange of hands. I frown at it. It makes me sad that some poor tree gave one of its branches unto this absurdly decorated afterlife.

Poor thing.

When I lift my gaze, Sally looks insulted.

Genny laughs.

"It *is* ugly, Sally. Maybe try faux peacock feathers next time. Jazz it up a bit."

"But there's a bell," Sally says, her soft tone injured as she gestures toward the bottom.

I giggle, then stand.

Sally's disappointment vanishes the moment she hears me laugh. Once she's reseated, I recount the events of yesterday, starting with the lunch mishap, and ending with my final encounter with Leah.

When I'm done, I smile. A huge weight has been lifted. "I am *not* a filler piece, Sally. I will use my past to make a difference."

Sally smiles proudly, practically bouncing in her seat at my revelation.

Adam also grins.

Lukas, however, doesn't seem to react. His eyes are trained on me as I speak, but his expression remains impassive.

Genny, to my dismay, scoffs in blatant protest at the mention of my shared moment with Leah before reaching forward and yanking the stick from my grasp.

"Seriously?" She jerks out of her seat, fingers clenched tightly around the base, tone incredulous. "After everything she's done, after all the shit she's shamelessly put you through, you're willing to let it go? Just like that?" Genny shakes her head, as though trying to rid her mind of the possibility, before continuing. "Because of one"—she curls her fingers in quotation—"'woe is Leah!' moment?"

Her expression hardens. "That's bullshit. I don't believe it."

"Language!" Mrs. Rodriguez chastises from three rooms away.

Genny's eyes roll in unspoken (for once) frustration. I calmly take back the Speaking Stick and look directly at my best friend so my words cannot be mistaken. "Who are we to judge someone else's pain, Genny?" I don't feel sad, yet my eyes well with tears. "Who are we to decide a person's worth, based on what we see? Because between all of us"—I break to signal toward the others the room—"who could possibly understand more that how a person seems is often just a projected image of how they need to be seen to get by, not necessarily who they really are?"

Genny's head jolts at my adamant tone, her pink bangs falling loosely over her right eye. She pushes them away and after several seconds of us staring at each other, her brows clamp together. She reaches in my direction for the stick so she may speak.

Reluctantly, I hand it over.

"Like I said yesterday, I am who I am. And who I am

not is someone who makes it my mission to better my own pitiful existence by bullying others, like the very person you're suddenly so focused on protecting. She's a shit human being."

My anger flares. Because she's so focused on Leah, she's not hearing what I'm saying. And I'm so tired of not being heard. I laugh without humor, yanking the stick back into my possession.

Sally jerks upright and out of her chair, and as much as I would like to think it's to calm the brewing storm, I have my suspicions that her main concern is protecting her Speaking Stick from irreparable damage.

Her tiny frame enters my periphery as I respond, "Well, Genny, I'm sad to inform you that we all can't be as perfect as you." There's a shared inhalation around me, but I keep on going. "Healing is a process, consisting of many stages. Yet you expect everyone to be at your level. And that's completely unfair when some of us are just getting started."

Equal parts pride and panic drive my erratic heartbeat. Sally ceases her movement to watch both of us while I stand with the stupid stick gripped so tightly in my hand it tremors.

The living room is silent, save for our breathing.

Genny's brow lifts into two perfectly formed arches, and then...she smiles. No, she beams. A full-on, blinding grin. She makes no move toward the stick, instead bucking the rules and stating without permission, "So, my lioness awakens."

I try to fight it, but can't help it—I grin back in her direction. Together we take our seats, no words necessary. Graciously, I hand the Speaking Stick back to Sally, who lovingly strokes its feathers on her way back to her chair.

From then on, the session proceeds pretty typically. Here are some highlights.

Sally to Adam: "Have you attempted to make contact with your family?"

Adam: "Hell no."

Sally shares a heartfelt lecture with regards to the importance of closure.

Sally to Genny: "When was the last time you used?"

Genny: "Heroin? Not since entering Sacred Heart over two years ago."

Sally: "Your question concerns me. Is there another drug you struggle with?"

Genny: "No. Well…I *did* down an entire six-pack about half an hour ago in preparation for this session. Since it was purely strategic, I don't think it counts as an addiction."

Me: *giggles*

Sally: "Well, six is better than the twelve you downed last week. I must be making progress." *grins as she writes*

It's not until Lukas's turn that I actually start paying attention.

"Lukas." Sally turns her full attention to him, placing her pen gently on top of her notebook. I recognize the gesture. It's her silent illustration that he can speak without fear of being recorded. "Would you like to discuss the events that led you to Sacred Heart?"

Lukas's dark brows slant, and he grips the back of his neck, focusing on his well-worn boots as he speaks. "Not here."

We try (and fail) to hide our surprise. In all our sessions, he's never indicated any possibility of opening up about his past. Genny's eyes find mine, and she smiles, most likely planning the intricate details of the Wildflowers ceremony as Sally speaks.

"We can speak privately in my office, if you like?"

He shakes his head. "No."

Sally smiles gently, as she has done with all of us when we haven't felt ready to talk. I respect her ability to look genuine and not hurt when we won't open up. She clears her throat and offers softly, "Well, whenever you're ready." Her eyes linger on him momentarily before she addresses the group.

"Thank you for finding the courage to share with me some pieces of yourselves. I know it's daunting, and I know you don't know me, but with each session I grow closer to knowing and truly understanding each of you. We can travel this road together, if you'll have me on your journeys. I can and would very much like to help, but only when and if you find it within yourselves to trust me. I know it's not easy, but I'm here for you. Always."

I offer her a shy smile in thanks as we all rise to our feet. She returns it with her own before exiting the living room.

Genny has no problem with retaking control of the group. "Wildflowers." She dips her head in reverence, and it's all I can do not to laugh. "The ceremony shall commence in T-minus thirty minutes."

As one, our eyes flit to a well-known key ring suddenly sprung from her pocket, dangling from the tips of her fingers. "Mrs. Rodriguez said we could borrow the truck until eight."

And just like that, in a '65 Chevy in need of massive repair, we're gone.

9

Genny dumps the contents of her backpack onto the grass in front of us, and we gawk openly.

"You were not kidding about the s'mores," I say through laughter.

When a Toblerone lands on the heap of graham crackers and marshmallows, my head jerks upward in question. Genny answers with a shrug. "It's the best I could do. Mrs. Rodriguez, with her five food groups, clearly missed the memo about a sixth having been mandated by youth everywhere. Or maybe not, since I found her chocolate stash a couple of months ago."

I gasp, appalled. "You've been holding out on us."

She waggles her eyebrows, then in Limp Bizkit "Nookie" style offers her response. "I did it all for the *nougat*."

We allow her to go on for the full chorus, but when she

brings her hands to her mouth to begin an impromptu and completely irrelevant beatbox session, I cut her off with a stern shake of my head. "No. Stop it."

She stops, but the distant look in her eyes tells me she's still reciting lines in her head. My deadpan stare remains on her until she finally gives up. "Fine," she growls.

"Ceremony?" I prompt, crossing my arms over my chest. "We only have an hour, Limp."

I rub my upper arms, chilled by the night air. While my gloves may provide some warmth to my hands and fore-arms, I'm only wearing a tank top. In the moment, I wasn't really concerned with grabbing anything warmer, but now with goosebumps rippling over my skin, I realize my hasty mistake. My lower body is golden, though. Fleece pajama pants are the best invention ever, even if they do have pickles topped with Santa hats all over them.

Don't ask. I picked them out at a second-hand store. They called to me and I took pity on them.

Genny, however, is expertly shielded from the chilly spring night with a cardigan. Gray kittens cover every single inch of fabric, all in different positions. Some even paw at balls of yarn.

I squint at the painful sight and frown. It's quite tragic.

Tearing my gaze from her, I look around at the other Wildflowers to realize it's not only Genny who's dressed for the elements. Adam is wearing an extremely worn bomber jacket and Lukas is donning a thick, black hoodie that looks rather cozy and enticing. Or maybe that's just him.

I exhale in defeat. So, I'm the only underdressed idiot in the bunch. Awesome. Teeth chattering, I look to Genny again and repeat, "Seriously, Genny. Ceremony. Right *meow*. Some of us are freezing out here."

Genny smiles graciously, then motions to her cardigan before offering me a well-deserved deathblow.

"My Gee-Gee made me this." She pauses. "Before she died." And as if that wasn't dramatic enough, she throws in, "Leaving me with no kin."

Knife. In. My. Heart.

I'm *such* an asshole.

My mouth flies open, ready to spew an apology, but she cuts me off with an impish grin. "I happen to think it's *purrrrrrfect* for tonight."

Our chuckles ring through the air, then she clasps her hands together and her expression solidifies into one of respect, ready to start the ceremony.

"So, first, introductions are to be made."

Adam and I grin at each other, then watch Genny as she kneels down and unzips the front zipper on her backpack to extract a flashlight. Lukas looks on silently, but his eyes are lit with curiosity. I begin to bounce from one foot to the other in attempt to keep warm, rubbing my biceps.

Genny rises, flicks the light on, and signals with a jerk of her head. "This way." Single file, we follow her through the long blades of grass. Interspersed are several patches of light purple and pink wildflowers. I try not to step on them as we walk.

Several minutes later, we finally arrive at our destination. On a muddy bank lining the pond, our small patch of wildflowers is in full bloom, the stark white petals differing from the many other colorful blossoms that have overtaken the field behind us. They bend and bow with an oncoming breeze, and I smile, picturing them waving at us as if cheerfully greeting old friends. Genny grins with similar recognition.

Slowly, she crouches to the ground, lovingly curling her fingers around the blossom of the closest wildflower. "Lukas."

He begins to take a step forward, but halts suddenly, his expression taut across his face. He stares at the ground in contemplation before turning to face me.

Taken completely by surprise, I can do nothing but gape as he curls his fingers under the hem of his hoodie and whips it over his head in one swift movement.

It's quite possibly the sexiest thing I've ever witnessed.

To make matters worse, I'm ogling the movement of his muscles beneath his white T-shirt as he wordlessly shoves the hoodie in my face. Even Adam is helpless facing this glorious display. He exhales sharply next to me, and I elbow him in the ribs. And then, the impossible happens.

Because standing in front of me, Lukas holds my eyes for a brief moment, then—I kid you not—he shakes his head and...*grins.*

Teeth flash, and Lord help me, a dimple sinks deep into his left cheek. Adam and I sigh in unison, which only serves to broaden his smile.

And in this moment, I know I'm totally and utterly screwed.

My entire body crackles as I take hold of his offering, the body heat trapped in his hoodie instantly warming my hands. It smells like him. And I know with absolute certainty I was right.

A simple smile from Lukas White is most certainly enough to sustain a thousand broken souls. *Mine included.*

He looks back to the ground. "You're cold."

"Thank you," I respond, smiling meekly in appreciation.

He silently acknowledges my gratitude with a dip of his head before turning back to Genny. She's looking at me, her grin unconcealed.

When Lukas slowly kneels beside her, I lift the hoodie to slide it over my head. Adam chuckles beside me, elbowing me in the ribs this time while I'm defenseless. I curse him from within the heavenly confines of the hoodie before poking my head through the neck hole and pushing my arms through the sleeves.

Ignoring us, Genny wisely continues with the introductions. "Lukas, these are our wildflowers. Our namesakes." She gestures to the field behind us, brimming with colored blossoms. "You see, every one of these flowers will eventually succumb to the seasons' brutality. Mark my words, all will be worn down by extreme heat and by the middle of summer, they'll be gone. Every single one."

Her hand stalls on the white flowers still dancing happily in the breeze beside her. "Except *these* badasses, because they're stubborn. Resilient. They will last long after the others are gone. Like us, they continue to flourish in defiance of the demanding seasons. Their strength and ferocity stem from below the surface where their roots are forever tangled, interwoven in such a way that for the remainder of time they will bloom together, and when winter finally prevails, they perish as one. But even in death they remain connected, thriving within the comfort only they can provide each other, until spring brings them to life once again."

Genny angles her head and smiles lovingly at the wildflowers, then cups an open blossom between her hands. After a silent moment shared between the two, she releases it and looks to Lukas. "Wildflowers, this is Lukas. He's one of us."

Without another word, she rises and steps away, allowing ample time for Lukas to familiarize himself with the flowers in question. My teeth sink into my bottom lip as I watch him reach forward and timidly brush the velvety petals with the tip of his finger. His hardened expression relaxes, and when the flower cheerfully waves back at him, the corner of his mouth lifts, softening it further.

God, he's beautiful.

I take a quick sharp breath, to make sure I can still breathe.

He gives the flower another gentle stroke, then gingerly trails his finger down the stem. Once through, he remains crouched in a silent moment of kindred connection, then after another meaningful touch of the white petal, he rises.

And I as watch the encounter, the oddest thing happens. Or maybe I just imagine it.

But I could swear that the flower stills, then with all its tiny might, lengthens its stem to follow him as he stands. She stretches herself to her limit, but sadly, she cannot follow. Eventually she concedes, drooping in defeat when he turns away before giving him a despondent wave goodbye.

I offer her a sympathetic grin.

I know how you feel, my friend.

As soon as Lukas has risen to his full height, Genny pins each of us with a lengthy stare. "We, the four of us, are bound together by our own horrific pasts. But within this group, we find solace in each other because only we can truly comprehend the devastation endured. And the devastation we will endure. Because the truth is, winter is inevitable. But I find comfort in the fact that we have each other to hold on to until spring finds us once again."

She glances at the patch of white flowers then back to Lukas. "So yeah. The very definition of being a Wildflower is just that. We're bound so closely that your pain is our pain. Your story is no longer just yours to bear—it's ours. And when winter strikes any of us, we perish together knowing we will rise together as well. We are four, but we are one. And together, there's nothing we can't overcome."

Genny's face splits into a wide, shit-eating grin as she concludes, "Plus, I'm Genesis. I'm the creator. So, you really don't have a say. You just are."

I roll my eyes and shake my head.

Adam barks a laugh.

Lukas remains silent, but his gaze drops to the wild-flowers before it lifts to meet our eyes. And when he finds mine, I know her message has been received loud and clear. Vulnerable Lukas looks back at me.

And although we've always known he would, he now has finally accepted his fate.

As the Fourth and final Wildflower.

10

As we trek back to our fire pit, the cicadas fill the silence with a beautiful symphony. I inhale deeply with the breeze, taking in the floral scent surrounding us. With my hands deep in the hoodie's toasty front pockets, I glance over my shoulder to make sure Lukas isn't suffering without it.

His piercing eyes lock onto mine, sending a jolt through my heart. It stammers within my chest, then begins to race. I offer him a smile, but instead of getting one in return, he breaks eye contact and runs his hand through his hair.

I look forward, remembering and replaying the one and only smile I'd seen given by Lukas White. And as the moment repeats over and over in my mind, it dawns on me.

Oh my God.

Maybe that smile wasn't meant for me at all.

Maybe it was meant for Adam.

I gasp internally at the revelation and glance at Adam and Genny, arm-in-arm ahead of me. Adam throws his head back in laughter at something Genny says, and my lips pucker.

Could it be?

I mean, Adam is hot. Definitely. With those high cheeks bones and rounded lips, his face is perfectly sculpted. And he's nice. If Lukas is into Adam, then yeah, it's obvious they would be perfect together. Yin and yang. Outspokenness and brooding silence. Light and dark. Skinny jeans and boot cut.

I'm so stupid.

I deflate with the realization that he's completely out of reach. Unobtainable. Can it really be that my heart is so traitorous it would lead me down another path of longing for unrequited affection?

If that's the case, my heart is seriously an asshole.

My eyes roll in frustration just as the sound of booted feet falls into sync with mine. My heart, the asshole that it is, kicks up in response to Lukas's being near. I shake my head to clear my thoughts, then plaster a grin on my face and direct it in his direction.

His eyes are trained on the ground (so much for his advice to me earlier), but he asks, "You warm?"

"Yeah. Thanks."

I look ahead again, surprised by my response. Maybe monosyllabic communication is contagious. But before I can test my theory, we arrive at our fire pit, and Genny has the fire blazing wildly in no time. Then she, no joke, falls onto the heap of marshmallows, graham crackers, and Toblerone as though she hasn't seen food in a month. Adam reaches forward, ripping open the packages as they're handed to him in order to speed along the process. Lukas begins the s'more assembly, while I unthread hangers, perfect roasting tools. We work silently as a unit and before I know it, marshmallows are burned to the point of almost being inedible, melted chocolate is sandwiched between graham crackers, and we've each stuffed at least two s'mores into our mouths.

Much like in group, we sit in an arc formation—ordered by our Wildflower initiation dates—and watch the flames as they dance in front of us, content in our existence together.

Until Adam breaks the silence.

"My parents were the best parents a kid could ask for. I never wanted for anything. I loved them more than anything, and they loved me completely…right up to the moment they found me making out with Seth Wright in my room. Someone I also loved, and thought loved me, too." He laughs silently, though there is no amusement in his expression. His solemn eyes remain focused on the flames in front of him. "My parents flipped. They banned me from their home, and I was whisked away to Sacred Heart as punishment for my deviance and forced to transfer schools. And Seth, well, I guess he was so freaked at being outed by my parents, he was literally scared *straight*, or at least into pretending to be like he was before we met. Regardless, what I thought we had together obviously wasn't worth fighting for, because I never saw him again. I was left with absolutely nothing. No one. Just for being who I am."

He directs a weak smile at the ground then looks me in the eyes, his clear, blue gaze unassuming, honest. "I don't really know what's worse, Chloe. I really don't. To experience the feeling of being loved only to find out it didn't actually apply to you, or never receiving it at all."

I toss the rest of my uneaten s'more into the fire and answer truthfully, "Me neither. I mean, either way it all pretty much sucks, right? I don't think your pain is any less than mine. It's just…different. It still hurts, all the same."

"Yeah." Adam nods, finishing off his third.

Genny takes this moment to join in. "To quote Mary Poppins, my parents were 'practically perfect in every way.'" She shrugs. "I started using for no other reason than the fact that I could. There's really no other explanation. I was a kid, caught up in doing what kids my age did. At that time, it was purely recreational: weed, coke, X. I wasn't angry, not then. It wasn't until their car accident that I started abusing. That's when I switched to heroin." She runs her thumb over her scars before leveling me with knowing eyes. "I was constantly pummeled by voices in my head, each one serving as a constant reminder of my grief. I suppose it was easier for me at the time, to try to block the ugly truth that I had wasted my last year or so with them being high. The fact that I couldn't remember them coming to my room to wish me something so simple as a 'goodnight'…those are moments I would give anything to experience again."

Tears well up in her eyes when she meets our stares. "I'll never get that time back. And to make matters worse, when I moved in with my grandmother, with Gee-Gee, I was so fucking angry. I hated her, but only because I hated myself. Then she was gone, I was addicted to heroin, and I had nothing to show for our time together except this hideous cardigan that I happen to love because she made it for me."

She looks at the sleeves, turning her arms back and forth to see the different patterns. The longing I see in her expression slices my heart in two. "Yet, Gee-Gee will never know. This is how I know she loved me, but she'll never know that I know, that I love her, too."

Genny shakes her head. "Such a waste. So many missed opportunities."

From beside me, Lukas watches our interaction with interest, fully aware of our backstories from group. And although we've already heard it, I understand Genny's need to recount her story. Healing is a process, and souls are fragile things. Although a soul can be mended, fissures remain, leaving it susceptible to completely shattering at any time. Sometimes the only way to keep that from happening is to talk about the past, the crushing weight of the memories lessened with each word.

Although, this is the first time Genny's ever mentioned Gee-Gee. A part of me wonders why, but a greater part feels an overwhelming sense of pride that she chose us to share something with, something that was so clearly protected—hidden—within the confines of her heart.

Lukas, too, tosses the remainder of his s'more into the flames, but just as he brings his chocolate-coated thumb to his mouth, I force myself to look away.

Then, taking my cue from Genny, I share my story too.

"My parents definitely weren't perfect, but I was born into a life of privilege. My father was the CEO of a global tech company, a multi-millionaire, my mother his trophy. How I was conceived I'll never understand. The two of them rarely spoke to each other. He was never home, and she was perpetually planning her next cocktail party, both on paths that never seemed to intersect."

I shrug, sadness weighing my shoulders. "For as long as I can remember, I simply didn't exist in my parents' eyes. Not when I won the fifth grade science fair, not when I cried myself to sleep because I wasn't pretty enough to make the cheerleading squad, and definitely not during pivotal moments of indecision when some guidance, or limits even, would have been useful: like whether or not losing my virginity at fourteen was a good idea, or whether or not being taken advantage of while too drunk to peel my eyes open, much less fend off an aggressor, was considered rape."

Three sharp intakes of air sound around me, but I'm more than prepared for their reactions. Although Genny and Adam knew about my attempted suicide, I gave them only partial truth. I didn't just do it to get my parents' attention. Until tonight, I've never told anyone this part of my past, but right here, right now, it seems right to share it.

"I kind of lost it after that. I was completely numb. It

was the only way I could look at myself in the mirror. I was disgusted in my own skin, and if I could have peeled every inch of it from my body, I would have. After weeks of hiding the pain, the absolute revulsion, I couldn't take it anymore."

Slowly, I tug the gloves free from my arms, one after another. After setting them by my side, I extend both wrists toward the light of the fire, displaying the purple lines trailing upward along the skin of my forearms. Genny and Adam have already seen the scars, but I've never shown them to Lukas. Shame and regret heat the blood in my veins—a warm flush to creeps along the tops of my cheeks. I avoid the eyes of the others, tracing one of the scars lightly with my finger.

So, this is what being vulnerable means.

I exhale a light breath. "I went to my parents' room one night, fully ready to tell them what I had done, what had been done to me, and how much I needed their help to deal with it all. But I never got the chance. Because as I stood there, as I listened to how my mother got pregnant only to secure her future and how I meant absolutely nothing to my father, it completely broke me. I was done fighting to be noticed, to be a part of their lives. So, I gave up and gave them what they wanted."

I glance at Genny, the light from the fire reflecting in her unshed tears. Adam's expression is much the same, and for a change, *I* feel the need to console *him*. I reach to the side and grip his hand, and in turn he squeezes my fingers softly, offering his encouragement and support.

I give him a wobbly smile in thanks, but the warmth of

another finger touching the scar draws my attention away from Adam's glistening eyes.

"They should have protected you, kept you safe." Lukas's baritone voice is soft, but clear. "I tried to protect someone once."

He continues tracing up and down my scar, his eyes on my arm as they track the movement. "I was abandoned on the street, found on the brink of death, wrapped in a blanket beside a dumpster. I was a 'miracle baby,' or so they said. I've read the articles, trying to track down clues about my mother, but all I found was the fact that once the hype of my survival was gone, so was I. After my fifth foster home, I gave up trying to adapt. I stopped speaking completely. To foster parents, to state-provided therapists, to anyone really. Until *her*."

Lukas's eyes lift from my arm to meet mine, and the pain reflected in them shatters my heart. I feel so insignificant within the depths of his agony, but I can't look away. My eyes remain locked with his, silently willing him to continue speaking. And seemingly lost in the moment, he does.

"It was in my last foster home. I was fifteen. Michelle was eight. She was such a tiny thing—she followed me everywhere. Never said a word, she just...followed. She would stop walking the minute I turned around, finding refuge behind any available corner, and I would wait for her curious eyes to eventually peek around the wall at me. We were cut from the same cloth. I could read her mind as though it was my own. She was scared, but for some reason, she trusted me. And I trusted her. I can't really explain it."

Lukas shakes his head, and I feel him pulling away, so I release my grip on Adam's hand and turn in Lukas's direction. Giving him my full attention, I reach forward, and brazenly take both of his hands into mine. Surprisingly, he laces our fingers together, his brows drawn tightly as he inspects our joined hands.

After some fidgeting, adjusting his grip, rethreading his fingers, he continues. "She was the first person I spoke to in years. It started slowly, a word here and there, then full sentences shared between us. Simple stuff really, but it was nice to have someone to talk to. It wasn't long until I was reading her stories every single night. I stayed with her until dawn just to make sure I was the only person who tucked her in. I wanted to make sure she felt safe. I just...I had seen so much shit happen in other homes, I refused to let it come near her. I wanted to protect her."

When Lukas looks up, a tear escapes and trails down his cheek. "But I couldn't. After months, I was exhausted. One night was all it took. I fell asleep and left her alone. When I woke, I ran to her room, and..."

He shakes his head, chin trembling. "It's burned into my memory. I see it every single night when I go to sleep. The hem of her nightgown around her neck, our disgusting *foster* parent hovering above her, hands where they shouldn't be, violating her. And God, the fear in her eyes. I just...I just fucking lost it. I pulled him off her and beat him until he was unrecognizable. I would have killed him if the cops hadn't showed. I *intended* to kill him."

Lukas grips my hands tighter, too tight, but I take the pain willingly, for him. Because I understand the need to be heard. And this is his moment, every single agonizing recollection of it. "They hauled me away on assault charges. I spent eight months in juvie then was released to Sacred Heart until I age out and the state can safely wash their hands of me."

Another tear falls. "I don't think I'll ever know what happened to Michelle. I tried to track her down, but there's no record of her anywhere. All I know for sure is I failed her. I didn't protect her."

Lukas presses our palms together, his and mine. "You should have been protected, too."

His face crumbles in defeat, and I do the only thing I can think to do. I wrap my arms around his shoulders and squeeze him so tightly even I have trouble breathing. I simply hold him as he cries, his tears dissolving into the fabric of his hoodie, and I hold him just as securely when the other Wildflowers join our embrace.

Together, as one, we absorb his pain.

Without question, as we're knotted together in a sea of arms, we relinquish and redistribute every ounce of wrongdoing, every ounce of injustice, every ounce of pain equally among the four of us. We take everything he has so vulnerably offered as though it's our own. It's the only way to make the enormity of that much pain bearable. And as we hold on to each other, flashes of Lukas and his inherent need to protect the vulnerable flood me.

In fact, since he entered our lives, I can't remember a time when he hasn't protected each of us.

I finally *see* him, and now I understand exactly what he needs. What we were meant to provide him.

Not a group of people meant to guard and protect, but a family in which he finally belongs.

So, we give him us.

And as he clenches the fabric of his hoodie in his two trembling fists, I know he willingly accepts our gift.

SUMMER

11

The heat of summer is upon us, and we have a gazillion *keep-the-kids-busy-and-out-of-trouble* projects queued up. I'm currently working with Genny on the third item on Mrs. Rodriguez's list: repainting the wooden fence lining Sacred Heart's property. All two acres.

We've done exactly two planks in as many days.

It's going to be a very long summer.

Adam has it much worse though: he's sentenced to garden upheaval and lawn maintenance.

Poor guy.

Meanwhile, Lukas has been given the task of repairing the practically unsalvageable Chevy in order to squeeze out its last remaining miles, and we use every single one of them to our advantage. Because though we may be somewhat separated during the day, at night we come together, borrowing the

Chevy to visit the wildflowers and swim in our pond.

I wipe a bead of sweat from my forehead with my bare arm, noting how free I feel, no longer bound by the need to wear my gloves. While I did wear them to finish out the school year, I don't wear them anymore. *Not here, anyway.* I shed that necessity in the tears I shared with my Wildflowers that night and there is no way to adequately describe the peace I've felt since.

April and May flew by in the blink of an eye, and a few other changes should be noted.

Surprisingly, Leah Allen gave us a wide berth the remainder of the school year. While she still played 'the bitch' to perfection, I, thankfully, was no longer on the receiving end of her displaced anger. None of us were. She even called off Eric Warner and her other minions, declaring a ceasefire on the rightful possession of the Jesus Table during lunch.

Unsurprisingly, the four of us Wildflowers became inseparable, closer than ever. And although smiles from Lukas were still rare, whenever they surfaced, they were genuine. As it turns out, Lukas White is pretty funny.

Who knew?

But even though so much happened this spring, a crucial change has yet to happen. One I still struggle with on a daily basis.

Because the night of the ceremony, when we held Lukas in our arms as he cried, the heavens split wide open to proclaim in excruciating clarity what I already knew, but refused to accept: my feelings for him had no right to exist.

It was no longer of consequence if I had feelings for Lukas, or if he had feelings for me, or for Adam.

These questions were senseless and irrelevant and needed to be banned from my mind. All my feelings needed to be pulverized until they were no more, unable to threaten the fragile threads weaving the four of us together.

My head was completely on board with this plan, knowing the inescapable damage that could be done otherwise.

My heart?

Well, what can I say?

It's still an asshole.

Which is exactly why I said yes when I was asked by Tommy Ledbetter if I'd like to go out with him to see a new rom-com this weekend. I needed the distraction. Plus, I really, really wanted to go to a movie. Lame, but true. We don't get out much.

Granted, the acceptance of his invitation was not so much mine as Genny's, since she was called upon to speak in my place. I just stood in the cereal aisle of the grocery store dumbstruck and unable to form a coherent answer. After Tommy left with the house phone number in his pocket and a smile on his face, Genny informed me the boy had been hopelessly vying for my attention at school on a daily basis. Something I may have seen, had I been, you know, "looking up." Yes, I'd definitely improved, but to expect a complete change overnight was insane.

And…Tommy Ledbetter?

I crinkle my nose in thought.

I mean, I guess he looks familiar. Maybe?

The question of his existence is still plaguing me when Genny speaks, yanking me into the present. Finishing an upstroke, she turns to me, her entire face splattered with white paint.

"Big date tonight. Finally a night out for all of us," she says, then wipes her cheek and grimaces. As much as I would like to laugh, I'm sure my appearance is much worse.

"Yeah," I dazedly respond. "Awesome."

I vaguely remember asking Mrs. Rodriguez if I could go to the movie with Tommy, and she approved. Right before she mandated that the other Wildflowers must accompany me on my…"date."

Honestly, it's all such an awkward blur.

But I'm okay with it. After my last questionable outing, I actually welcome having those I trust on standby.

"Good," Genny affirms, "because you have like, an hour to get dressed. The movie is at six thirty."

I launch myself off the ground. "No way! You're kidding, right? It's tonight?"

Her expression is disturbingly content. "No."

"No, you're not kidding, or no, it's not tonight?" I inquire, my tone half-frustrated, half-freaked the hell out.

Genny makes a poor attempt to hide her smile. "No, I'm not kidding. Yes, the movie is tonight, and Tommy called about an hour ago to confirm." Her mouth curves downward. "I guess I forgot to tell you."

"Oh my God!" I whirl around, paintbrush still in hand, and start running in the direction of the front door. Just as my canvas shoes hit the wooden deck, Lukas and Adam emerge from the house, and struck by the sight of Lukas dressed and ready for *my* date, my brain shuts completely down. Along with my coordination. And given I'm sprinting full speed, my legs buckle, my feet misstep, and before I know it, my body is sprawled out on the deck, paintbrush still in hand.

Face, meet wood.

Nice, Chloe. Real nice.

"Oh my God. Chloe, are you okay?" I recognize Adam's voice, though it's muffled by suppressed laughter.

I inhale despite my mortification, then set my chin on the plank beneath me, immediately greeted by a pair of black boots and the frayed hem of boot-cut jeans. I close my eyes, internally cringe, and release my breath. I open my eyes just in time to see Lukas White grinning down at me.

His inky hair is spiked every which way, his black T-shirt stretched across his massive chest, and that stupid dimple is winking at me as he tries not to laugh. Slowly, he crouches in my line of vision, his eyes twinkling with amusement. He extends his hand, but before I can take him up on his offer to help me up, he reaches forward and gently pinches a stray strand of my hair between his fingers to tuck it behind my ear with deliberate care.

The gesture is so tender, and it makes me remember

how sweet he was with the wildflower during the ceremony.

He's such a paradox. There is so much gentleness within him, but he hides it away.

My heart flutters in my chest, and I silently curse its action.

I place my closed fists on the wood, but before I can press myself up, two hands curl around both my biceps and easily lift me off the deck. Once I'm on my feet, the familiar scent of his soap wafts around me.

He angles his head in concern. "You okay?"

I nod. "Yeah. I just…" I glance at the brush in my hand. "I was painting."

Lukas looks behind me at Genny, whose heinous cackles are still echoing in the air, then back to me. "I thought you and Genny were painting the fence, not the deck." He grins shamelessly, and the sight steals my breath. "Interesting technique."

I avert my eyes and meet Adam's over Lukas's shoulder. No longer concerned for my well-being, he's given his laughter free rein. I glare at him, privately noting that I very much approve of his loose white button-down/black skinny jeans tucked into combat boots combo, then redirect my gaze to Lukas. "I was painting the fence, until Genny reminded me that we're going to the movies tonight." I shift my weight to my other foot then lie. "I was so excited, I just tripped."

Lukas's smile widens. "Date night with Timmy?"

"*Timmy!*"

Adam shouts the name in perfect Timmy Burch pitch as he moves to stand next to Lukas, both with boyish grins lighting up their faces. I've never really understood *South Park*.

Narrowing my eyes, I angle my head in their direction. "It's Tommy."

"*Timmy!*" Adam cries again, then I'm forced to watch as both of them break into an extremely immature fit of the giggles.

Even Genny joins in as she walks up behind me. "You're all ridiculous," she scoffs. And of course, I'm not taken the least bit seriously. Not that I can blame them. I'm sure the half-grin on my face negates any and all threat.

Adam reaches for the paintbrush still in my grasp. "And you, my dear, are a mess." With his free hand, he drags his thumb along my chin and holds the brush in front of my face.. He redirects his gaze at Genny and adds, "You're even worse. We'll clean up out here—you two clean up in the house."

I nod, then take off again, swinging the door open and flying inside with Genny on my heels.

Thirty minutes later, we're both showered and paint-free. Genny's wearing an old Pink Floyd concert tee, bell-bottom jeans that practically cover her Chucks, and a wallet tucked into her back pocket with a long chain hooked onto her front belt loop.

I smile, partly with pride, but mostly in appreciation of her obvious attempt not to scare poor Tommy.

My hair is partially dry like hers, though my waves are

more pronounced as they flow down my back, and I'm wearing a simple rugby-style T-shirt with navy and white stripes, dark blue skinny jeans, and my white, generic Keds. My makeup is minimal, much like Genny's, with a light shadow and mascara on my eyes, and a clear, shiny gloss on my lips.

It's not much, but I feel pretty and comfortable in my skin.

"You look gorgeous," Genny states, linking our arms together and leading us to the door.

I laugh. "I don't look any different."

She grins. "Oh, but you do. You just don't realize it."

As soon as we step outside, the boys turn in sync to face us. Adam beams with pride, his eyes tapering at the sides with his smile. "You ladies look beautiful this evening."

Genny rolls her eyes then releases me to take Adam's offered arm. Together, they head toward the truck, leaving me to fend for myself under the scrutiny of Lukas's stare. He quirks an eyebrow and his mouth follows suit, lifting at the corner.

I blush, nervously tugging at the hem of my shirt before once again meeting his studious gaze.

How can just his silence fluster me? "What?"

He shakes his head, still lopsidedly grinning. Wordlessly, he reaches forward and lifts my hair over my shoulder. I try not to shudder when his fingers trail down the fabric of my sleeve and cross under my elbow, but lose the battle when his thumb touches my forearm.

He drops his gaze and my eyes follow…

Oh. Shit.

My gloves. My lack of them.

Panic worms its way through my stomach. Foolishly comfortable here at the house, I hadn't even thought to hide my scars when going out… They'll be on display. People pointing, snickering, frowning, pitying. Instinctively, I move to cover them, but Lukas gently holds my wrist with his other hand.

Fear clogs my throat, and I shake my head in refusal.

No. I can't do it.

"Look at me, Chloe." His tone is stern, but not cold.

Although my head is still moving back and forth, I somehow manage to peel my gaze from my arm to meet his eyes. My chin quivers uncontrollably, and all I can think about as I look at the boy towering over me is how impossibly strong he is and how incredibly weak I am.

I don't want to be weak.

I've been living in a bubble, but it's not the real world.

I'm not ready. And I hate it.

Hate me.

His gaze is surprisingly tender, and I want to hide there in the softness of his understanding. He tightens his grip on my wrist then shakes his head. "No more hiding."

"I…I…c-can't…" I need air. Now.

Lukas answers in a soft, pleading whisper. "But you can."

Stubborn tears claw at my throat. *Fight it, Chloe. Fight it.* "Why?" *Why should I?*

"Because you have nothing to be ashamed of. These scars"—he lifts both my arms into my line of sight—"are a part of you that should never be denied. They're your battle scars, and they should be worn with pride. When I look at them, I don't see the mark of a frightened girl, but of a warrior. I see someone *I* strive to be. I just…"

He releases his hold on my arms, then runs his hands through his hair. "When you cover them, I can't *see* you. And I need to see you, Chloe. I can't explain it, I just do."

His admission steals my breath, but I force myself to remain impassive, silently allowing him the time he needs to speak. After a couple of seconds, Lukas shakes his head. "I'm sorry. This isn't about me or my needs. It's about you."

He rests his hands on my shoulders then presses his thumbs underneath my jaw, tipping my head so I'm given no choice but to meet his eyes. "You're scared. I understand that. But can you honestly look me in the eyes and tell me these past few weeks without those gloves haven't been liberating?"

I'm still barely breathing.

"You don't need them for comfort. You don't need them to conceal a goddamn thing. What you need is to look the world straight in the eye, give it the middle finger in honor of your shit past, and laugh your ass off because you came out on top. Then, just for spite, you need to laugh a little more, because you came out so far on top, the only person who can look down on you from where you're left standing is you. No one else."

Wow. Okay.

So, Lukas had absolutely no problem communicating that.

In these moments, I see the protective big-brother heart that Michelle must have seen. She had him in her life a short time, but I doubt she's forgotten him. Her guardian angel. *Her avenging angel.*

A hint of amusement tugs at my lips, and although I find myself wanting to say, "Sir, yes sir!" what actually comes out is a defiant, "I can give the world the middle finger."

Lukas grins then drops his hands to gesture to space around us. "I know you can. So, let's see it."

Breathy laughter escapes me, and I roll my eyes. Slowly, I lift my arm and deliberately extend my middle finger for the whole wide world to see.

Behind Lukas, the door of the truck swings open, and the sun reflects off Genny's pink hair. "Well, fuck you, too!" she shouts. "Now, Lukas, if you're done corrupting our precious Wildflower, we have a movie to get to or we're going to be late for our date. Plus, I need popcorn, stat."

"*Timmy!*" Adam eloquently adds.

Lukas chuckles, falling into step with me in the direction of the Chevy and leaning into me as we walk.

"Speaking of Timmy…"

"Tommy," I correct.

"Just so you know, if he so much as glances at you in a way I feel is disrespectful, I will end him."

I laugh. "Aren't you like, on probation or something?"

"Yeah," Lukas admits, shoving his hands in his pockets and looking wistfully up at the sky. "But some people are just worth fighting for."

12

We coast into the movie theater's parking lot, the four of us crammed into the cab like sardines. I start to make a clown car joke as Lukas kills the engine, but I'm shocked into silence when the truck protests with a backfire of deafening proportion. The near explosion startles a group of young girls passing by the front of the truck. A collective shriek sounds, then several pairs of eyes narrow in our direction. As soon as Lukas waves his apology, every single one of their faces breaks into a stupid, dopey grin.

I gag and roll my eyes.

Next to me, Genny does the same, and I silently thank her for her support.

Meanwhile, Lukas proclaims his innocence with a flash of his palms while choking back laughter.

Disappointed by his lack of participation in our theatrics,

I turn to glare at Adam, but my anger falls short.

Adam is the most easygoing person I know. But this—a clenched jaw, narrowed eyes, pinched lips, and a hardened glare burning a hole through the window? *What the hell?*

My face falls in confusion, and I turn to follow his stare. My eyes skate over the parking lot, until they lock on a group of people loitering in front of the theater.

When I turn back with a curious expression, a muscle ticks along Adam's jaw and his stare lingers on the group before he faces me. And though his expression is furious, his eyes are raw, broadcasting an undeniable emotion.

Heartbreak.

He doesn't have to say one word for me to know who is in that crowd.

Seth Wright.

Anger boils within me. It heats my face and scorches my blood, the torment in Adam's eyes serving as an accelerant. Instinctively my fists clench, and as though sensing my need for retribution, Adam gives his head a minute shake.

Genny makes a threatening gesture at the young ladies still ogling Lukas and watches in supreme satisfaction when they scatter. With a grin, she turns to me, but her smiles quickly fades. "You okay?"

"Yeah. I'm just nervous," I lie.

Adam looks again to the crowd, and I lean forward, snatching my purse from the floorboard in frustration. "Let's get this over with."

Genny's eyes widen in shock. She angles her head, and

when I offer no response, she looks to Lukas for answers. He shrugs his reply, and if circumstances were different, I would totally laugh at the silent, yet incredibly awkward exchanges occurring between us. It seems our group, usually so in sync, has difficulty functioning outside the walls of Sacred Heart. A simple trip to the local movie theater has thrust us into a tailspin.

"Well then," Lukas announces, his dimple sinking into his cheek.

He opens his door, prompting Adam to do the same. We all pile out of the truck, and once our feet hit the ground, I make my way to Adam.

"We don't have to go in. I can reschedule. It's fine. We can do it another night."

Adam's lips pinch tightly, and he shakes his head. "No. I was bound to run into him at some point. I hoped I wouldn't, prayed for it actually, but obviously that prayer fell on deaf ears."

Yeah. I get that. I mean, one good thing about being so far away from home is that I don't have to worry about running into my last…"date."

Adam forces a smile then wraps an arm around my shoulder. "I can't complain, really. I mean, three others were answered when I met you guys."

My heart squeezes and just like that, the need to murder Seth Wright floods me all over again.

As the four of us approach the ticket line, I breathe a sigh of relief when the loitering group (including Seth) enters the building. The rigidity of Adam's muscles lessens, and he releases me, stepping ahead to request our tickets.

He distributes them and with tickets in hand, we turn... and run smack dab into Tommy Ledbetter.

His brown hair curls at the ends, falling across his forehead and brushing the rounded lenses of his glasses. He smiles shyly at me before his eyes drift to my scarred arms. And, as if they have a sixth sense, the Wildflowers tense around me.

To his credit, he says nothing. He simply lifts his stare, still smiling, and I grin back at him. After an awkward moment of silence, he introduces himself to the boys. And to their credit, no *South Park* references are made. After shaking their hands and giving Genny a friendly side-hug, he hangs back with me while we enter the concession area.

Tommy and I watch as Genny over-ambitiously purchases a tub of popcorn that could feed a small country and fall far behind the other three as we make our way to the indicated theater. Ridiculous. Three teenage chaperones. It's laughable.

"You look really pretty tonight, Chloe," he states, opening the door, chivalrous.

I smile, glancing at my attire. "Thanks." Tucking a stand of hair behind my ear, I add, "You look great, too." Shaking my head, I awkwardly amend, "I mean, not that you said I look great or anything."

Oh my God. What is wrong with me?

He laughs, still holding the door as I pass him. "I'm

officially rephrasing. Not only do you look pretty, you look great."

His voice carries a slight tremble. *He's as nervous as I am.* Not only do I find it endearing, it's incredibly comforting. I aim my grin at the floor, my hair falling like a curtain to conceal it.

The theater isn't as full as I imagined it would be, and finding seats proves easy enough. I take note of the familiar cackles and murmurs, pegging the rest of the crew to be a good distance behind us. Surprised, yet thankful they're not directly behind us, I settle in.

The first half of the movie is pretty standard. Boy meets girl. Girl is pretty, but not enough to get the boy's attention. Or so she thinks. Then in an incredibly lame attempt—totally my opinion here—she completely alters her appearance in order to get his attention.

And it's at right about this point when I start to lose focus on the movie.

Tommy yawns next to me, lifting his arms into a wide stretch, deliberately resting one along my shoulders.

As soon as his fingers curl around my upper arm, several kernels of popcorn whiz by my head. Some lodge into my hair, while several others plummet to the ground by our feet. Tommy doesn't seem to notice.

I roll my eyes, summoning every ounce of patience I possess before turning around. Three pairs of eyes avoid mine, studiously trained on the movie. I narrow my glare. When none of them dare to make eye contact, I whip back around and relax into Tommy's hold.

Around the time the on-screen couple shares their first kiss, I rest my head on Tommy's shoulder out of sheer boredom. Just as I begin a thorough examination of my nails, an entire bucket's worth of buttery goodness is launched and lands into our laps. Tommy gasps, surprised, probably holding back an expletive. Catching onto our "chaperones'" little game, I stay calm, refusing to give them the satisfaction of the response they're so clearly trying to instigate. After releasing a defeated breath, Tommy removes his arm to silently wipe the popcorn from his legs, prompting a subtle cacophony of snickers behind us.

Unable to do anything else, I lift my head, shrug apologetically, and smile to hide my frustration. "I'm so sorry. It seems my friends have only recently graduated kindergarten."

I grab a handful of popcorn from my lap, tossing some into my mouth. Tommy laughs softly. "Nah. I get it." He folds his hands and sets them on his thighs. I look down and pray the grease hasn't ruined his khakis.

For the remainder of the movie, Tommy sits ramrod straight with his hands knitted securely together in his lap, and all I can focus on is how disappointed I am. *He gave in so easily.* I mean, it was just some kernels of popcorn.

By the time the credits roll, my mood is sour, and my stomach hurts because Genny put entirely too much butter on the popcorn. Tommy and I rise from our seats in unison, then slide out of the row. Once I'm free, I glare upward, waiting for Genny, Adam, and Lukas to make their way down the steps. When I'm met with their shit-eating grins, my scowl deepens.

I'm too frustrated to say anything.

I turn on my heel, giving my "friends" the cold shoulder, and smile angelically at Tommy. His returning gaze is one of apprehension. I have no idea if it's residual anxiety from the popcorn assault, or if he's figured out that I'm about two seconds from losing my shit.

Honestly, it doesn't matter. The night is a lost cause at this point.

We head out of the theater where Tommy, unsurprisingly, wishes us a collective and uneventful goodnight before racing to the safety of the parking lot. I watch until he's safely to his car then whirl around with my hands on my hips, glaring angrily.

At Genny.

Her eyes flare wide, and she brings her hands dramatically to her chest, as though appalled at my insinuation. "What? I had nothing to do with it."

When I cock my head, she amends, "I swear to you, any alleged shenanigans, that may or may not have occurred upon the invasion of your personal space, were not *my* idea."

I deliberate, eyeing her intensely. When she doesn't falter, I lift my chin in approval and slide my eyes to Adam.

He chuckles while shaking his head. "Nope. Try again."

His thumb flies to the side, openly incriminating Mr. Tall, Dark, and Broody.

Lukas? What?

I dismiss him entirely and reroute my silent accusation back to Genny. She laughs then jerks her head in Lukas's direction.

When given no other choice, I finally glance at him. With brows raised and hands shoved deep in his pockets, the subtle grin on his face is all I need. Although slight, it's an open confirmation of his guilt, and his total lack of shame for his actions.

Why would he do that to Tommy? But as I begin to ask the question, the door of the theater flies opens and the sound of boisterous laughter distracts me. My eyes glide smoothly over Lukas's shoulder and lock on the same group from earlier. Adam tenses, and even though it amounts to only a miniscule shift in his demeanor, its effects are immediate.

Suddenly, I'm in his bedroom, present in the exact moment his entire world is upended. Bonds severed, trust violated, and love forsaken, the impact of all three losses whirling so out of control, there's nothing left for an innocent heart to hold on to.

I feel the pain carving into his heart, into *mine*. Fury. That's what fills me until it's no longer containable. I angrily shoulder past my group and stomp toward Seth's. *It's time to know who you destroyed, asshole.* Several people turn to watch, and they look amused…briefly.

My swift steps soon come to a grinding halt, and completely disregarding the six-foot-something men towering over me, I inquire, "Which one of you is Seth Wright?"

I'm seething—my fingers are curled so tightly against my waist they bite into my skin. The heads previously aimed at me swivel on their necks toward the person in question. With eyes the color of honey and just as warm, Seth studies me. He raises his hand. Apprehensively. *As he should.*

He is rather easy on the eyes. Dark brown hair styled into an off-center peak, equally dark lashes framing light brown eyes, and a grin that's surprisingly captivating.

And strikingly sincere.

Jerk.

"That would be me." He steps forward just as the sound of several scampering feet from behind alerts me to the Wildflowers' presence.

"Chloe. Stop," Adam says, breathing heavily.

As soon as Adam's words leave his mouth, Seth's entire body seizes in recognition, and his easy smile wanes. I watch from below as his eyes find Adam's, fully expecting a spiteful glare and an explosion of intolerant slurs to be directed at my friend. And with my hands balled into fists, I'm more than ready for them. I'll gladly take on *all* these assholes. Badass Chloe, it seems, has resurfaced.

But none of that happens.

Seth's shocked stare softens into undeniable admiration, and his lips curve into a shy smile. He shakes his head in subtle disbelief, then seemingly transfixed by Adam's presence, wordlessly bypasses me with a single step in his direction.

I turn, my fury dissipating. *What's happening?*

Adam's jaw is set as he stares at the ground, refusing

to look at Seth. Undeterred, Seth continues walking until they're standing Nikes-to-Docs, and when Adam further denies Seth his eyes, Seth lifts his arm.

Lukas tenses next to me, no doubt watching Seth's reaction for any sign of violence, his entire body on high alert. But when Seth tenderly cups Adam's cheek and strokes it gently, Lukas relaxes. Genny moves to my side and in unison, the three of us step to the left to better see their faces.

When Adam's eyes finally rise, they're full of unshed tears. His chin quivers and he swallows deeply, the pain of Seth's betrayal so clearly evident in his tortured stare. Several seconds pass, neither saying a word as they stand in silent conversation.

A tear escapes, coursing its way down Adam's cheek, and he looks away, ending their exchange. But not for long, because as soon as his head shifts downward, Seth captures his face with his other hand and forces Adam to meet his eyes. Seth's gaze is intent as it peruses Adam's features. It's as though he's in awe that Adam is standing in front of him.

Then he levels his eyes with Adam's, his voice trembling when he speaks. "I couldn't find you."

I draw in a sharp breath. *Oh my God.*

Four simple words.

"I couldn't find you."

Adam's parents lied to him. One look in Seth's tear-filled eyes is enough—the truth is undeniable.

He's been looking for Adam all this time.

Adam takes a slow breath. With his hands still framing

Adam's face, Seth leans forward and gently grazes Adam's lips with his. Adam hesitates at first, but when the sincerity of the gesture can no longer be questioned, his entire body relaxes into the kiss. It's tender and patient—Seth wordlessly conveys what he's been denied the chance to say. It's as if each brush of their mouths is offering an apology. When Seth ends the kiss and says, "I've missed you so fucking much," I see resolve in his eyes. A promise.

A sniffle beside me draws my attention. I glance sideways to see Genny, tears cascading down her face, and let me just say, she's not a pretty crier. I bite my lip to stifle a giggle and wipe my own eyes before taking her hand into mine.

Without thinking, I do the same on my other side, my delicate fingers curling around Lukas's muscular hand. His entire body bristles, probably surprised at the uninvited contact. With tears still brimming, I look at him and smile, hoping he'll accept my invitation. His eyes linger on mine, searching. When he seems to find whatever he's looking for, he grips my hand securely and with surprising intimacy, threads our fingers together. A hint of a smile, and I grin reassuringly in return.

Cheers erupt from behind us. I look over my shoulder to where Seth's group still stands, and my grin widens when I see every single one of Seth's friends with the same dopey, love-struck grins plastered on their faces. One of them even winks and tosses me a thumbs up, and I laugh before turning back around.

Glancing back at the happy couple now woven together

in a tight embrace, a thought occurs. I just wasted ten of my hard-earned dollars on a stereotypical movie with cheesy lines when the most beautiful love story is happening right now in front of my eyes, unscripted and absolutely free.

I'm still grinning when Lukas leans down, his eyes glued on the boys in front of us. The warmth from his cheek radiates against mine—I try not to hyperventilate, because this is Lukas—and he whispers, "That's why."

My brows draw together in confusion, but he answers before I even have time to ask. "I've never seen love, but I'm pretty sure the look in Seth's eyes when he saw Adam was exactly that."

Still uncertain, I turn my head slightly, just enough to meet his eyes. My breathing stalls. He seems to struggle to find the words, but after a frustrated shake of his head, he manages to continue so only I can hear. "You deserve to be with someone who looks at you the same way. With absolute reverence, each and every time he sees you, from the very first look right up until the last. Tommy didn't, and he didn't fight for you when challenged. He just let you go." He shrugs. "So yeah, I pelted him with popcorn because he didn't deserve the privilege of sitting next to you in that theater."

His mouth quirks upward at the corners when he adds, "Plus, it was fun."

I roll my eyes with my whispered reply. "Great. So what you're saying is, if a guy doesn't look at me in the way you find acceptable, more shenanigans are to be expected?"

"Exactly."

My eyes narrow, but my stubborn grin proves difficult to hide. Lukas's gaze drifts to my mouth, noting my attempt, then lifts to meet mine. There's something reflected in it, but before I have the chance to explore it further, he disengages his stare and rises to his full height. And God, how I feel the loss of his presence so close to me.

Genny has long since released my hand, abandoning me to make small talk with Seth's friends. But Lukas's hold remains, his grip warm and reassuring.

I consider his words, then wonder…is this Lukas's way of telling me he won't let me go? Then I think about how utterly ridiculous the notion is and mentally slap myself back to my senses.

Just like he guarded Michelle, this is him telling me he'll guard me, too. Us. Our group.

Lukas drops my hand, shocking me further when he wraps an arm around my shoulder. It's reminiscent of Tommy's attempt earlier, but it feels more protective.

I've never been held this way.

Silently, I snuggle into Lukas, place my head on his chest, and listen to his steady heartbeat while watching Seth and Adam make up for lost time.

And as I'm tucked in closer to his side, I grin, taking great pride in the fact that absolutely no popcorn was harmed in the making of this moment.

13

At the local supermarket, Lukas and I wander the aisles aimlessly, making the most of our freedom from summer duties. He pushes the cart slowly, his thick forearms crossed over the handle while I toss random things in as we go. We smile faintly when we catch each other's eye, which is often, and every single time the capillaries in my cheeks explode. We walk together in silence. It's not awkward, but nice, comfortable.

Just as a box of saltine crackers lands safely on our pile of groceries, I decide it's time to start a conversation. "Two hundred dollars seems like so much money, but it doesn't really buy a lot, does it?"

Lukas considers the basket, layers upon layers of generic products and the makings of cheap meals—*Sloppy Joes included! Yay!*— and replies, "It buys enough, I think."

"Yeah." I survey the lot as well. Grinning, I add, "I think that's why she always sends us. Who knows what Genny would come back with? Probably something bizarre that no one would even like, like two hundred dollars' worth of Twizzlers."

Lukas laughs, crossing his arms and leaning over onto the shopping cart again. "Nah, it'd be chocolate."

I chuckle. "For sure."

I point at some Goldfish, and he shakes his head, indicating the knock-off brand on a lower shelf with a dip of his chin.

I chuck one bag of those into the basket as he asks, "Was it hard? Going from having so much money to having none?"

I frown, thinking, then shake my head. "No. Not really. Feeling loved is worth so much more." My steps halt and I turn to face him. "Why do you ask?"

"It's weird to think about, I guess. That you had a completely different life before Sacred Heart. Posh house, fancy cars, expensive wardrobe, all that shit. Yet here you are, in a store with a delinquent"—he waggles his dark eyebrows and grins—"wearing secondhand clothes while failing miserably at trying to contain your excitement over something so mundane as Sloppy Joes mix."

I gasp, laughing. I thought my poker face during that acquisition was truly stellar. "Hey, Sloppy Joes are the shit. Grilled cheese, too," I say, knocking his shoulder with mine.

Still smiling, he nods and pushes the cart forward. I step in time with him, adding in a thoughtful tone, "I don't mind the clothes. I don't miss the house or the cars. The years I spent there were nothing but an emotional vacuum. I wasn't really attached to anything or anyone. In fact, I didn't really have anything I considered valuable until I was placed with Mrs. Rodriguez."

I give him a shy, sideways glance, and the curve of his mouth tells me he understands exactly on what, or on *whom*, I place value. I quickly look away, directing my eyes to the scuffed flats on my feet as we walk.

Two aisles later, I ask, "What about you?"

He grabs a one-pound plastic bag of Frootie Tooties, and I giggle because the name is pure ridiculousness. *Tooties.*

He chuckles and tosses the bag into the cart. "Well, I had nothing to lose when I came, if that's what you're asking. I don't really think I've ever had anything I could call mine. To me, 'mine' alludes to holding on to something forever, and I never really stayed in a place long enough to find something worth keeping. Never took anything with me, never left anything behind."

Lukas leans forward as he pushes the cart. His posture is relaxed and unassuming, as though his admission wasn't completely tragic. My brows descend, and I mentally store his statement to address at another time. "No, I mean, was it a lot for you? Being surrounded by so many people? You just…" I worry my bottom lip, "You just seemed as though you wanted to be left alone when you first came here."

This time he stops mid-aisle to face me. "Yes and no."

He shrugs. "I was still pretty messed up in the head when I first got to Sacred Heart. And I was wary. I didn't set out to form any relationships, that's for sure."

Ouch.

For some reason, his words sting. He must see it in my expression, because he's quick to say, "But the longer I stayed, the harder it was to keep myself separated. I found myself curious about what it would be like to feel part of something for once. You all were, *are*, so tightly woven, so protective of each other, it's hard not to want to be included when what's happening in front of you is everything you've ever wanted."

"You were always a part of us, Lukas. You know that, right? That you always had a home in us. We're friends." I swallow the knot of sorrow constricting my throat. "We're family."

He nods firmly. "Yeah, I do."

I smile at him, fighting the urge to wipe an escaping tear. Hastily, my eyes fall to the ground, trying to hide my reaction. I'm sure Crying Chloe would do nothing more than freak him out, and he's come so far these past few months, I refuse to lose him now because of a few ill-timed tears.

So, I train my gaze downward and will myself to get it together. Seconds pass, then warm fingers grip my chin and slowly tilt my head up. I look toward the ceiling, then side to side, refusing to meet Lukas's stare.

Childish, I know. I can't defend my actions.

His chuckles draw my attention, and I finally meet his

eyes. They crinkle at the sides in silent laughter. I narrow mine, which earns me that dimple—a big smile. Then I roll them, and he barks a laugh.

All will is lost.

My mouth surrenders and gives him a smile in return. The tear also revolts, rolling down my cheek.

Lukas gently swipes it with his thumb then says almost too quietly, "Please don't hide what you're feeling from me."

Another traitorous tear falls, and he wipes it away immediately.

I shake my head, "I'm sorry. I just…I feel too much sometimes. I can't explain it, but I feel your pain, Lukas. I do. And it breaks my heart."

I laugh, embarrassed, then my face crumbles as I start to cry.

He gathers me in his arms, pulling me into his chest, and holds me tight. And there we stand, in the middle of the cereal section, right beside the Frootie Tooties, me sobbing uncontrollably in his arms.

Embarrassing? I think yes.

This is what I needed all those years ago. Touch. Compassion. Comfort. Lukas has led such a solitary life, and I'm sure he's horrified by my melting into his arms. The need to be held as I cry and somehow he gets that. *Not that I'll ever be able to say that to him.*

Minutes pass, and eventually I release him, backing away, my face a snotty, hideous mess. I lift the bottom of my T-shirt, blot my face, then squeeze my nose into the fabric.

When I finally manage to look up again, Lukas says nothing. He simply removes the strands of hair clinging to my damp cheeks so I can better see. Not that I want to. I kind of want to get the hell out of here, but we have a full cart and people at home expecting groceries.

Breathe, Chloe.

After finally managing to gather my composure, I repeat, "I'm sorry."

Lukas captures my face in his palms. "I refuse to accept your apology. *Never* apologize for feeling. Feeling is human, and humanity these days is something rarely seen. Thank you"—he levels his gaze with mine—"for reminding me that it actually exists."

I nod, sniffling while he wipes tears away, then glances around. *God, we've got an audience.* Some watch with smiles on their faces. Some look like they're ready to beat Lukas to a pulp. *How is that strangers want to protect me but my father never cared?*

I laugh, signaling to all that I'm okay, and watch as they slowly resume their shopping. I look back at Lukas, and reluctantly I force myself to step out of his hold.

It's too much. Not him, but me, my own longing for intimacy. Intimacy with him. Moments in his arms like that make me want more. And it's not right. Not now. Maybe never. I really need to wrap my head around that.

"I'm okay," I assure him, scrubbing my face and inhaling deeply.

He waits patiently, and once I've collected myself, we

turn to continue shopping in silence.

By the time we hit the boxed dinner aisle, the need to speak is overwhelming. So, I decide to pick up where we left off. "You've been at Sacred Heart for a while now. Did you find anything worth keeping yet?" I inquire, grabbing a box of Panburger Partner.

He grins. "Yeah, I think so."

"Is it a lamp? Mrs. Rodriguez does have some pretty kickass lamps."

He lowers his forehead, laughing while watching his feet, then rests his chin on his arms. "No. Not a lamp."

I smile dreamily and offer my advice. "You should take the one by the couch."

He grins. "The one with the pelican for the base?"

"God, it's awful." I laugh, picturing its chipped beak. "Surely she'd never miss it."

We both break into laughter as we roll to the checkout aisle, finally finished with our shopping. I check the list, making sure we didn't miss anything, which we didn't. Once everything's bagged and the total is announced, we're ten dollars under budget—go us!

I proudly present my hand for the change, but Lukas captures the attention of the cashier with a flash of his finger, a signal to wait. He scans the surrounding options, then digs out a light-up ring from the plastic fishbowl near the register. It's rubber and resembles a yellow, prickly alien life form.

"And this." He hands the cashier the ring, while I eye him, curious. Lukas disregards me as he addresses the cashier, who is indeed blushing, a common side effect when in close proximity to Lukas White. *No one is immune.*

And he has absolutely no idea.

With my hand still extended, I accept the now eight dollars and some change while Lukas happily pockets the ring. The cashier's eyes flick down to my arms, then quickly rise to meet my eyes. She smiles kindly, and I give her a thankful grin in return.

After the bags are loaded back into the cart, we head to the truck that Lukas has surprisingly managed to keep running all summer. Together, we haul the groceries into the bed. Lukas slams the tailgate shut while I return the cart to the nearest cart corral.

More than ready to extract myself from the embarrassment that was this shopping trip, I turn and my entire body goes still.

Lukas stands before me, his arm propped on the side of the truck, booted feet crossed at the ankle as he leans. His mischievous, lopsided grin is blinding and on full display. His hair is haphazardly styled, his navy blue T-shirt hugs his upper body, and his well-worn jeans are slung low on his hips. I wish I had a camera, or at the very least a cell phone like every other kid my age, just to capture his beauty. Although it's not his physical attributes I'd be seeking to eternalize.

I would attempt to catch the emotion. Like, the playfulness in his eyes and the ease of his smile. The childlike innocence, joyous and full of life, and the relaxed posture and easy expression I so rarely see. The impact of this, of him, renders me utterly breathless.

Yet again.

I sigh helplessly, doing the best I can. I take a mental snapshot and store it in my memory as I slowly walk to where he's standing. When I'm about two feet away, I see it—he's holding the ring he just purchased.

I bite my bottom lip, and grin.

"Well, it's not Sloppy Joes, but I thought this might brighten your day." He pinches the ring, and a multi-colored light show flickers beneath its rubber surface.

"Get it?" he prods. "Brighten?"

I laugh, stepping forward to take the ring. "You're so punny."

He chuckles, catching my wrist in his free hand. The light-hearted moment passes, morphing into something much deeper, more intense. We look deeply into each other's eyes.

He angles his head, his eyes so piercing it feels as though he's looking into my soul. Our gazes remain locked even as he slides the ring onto my forefinger. I inhale sharply when he covers my hand with his, surprised by the gesture, then release my breath, comforted.

Pleased with my reaction, his lopsided grin transforms into a full one. Then, his voice low, he decrees, "To remember the day you filled my heart with your tears."

Oh Lukas.

He leans in, his clean scent wafting around me as he places a kiss on my cheek. And for the second time today, all air is stolen from my lungs. His lips are soft against my skin, and their warmth sets my cheeks ablaze. My heart hammers and short breaths saw my chest. Much too soon, his lips are gone, their heat redirected to my ear as he whispers, "Thank you."

I nod against his cheek. His shoulders shake lightly with laughter as he rises. He takes a step backward, but doesn't let me go. Threading our hands together, he pulls me close and leads me to the passenger side of the truck.

Once I'm inside and alone, I absently touch the rubber bristles of the ring, lost in the moment as Lukas rounds the front of the truck. I drop my stare, momentarily mesmerized by the bursts of color.

Then, I smile.

Well, one thing's for certain. Although I love this ring and will treasure it always, I don't think I'll ever need a reminder to remember today.

Every single moment has been irrevocably woven into my heart.

14

I inhale deeply, savoring the serenity only the heat of summer can bring. Spring is nice, but summer, well…it cleanses my soul. The warmth, and the sun's luminous, constant shine—I feel renewed vigor every moment I spend outside.

Clad in a modest one-piece bathing suit, I'm lying on a dampened towel, the warm breeze tickling my exposed body, slowly drying the droplets of water on my skin. I'm in a prime spot next to our pond, and the soothing fragrance of soil and flowers fills my nostrils. I stretch my arms above my head and look into the clear blue sky, another wave of peacefulness washing over me.

My eyes follow a cloud that looks suspiciously like a Smurf, and I grin. Because right here, right now, there's only the elements and me.

I've never felt more at home. At peace.

More than the loss of my gloves, finding strength in this moment of solitude is nothing short of extraordinary. I use to define myself—my value, my worth—by others' eyes, but no longer.

I'm me. Take me or leave me, I don't really care, because outside opinions are no longer considered.

I love who I am.

I love Empathetic Chloe, because she's wise beyond measure.

I love Badass Chloe, because she takes a stand when it's necessary.

I even love Former Chloe, because she helped me learn what I needed to learn.

But most importantly, I love *Chloe*, the totality of all the pieces that make me, me. I feel myself blossoming just as Genny predicted, and honestly, I take pride in my growth. Change is quite possibly one of the most difficult things to accept. Many find security in routine, regardless of the damage it can cause. Instead of breaking a destructive cycle, whether internal or external, most will allow it to continue because it's constant and therefore, to some degree, comfortable. And when you're trying to find something, anything, to hold on to while your world is spinning out of control, it's easy to anchor yourself to the familiar, no matter how terrible it might be.

Speaking of Genny, I hear her spout a string of very unladylike curses, then squeal like a ten-year-old when Adam pushes her into the water. I laugh and roll over, propping myself up on my elbow just in time to see her head break through the water, hair plastered over her irritated expression. Unfazed by her impending wrath, Adam roars savagely and beats his fists on his chest, taking a running start before jumping off the edge of the pond. Midair, he tucks his knees to his chest and seconds later, lands a perfect cannonball. Genny is unceremoniously caught in the splash radius, furthering her annoyance.

Grinning, I sit up and flash an imaginary scorecard. "Ten! A perfect ten!"

Adam gives a celebratory pump of his fists and I laugh out loud.

That is, until my eyes find Lukas as he approaches, his sculpted bare chest and abs on clear display. Stunned stupid by the sight, I choke on my laughter as he plops on my towel next to me. He shakes his dark head of hair like a wet dog, launching droplets of water all over my drying skin.

I narrow my eyes.

He flashes that dimple.

I sigh internally then ask, "Really? I just dried off."

He gives no response, just scoots himself closer, still on *my* towel, and lies down. While *his* towel is right next to mine. I don't remind him of this because, well. Lukas, practically naked, lying inches away from me, why would I?

Duh.

He extends his arm and I lie back, my head comfortably pillowed on his massive bicep. Together, we look toward the sky and breathe in. We chuckle in unison, and I look to the side, noting our wildflowers are doing well in the heat of the summer. They're happy and full of life as they wave at us.

Several blissful minutes pass like this, until our tranquility is abruptly ended by Genny, who drops onto her towel next to us, muttering. I lift my chin, watching her yank her pink hair up into a haphazard ponytail, her tank top and jean shorts completely soaked. She glares at Adam—who's cheerful as ever—as he takes a seat, grinning an ornery grin. Darkened by the water, his blond hair falls nearly to his chin. It looks good. Or is it the gleam of love reflecting in his brilliant eyes?

I take a moment to look at him, overjoyed at the thought of another blossoming Wildflower in our midst. Several weeks have passed since our run-in with Seth, but not a day goes by that we don't see him. His visits are welcomed and encouraged at Sacred Heart, which I find hilariously ironic. After seeing just one shared look between the two, Mrs. Rodriguez needed no further convincing that Seth was in Adam's life for good. She welcomed him with an elated expression and open arms, just as the rest of us did.

I glance over at Lukas, whose faint smile tells me he recognizes the shift in Adam's demeanor as well. There's no sign of tension or jealously in his features, and I feel an involuntary but undeniable surge of relief. While I've lectured myself numerous times about the idiocy of wanting someone you can't have, I have yet to control certain responses when I'm near Lukas White.

When he leisurely reaches to the side and grips my hand

with his, my heart stutters in my chest, while he just relaxes and closes his eyes, as though the gesture is nothing. As commonplace as breathing.

I understand his behavior. At least, I think I do.

It must all be part of his healing process. I mean, witnessing Lukas's growth has been an incredible experience. Over the past few months, his smiles have become more frequent, his words more plentiful, and his willingness to touch and hold much more abundant and unapologetic, even when others are watching. His eyes often linger on mine, as though seeking something. While I'm unaware of what it is, he seems to always eventually find what he's looking for. I know the moment he does because his features relax and resolve gleams in his eyes.

It's purely therapeutic—he needs to learn that these actions are, and should be, given freely here and they will be reciprocated. It's a normal part of life to communicate through closeness, to exchange glances, hold hands, embrace. Those are things he's never granted himself, and he's learning and practicing them willingly now. With me.

While I feel privileged he trusts me enough to get close to me, I'm constantly having to remind myself what this *isn't*. Thinking or wishing these gestures are more than what they seem will only serve to damage our relationship. And I can't let that happen.

It's a constant battle, but I keep it up, because Lukas laughing so openly at something Genny says to Adam is worth the sacrifice.

He needs to heal. He doesn't need a girlfriend, let alone one that's practically a sister. And he definitely doesn't need my issues hindering his progress.

I turn my gaze back to the sky, inhaling contentedly as silence descends on us. That is, until Genny breaks it.

"Chloe, what's your worst fear?"

I lift my head and look at the three other Wildflowers, all of them gazing up at the sky, before responding. "I don't know."

Genny laughs. "Yes, you do. Stop thinking and say the first thing that comes to your mind."

I pucker my lips in contemplation, then answer. "Time."

She shifts next to me, and I know without looking she's propped up and staring at me. "Interesting," she offers. "Why?"

I shrug, still looking upward. "I guess because time is so defining. It dictates every single aspect of our lives. Time to get up, time to be at school, time to go here, time to get there. It's a limitation constantly used to define our existence. It's stifling."

Suddenly perturbed, I lift my weight onto my elbows. "I mean, why can't we just be? Why are we constantly rushing, always trying to beat the clock? It never stops. Ever. And that scares the shit out of me."

Genny barks a laugh. "Until it does."

I train my gaze on her, and she continues. "That's my worst fear. That when my time is up, when I leave this earth, I will be…forgotten. That I'll have left nothing to mark my time here. I mean, what if I have nothing to show for my life?"

"You have plenty of time to make your mark," I counter, shaking my head.

Genny sighs. "You know I can't see my future?" She smiles solemnly, not looking at me, but through me with her rhetorical question. "I've never admitted this out loud, but you know how people picture their wedding day or their kids or some stupid future shit like that?"

Her eyes meet mine. I nod. "Yeah."

"Well, I don't see that. There's nothing. It's blank."

Wow. I'm literally stunned. *How can it be blank? What do I see in mine?* But as I'm about to inquire further, Adam speaks. "Complacency."

I turn to see him plucking blades of grass, deep in thought. "Society is all about conformity. People try to change themselves so they can fit in, and they exclude anyone who doesn't. The sad thing is, a lot of people don't do this completely consciously—they're bound to that mentality by nothing but their own complacency. Prisoners, unaware."

Adam looks at each of us before concluding, "To actively ridicule and be intolerant is unjust. But it's people's inability to take a stand, their blind tolerance of hate and bigotry… That's what scares me the most. Nothing worth fighting for comes with ease, otherwise there would be no battles. No protest. No change. Yet so many accept the norm because it's the path of least resistance. What they fail to see, no… what they choose not to see, is the collateral damage they create as a result of their silence. Of their complacency."

When his troubled eyes meet mine, I give him a small smile, because I need him to know I'm anything but complacent. His mouth curves in thankful recognition before he tucks his hair behind his ears.

Just as he does, Lukas murmurs, "Losing control."

Genny gapes at me. I return her shocked expression before redirecting it toward Adam, whose jaw has also dropped. We all remain silent as we await his words, fearful of shattering the moment.

As we've learned, it takes a while, but eventually, he explains. "Anger dictated my life. I was pissed at everything, because I had been given nothing. I'd only ever known emptiness, and the one time I had someone I cared about, well, we know how that turned out. I lost control and as a result, I lost Michelle. Then I met the three of you, drawn to you all by the bond you share. And now that I'm a part of it, I live in constant fear that I'm destined to repeat the pattern." He heaves a heavy sigh. "Nothing deserves nothing, yet you three are everything to me. I'm terrified I'll lose control again, and in turn, I'll lose you too."

We exchange wide-eyed glances before looking back at Lukas. His eyes remain closed, and his hand envelops mine. I give it an encouraging squeeze, then swallow before speaking. "You didn't lose Michelle because you lost control, Lukas. You rescued her. She was living a nightmare before you found her, and what you did saved her. She was removed from that home, right?"

Lukas's nod is almost imperceptible. "Yeah, but who

knows what shithole she landed in after that? If I would've maintained control, I could've stayed by her side and made sure she was safe."

I shake my head. "You don't know that. You assume she landed in a shithole home, but it's just as possible that she ended up with a family that adores and treasures her, all because you took a stand. You did what you had to do, what any good person would do, in that situation. But you can't protect everything and everyone, Lukas. That's too much of a burden for one person to carry."

Adam chuckles, adding, "Yeah, it is. No wonder you were so pissed all the time."

Lukas's lips curl into a small, relenting smile, and only then does he open his eyes. He blinks a couple times, then looks at me in that soul-searching way he so often does. I smile in return and watch as his gaze softens and the tension in his shoulders relaxes.

"You can't control everything, Lukas. Sometimes you just have to let life happen," Genny says. She cups a dandelion near the ground, closing her hands over the fuzzy white ball. "Take this dandelion, for instance. I know the flower is protected inside my grip, safe from harm, but it's also cut off from the elements sustaining it. If I keep it contained like this, the seeds will eventually die."

She releases the dandelion and leans, pursing her lips and blowing softly. Right then, a light gust of wind kicks up, lifting and carrying the umbrella-like seeds. She watches them briefly, then looks at Lukas. "Oftentimes, the best way to save a life is to do what you can, then release your hold when the time comes. You may have lost control that night, but you showed that child, without a doubt, that she was worth fighting for." Genny pins Lukas with an earnest stare. "And like the seeds of a dandelion, she will carry that belief and blossom no matter where life replants her. All because of *you*."

Her face splits into a daring grin. "So enough with self-hatred and guilt. We get it. You're pissed at the world. But it's time to let that anger go and trust in us, because that's no longer your burden to bear. The Wildflowers protect their own, so from now on, consider the weight of that responsibility spread equally between four of us instead of you alone."

Adam barks a laugh. "Um, where was this nonbelligerent flowerchild ten minutes ago? Because I'm pretty sure the string of f-bombs that escaped your mouth over there"—he points to the pond—"is in complete contradiction with your peaceful floral presentation."

Genny plucks another dandelion and tosses it at Adam's head. He gasps, though humor fills his eyes. "You just killed an innocent wildflower!"

She smiles. "Yeah, well that one volunteered its life because your stupidity was killing it anyway."

I laugh, but eventually their banter is drowned out by a familiar sound.

Tick.

Tick.

Tick.

The presence of a specific countdown I'm constantly trying to escape. Trying to ignore. Yet, as I take in the other Wildflowers, their ease and laughter, I feel a sense of impending finality. A time when we are no longer together. Because the truth is, it's inevitable. Undeniable. In a few short weeks, we'll start our final year of school. At some point in the near future, we'll all be eighteen, legally adults, and eventually ejected from Sacred Heart. That time will come. We won't have our daily interactions. Our lunchtimes together. Our evenings together, wrestling with our disappointments in and hopes for this world.

How will we survive without each other when we're eventually blown apart by winds outside our control?

Time.

I hate it.

15

"God, I'm starving!" Genny announces to no one in particular as we enter the house. Both she and Adam are still soaked from the pond, outlines of wet footprints trailing behind them on the wood floors. Lukas and I, however, are blissfully dry. We're both still in our swimsuits, though my bottom half is covered by a pair of worn jean shorts while Lukas's upper body remains unclothed.

"When aren't you?" I observe, because honestly, I'm beginning to think she has a tapeworm or something. Her mouth purses, and she tries to punch my shoulder, but I shift too quickly and she catches nothing but air. I give her a smug grin.

Her keen senses on high alert as usual, Mrs. Rodriguez pops around the corner, appearing out of nowhere like the ninja she is. Tendrils of loose gray hair frame her narrowed eyes as her stare locks on the foot-shaped puddles.

We all freeze—except for Genny. Instead, she wisely drops her towel to the floor. Our stares fall with it, watching as she not so discreetly uses the ball of her foot to press the towel behind her and cover her wet footprints.

The corners of Mrs. Rodriguez's mouth twitch, but she quickly regains control of her amusement. Once the floor is mopped dry and Genny and Adam take their rightful places on top of the towel, Mrs. Rodriguez nods.

Then she opens her mouth and blows our minds. "I was thinking we could have pizza for dinner tonight."

The four of us stare blankly back at her, at each other. Then, in unison, we scream at the top of our lungs as though we won the lottery. And honestly, we might as well have. The odds are about the same.

We're still jumping up and down when Mrs. Rodriguez tags on the dreaded, "If…"

Abruptly, all our movements cease to better focus on her demand. "I need two volunteers to help me bring up some boxes from the basement."

Both our index fingers fly to the tip of our noses as Lukas and I shout at the same time.

"Not it!"

Since a touch to the end of the nose is basically the nonverbal exclamation of 'not it,' it may seem redundant to most. But it's the basement we're talking about, and I will take every precaution necessary to make sure my ass doesn't end up down there. It's creepy as hell. Apparently,

Lukas feels the same way and decided to double up on the negation right along with me. I grin inwardly.

With their fates sealed, Genny and Adam scowl at us, and I wonder if they may be a little waterlogged because they're usually a lot quicker. Grinning sardonically, I do a happy dance in celebration while Lukas shrugs in apology. Mrs. Rodriguez aims her smile right at her volunteers, clearly familiar with the rules of this game. Just another reason to love her.

"Go get dried off, you two. Then meet me down there," she says, jerking her head in the direction of the basement door.

Defeated, both Genny and Adam amble in the direction of their rooms. Mrs. Rodriguez then turns her attention to Lukas and me. "You two, order the pizza. Be sure to use the coupons in the drawer under the phone. And see if there's one for a dessert pizza. If there is, get one of those, too."

I widen my eyes at her request, still grinning. *I am so on board with this.*

She winks then releases a long, weary sigh. "It's just been one of those days."

I nod in understanding and look sideways at Lukas, but his tentative gaze stays on her. My brows pinch in confusion, but before I even make a remark, Mrs. Rodriguez is gone as quickly as she appeared.

Left alone with Lukas, I nudge his shoulder with my own. Though mine is much less massive. Kind of scrawny in comparison, actually.

His contemplative eyes fall to mine, and when they do, I give him a questioning look. He shakes his head then states, "She's been tired a lot recently."

"Really? You think?"

Has she been tired a lot lately? How have I missed that? And then the anxiety sets in. She's our strength, has given us all a home. Surely she's fine. But what if anything happens to her? What will that mean for us? Question after question surface, because I've never stopped to consider the possibility of what would happen if Mrs. Rodriguez weren't here.

After a few silent seconds, Lukas reaches to the side, clasps my hand, and threads our fingers together. I look into his eyes, and I have no doubt he can read my fear, my concern. He shakes his head and says, "I overanalyze. It's probably nothing."

Probably?

"Probably" doesn't make me feel better, at all.

Adrift in an ocean of worry, I follow him to the kitchen in silence. His back is to me, his hair completely a mess, and for once, it's not spiked to kingdom come with hair product. It's naturally unruly and sexy. I'm enamored by it, and my thoughts slowly shift from Lukas's observation of Mrs. Rodriguez to Lukas himself.

What would it be like to run my fingers through his hair? Would it be soft?

If he were to kiss me, would his stubble chafe my skin? Or would it perfectly contrast the softness of his lips?

His muscles flex as he walks—my eyes catch on the two

indentations above his board shorts. What would his back feel like if I traced it with my finger? Then, completely lost in my fascination, I do the most embarrassing thing I've ever done in my life. And trust me, there's plenty of competition for that number-one spot.

I lift my hand, about to actually find out exactly what Lukas's back would feel like, but then realize what's happening, and that it can *not* happen. So, instead of literally caressing him, I manage to stop myself halfway, index finger still extended, and as though he's the freaking Pillsbury Doughboy, I poke Lukas in the back.

His steps halt, and he angles his head, looking to see if the girl behind him actually did poke him.

For no apparent reason.

Which, she totally did.

I totally did.

Heat rushes into my face while I search for an excuse, any excuse. "I, uh…um, I just wanted to…" I offer lamely, my cheeks scorching.

His smile widens, and he turns to face me, leaning in close to whisper in my ear, "You can touch me any time you like, Chloe."

The deep rumble of his voice, the way he says my name, it makes my knees almost buckle. I grip his hand to keep from stumbling, inhaling deeply, then wishing I hadn't, because his scent lingers even after our time at the pond. His eyes skim over every inch of my face, his grin slowly subsiding as he gauges my reaction.

Deliberately, slowly, he flattens my palm against his chest, above his heart. The heat of his skin permeates my entire hand, and I shiver.

"Wow," I breathe, staring directly at his chest. "Second base and we haven't even gone on a date."

His smile reemerges and his shoulders shake with silent laughter, drawing my eyes upward. I grin at the sight of his dazzling smile. Although I wish it would make an appearance more often, I do feel a sense of pride this time. This one's mine.

When his laughter subsides, he curls his fingers around my hand and retorts, "I have no idea where *you've* been, but you and I have gone on several dates already."

My head jerks, and I snort at the thought. "Um, no, we haven't. I would remember going on a date with you."

"Hmm. Well, it's unfortunate that you don't remember. Because I do."

I scan his face. He's completely serious. I frown. "I think you were in the sun a little too long today, buddy."

He laughs softly and shakes his head. "Nope."

I fight the urge to feel his forehead, mainly because I like my hand right where it is, thank you very much. "When, exactly, was this first date? Because I kind of feel cheated out of the experience. Since it never happened."

"Movie night with Timmy."

He offers this answer as though the admission is nothing more than common knowledge. He might as well have stated water is wet or Reese's are made with peanut butter.

A succession of surprised chuckles sputters from my mouth. "What?"

"That night was our first official date. Our second was the day we had to run to the supermarket for Mrs. Rodriguez. And the last one was like thirty minutes ago at the pond." His eyebrows furrow. "I can't believe you don't remember that one. It *just* happened."

But as I watch him, completely dumbfounded and on the brink of hope, I spot it. The joking in his eyes. The laughter, likely all at my expense. Insecurity washes through me, extinguishing the warmth of the last few moments.

He's making fun of me. And honestly, who could blame him?

I swallow the hurt and yank my hand from his chest. "That's just cruel, Lukas." And cue the worst case of verbal diarrhea I've ever had. "I'm sure it's very funny to you. A stupid girl has a stupid crush, never saying a word, just blushing every time you're near, or getting goosebumps every time you touch her, or having a near heart attack every time you say her name the way you do. You just have to play along—it's so damn hilarious seeing her get all tripped up around you. Of course. Leave it to me to want someone who's emotionally unavailable, right?"

I hear myself laughing, and it's maniacal, and though I'm well aware I'm making a complete ass of myself, I'm unable to stop. Thankfully, it's at this point that I kind of dissociate with my physical self and my consciousness floats upward, all the while watching my self-implosion from the comfort of the ceiling.

"Right?!" I emphasize the question, and when Lukas just stares back at me with equal parts shock and amusement, I push on. I drop my voice as low as it can go. "I'm Lukas. I'm broody and detached. I offer little breadcrumbs of hope with my dimples and my random touches here and there that may mean something to others, but I'm damaged so they mean absolutely nothing to me."

His eyebrows lift at my insinuation, but for once, I don't care what he thinks, nor do I want to hear anything he has to say.

"You once told me to, and I quote, 'Look up so you can see the effect you have on those around you.' Well, mister"—I jab my finger into the bare chest I was so enamored with earlier—"maybe you should open your own eyes so you can recognize the consequences of your actions. If you don't mean it, don't do it, because the pain you're causing to someone who actually cares about you is excruciating." My incorporeal, detached self floating above it all would clap for myself if it could.

I give him one final glare, then step around him, ready to make a dramatic exit. But I only make it approximately three stomps before I'm whirled around so quickly, I lose my balance. A strong arm clamps around my waist, bringing me nose to nose with Lukas as I'm steadied on my feet.

He leans in, locking his eyes on mine, foiling my attempts to look at anything but him. My mouth pinched in protest, I finally stop fidgeting and just...look at him.

Only then does he speak. "You want to know why I touch you so often? Why I hold your hand or graze your skin or brush your hair out of your eyes?"

I scowl, my stubborn silence giving him the time he needs to speak. "Because your reaction is *everything* to me. When I touch you, I take that precise moment to look right into your eyes. To watch your face. Your expression. I search for every single response you so desperately try to hide. Because when I see your cheeks flush, or watch your eyes widen, or feel your pulse race beneath your skin, I find hope in the fact that someone like me can affect someone like you. And I cling to the possibility that someone like you might feel something, anything, for someone like me."

Lukas releases me and takes a step back, but I don't let him go. I move with him. Because he meant it. He meant all of it.

I've never felt closer to anyone.

He relaxes and gives me a shy smile with an accompanying shrug. "So, yeah. I'm not the best at communicating, but what I meant to say was that all those times we spent together were important to me. Every moment with you means everything to me. And it all started with the night at the movies, because that night I knew no one would treasure you the way I wanted them to, the way I would, if given the chance. I just—"

I launch myself into him, and silence his insecurities by pressing my mouth against his. I offer him all that I am, all that I ever will be in this one kiss, because he deserves nothing less. I try to relay with every brush of my lips that he matters, that he's important, that he's somebody. A living, breathing person who needs to experience love in the way it's meant to be experienced: as something inherent and fierce.

And thank God, Lukas wraps his arms tightly around my waist, pulling me closer. And in this moment I *feel* love, weaving us together and entwining our souls in a way I've never before experienced.

Not even with the other Wildflowers.

With him, I open completely.

Oh, the relief. It's immediate. I sink into him, parting my lips.

I have no idea how much time passes, but eventually we've somehow managed to migrate to the kitchen, my backside against the counter with Lukas's body pressed firmly against mine.

I put my fingers deeply into his hair, and I was right. It's as soft as velvet. His stubble is the perfect contrast to his lips. Not that I can feel much right now. My entire mouth is gloriously numb. *Yet, I've never felt so alive. So treasured and—*

Someone clears their throat, plucking me from this blissful moment and harshly snapping me back to reality.

"Get a room, assholes."

Both Genny and Adam stand shoulder to shoulder in the kitchen, now clad in dry clothes with wide, knowing grins. Lukas smiles and shakes his head. Looking over his shoulder, I watch as Adam nudges Genny in the ribs. She huffs and rolls her eyes, reaching beneath the front of her white tank to pull out what looks like a twenty-dollar bill. She tips it in Adam's direction, and he swiftly pockets the money.

After it's safely stashed, he winks at me. "Glad you finally caught on. Just in the nick of time, too. I only had three days left."

Completely ignoring the fact that my friends have been wagering on my love life, I ask the obvious question. "Am I the only person who wasn't aware Lukas and I have been dating? For weeks, apparently?"

Suddenly, Genny's eyes widen, she gestures, and I see Mrs. Rodriguez enter the room. I drop my hands just as Lukas takes a huge step back, taking a moment to adjust his shorts before turning around. I cover my mouth to hide my grin.

Thankfully, Mrs. Rodriguez is incapable of noticing anything else when she's on a mission. Incriminating things like swollen lips, ruffled hair, and rosy cheeks go undetected and unremarked on as she flits through the kitchen. She doesn't even bother looking at us, her gaze trained on the basement door.

"Genny. Adam," she says, snapping her fingers as she passes by. With her other hand, she points at Lukas and myself before pointing her finger in the direction of the phone on the counter.

Then she's gone.

It's amazing really, given her age, that she still has the ability to travel faster than the speed of light.

I shake my head then look at Genny and Adam. Their eyes bounce between Lukas and me, eagerly waiting for one of us to speak.

I shuffle next to Lukas and grip his hand tightly. When he looks to me, I match his unabashed grin with my own, then turn to address our crew.

"So, this is okay with you?"

I mean, it's the Wildflowers we're talking about. I know that a relationship that delves any deeper than friendship could prove to be catastrophic. They deserve their say.

Genny tilts her head and narrows her eyes in contemplation. Then she shrugs. "I have no problem with it. Just don't pull a Yoko and split up the group. No pressure or anything."

I swallow my relief, then turn to Adam. Still grinning, he asks, "Girl, are you daft? I've been trying to get you two together for a while now."

Laughter bubbles in my chest just as Lukas releases my hand. He curls his arm around my shoulders and pulls me into his side, placing a light kiss on the top of my head. I wrap my arms around his waist and exhale contentedly, reveling in how my body fits perfectly alongside his.

"Genesis! Adam!" Mrs. Rodriguez calls from the basement.

Their smiles drop, and they glare at the doorway.

"I'm sorry, guys. We'll take the next round," I offer.

Adam sighs. "I'm totally taking you up on that, that is, if we make it back alive."

"Let's get this over with," Genny says, linking her arm

in Adam's. As they hit the top of the stairs, Genny calls over her shoulder, "Don't you dare skimp on the toppings. Extra everything. I'm hungry and about to perform manual labor, so my mood is only going to get worse. Pizza will be the only thing capable of bringing me back to humanity."

I laugh as they descend, then turn to find luminous eyes staring back at me. They shine so brilliantly I have to force myself to breathe. *Has Lukas been looking at me like this all this time?*

I push up onto my toes, press my lips to his, then trail tiny kisses along his cheek to his ear. "We have to make up for lost time."

Six months, to be exact. It's disheartening to think about the amount of time wasted between us. I caged myself with invisible rules and boundaries that never really existed within the Wildflowers. I buried my feelings and attempted to hide my reactions, the very things that seem to have brought Lukas to life.

But I refuse to think about that any longer. Everything happens in its own time, and this time is ours.

My mouth spreads into a wide grin as Lukas chuckles softly. His arms encircle my waist, drawing me close, and his stubble tickles my skin as he whispers, "I've searched for you, Chloe Campbell. And now that I found you, I'm never letting you go."

My cheek presses into his. I lean back and place my hands on the sides of his face, leveling our gazes. I remember when his eyes were nothing but dark clouds and tumultuous storms, but that time is passed. Shining back at me now, there's only intense clarity and radiant hope. *He's breathtaking.*

"Well, what do you know? Genny was right."

He gives me a curious look, so I clarify. "You are light, Lukas. Pure and warm and brimming with life. As powerful as the sun."

He presses his forehead against mine. "But it's you who makes me burn."

Then he kisses me in a way that communicates exactly that.

16

I have no idea how we accomplished it, but somehow between passionate kisses, longing glances, and shy shared smiles, Lukas and I did in fact manage to order the pizzas, including the chocolate-chip dessert pizza Mrs. Rodriguez requested.

We figured it was best to keep her in a good mood.

Adam and Genny survived the basement, though they were intent on recounting every single near-death experience they encountered in the dingy room. Like the fact that a box fell, almost decapitating Adam. And the discovery of a black widow spider that launched itself at Genny's face.

Through her laughter, Mrs. Rodriguez clarified that the box was full of old pillows and the spider was not a black widow, but a harmless garden spider. Like that made any difference.

We ate together, and when our stomachs could hold no

more, we headed to the living room for movie night. We convinced Mrs. Rodriguez that *Deadpool* was a harmless superhero movie for kids, then got a kick out of her reaction every time he dropped an F-bomb. So like, every ten seconds. We were in tears by the time she left the room, crossing herself, and praying for our souls on her way out.

I gave her props for making it as long as she did.

The remainder of the night consisted of Lukas holding my hand, me resting my head on his chest, and his occasional light kisses brushing my temple. It was odd to feel so comfortable around him, touching him freely and smiling every time his lips grazed my skin. But I guess once the floodgates were lowered, we were drowning in the need to be as close as we possibly could. Maybe we found validation in our actions, confirming with each touch that our relationship had evolved from that of mere friendship, or maybe it was something as simple as two lost souls finally coming home.

Whatever it was, it was honestly one of the best nights of my life.

Which brings me to right now, standing alone in the bathroom while Genny snores away in our room. Unable to sleep and smiling at my reflection, I towel off my freshly cleansed face, wondering if my rosy cheeks are a result of the warm water or pure adrenaline-fueled excitement running through my veins.

My cheeks are totally cramping, yet I can't stop smiling.

There's a light tap at the door, and I say, "All clear," while looping my towel on its designated rack. Sharing a bathroom with two boys can be insane, so an "all clear" is our way of letting them know it's safe to enter. Unfortunately, it doesn't apply to Genny. She just barges in, regardless of the occupant.

Lukas steps inside, shutting the door quietly behind him. His eyes meet mine in the mirror, and he smiles wryly, standing next to me in front of the sink. An electric current fills the room, making my entire body hum, and I'm suddenly hyperaware of his presence.

Together, we reach for our toothbrushes, knuckles colliding. He steps back, gesturing for me to take mine first. After I grab mine, he takes his.

"Couldn't sleep," he offers, applying his toothpaste before offering the tube to me.

I grab it while admitting, "Yeah. Me neither."

We stare in silence, wide grins plastered on our faces as we begin to brush in unison. I don't know how many people actually brush their teeth for the full two minutes recommended by dentists everywhere, but two minutes feels like an eternity when you're trapped in the bathroom with someone you're hopelessly enamored with, watching each other brush and spit on repeat.

It's oddly intimate.

We take turns though, making the best out of the awkward situation and laughing quietly as we rinse our brushes.

After wiping my mouth, I turn to leave but Lukas has other plans. He steps in front of me, halting my forward movement, and his breath is warm and minty as it fans my face. "I felt it, too. I just wanted you to know."

When my face pinches in confusion, he says, "The time you felt something for me, I felt it, too." He shakes his head in frustration, searching for the right words. "I knew the moment I entered this house. One look at you was all I needed."

He meets my eyes. "I did try to fight it though. I forced myself to stay away, denying every single urge to touch you to see if you were real. I mean, you couldn't be real, right? It had to be all in my head, the fact that something as simple as a smile, or a glance, was enough to give me hope. So, I distanced myself, but only because I didn't dare believe."

He touches my cheek. "Without you even knowing it, each smile, each glance, thawed the ice I'd used to numb myself." He wraps his fingers around my wrists, displaying my forearms. "And these"—he lifts them higher, eyes on mine as he presses his lips reverently to each scar—"Your trust, your willingness to share them with someone as unremarkable as me, well. Like I said, there was no ice left after that."

Lukas looks at me with earnest eyes, his expression suddenly shy. "I just…I need you to know that. To know that you weren't the only one to feel, and not the only one completely in awe that this is happening between us. I mean, you feel it too, right?"

I nod. It's overwhelming, unbelievable actually, that two people can feel so much for one another in such a short amount of time. Yet here we are, helpless to do anything but.

And although I should reassure him, one word churns over and over in my mind, begging to be rectified.

"You aren't unremarkable, Lukas. You're everything." My voice breaks—I'm frustrated that I can't make him see what everyone else around him sees. I lift my hands and cradle his face, forcing him to meet my eyes. "You are extraordinary, and your life is invaluable. I don't know why you can't see it, but hopefully one day you'll realize how brightly you can shine. Because regardless of what you believe, it wasn't me who melted your walls—it was you."

Lukas tilts his head back to look to the ceiling. Dropping my arms, I watch the muscles lining his throat work as he swallows deeply, praying he's not reconstructing his ice fortress. After a number of excruciating seconds pass, he lowers his face, his eyes glistening. "If only it was that easy for me to believe."

He leans toward me, planting a lingering kiss on my cheek. "I don't think I'll ever see what you see, but I hope one day I can."

Then, without another word, he's gone.

Dazed, I glance at the open door, confused by his abrupt disappearance. But as I consider Lukas in his entirety, tonight may have been too much. He needs time to process such palpable, powerful emotions.

I get it.

And I respect it.

So, I don't follow him, though it kills me not to. I simply turn off the bathroom light and head to my room.

It's dark when I enter and suspiciously quiet—Genny isn't snoring. I look over to the twin bed across from mine to confirm she's still tucked in it. When her sleeping form rolls in my direction, I crawl under my sheets. Just as I flop on my belly and nestle my head into my bunched pillow, Genny's voice breaks the silence.

"He loves you."

I shake my head in the darkness. Love is such a strong word. "He *likes* me," I correct.

She mirrors my position, turning onto her stomach and tucking her pillow under her cheek. "No. He loves you. He has for a long time now."

I laugh and shake my head. "What? You're crazy."

The moonlight splintering through our blinds plays off her features, exposing her grin. "That I am, my friend. But I'm also not stupid. Or blind. That boy loves you, plain as day."

And I swear to God, she could be possessed or just sleep-talking, because as soon as the last words leave her mouth, she starts snoring.

With my cheek on my pillow, I listen to Genny impersonate a chainsaw, thinking about what she said, Lukas's admissions, and even my own earlier tonight. I replay the evening from start to finish, and by the time I'm through, a wide, shameless grin on my face.

Like Lukas, I was numb for a very long time. It took over a year at Sacred Heart for me to finally be able to accept myself entirely. My flaws, my strengths, my quirks, and most importantly, my scars.

Tonight was an emotional roller coaster, full of nerve-wracking ups and stomach-churning downs, but guess what? I felt every single emotion. And I did it fearlessly, arms thrown above my head, heart racing with each gust that stole my breath and each winding jolt I didn't see coming. It's a ride I almost deprived myself of experiencing. I'm not proud of my attempt to end my life, but I am proud I survived. And now? I'm finally thriving.

With my parents, there was no hope. No sign of love, let alone unconditional love. No wonder my world was so dark, so bleak. No wonder getting away from the darkness of my parents was what gave me the space to heal.

Does Lukas love me?

I don't know. I really don't.

I do love him, just as I love Genny and Adam.

And I also know with absolute certainty that somehow along the way, I learned to love myself.

Maybe there's a reason it took so long for Lukas and me to admit our feelings. Maybe one of us needed to take the plunge first in order to gain the necessary strength and confidence to persuade the other to take the same ride. And I know, without a doubt—every heartbreak I endured, every night I spent crying myself to sleep, every day I'd dreamed of a life like so many around me were living—I would relive every one of my agonizing experiences just to exist longer in this moment, right now.

I don't have to be angry anymore. I don't have to

hurt anymore. And I definitely don't have to be ashamed anymore. I'm choosing to see my past as a gift. It served to strengthen me, prepare me, and mold me in such a way that I'm now ready to utilize everything I've learned from it to guide someone else out of their own icy darkness.

And there it is, something I've never felt before. *Peace.* I inhale deeply, then grin.

I sure hope Lukas White enjoys roller coasters as much as I do, because he's most certainly in for one hell of a ride.

17

Lukas experiences his first massive drop in a week's time.

For the last ten minutes of our session, we've been listening to him tell Sally the story he shared at the Wildflowers ceremony. And although we've heard it before, it hurts just as much the second time around. He's definitely more guarded with Sally present. His tone is clipped, his eyes cautious. But even with his guard up, his courage renders me breathless.

When he's through, he relaxes back in his chair as though exhausted, and I more than understand the feeling. Vulnerability can be difficult and extremely taxing.

Sally sets her notepad on the floor next to her, smiling reassuringly as she folds her hands in her lap. "Lukas, I'm so proud of you for trusting me with that aspect of your past. I know it wasn't easy to share, but it needs to be acknowledged and discussed. And I need you to hear me when I say, you did nothing wrong that night."

He scoffs. "I went to jail, Sally. Obviously I did."

She shakes her head sternly. "No. You didn't. You were a victim protecting another victim. Plain and simple. You did a good thing, Lukas."

His head slices to the right in refusal to accept her words. "Well, she's gone now, so I guess I'll never know if I helped her or not."

Sally then leans forward in her chair. When she speaks, her voice is soft, yet daring. "Would you like to know?"

My eyes widen in surprise.

How can Sally possibly know something like that?

Next to me, Lukas shifts uncomfortably in his chair. Trepidation whirls in his thunderous eyes, yet tiny flecks of hope seem to glimmer from behind the clouds. Sally's utterly fearless as she holds his gaze, her gaze as impenetrable as his.

I want to reach for him, but I've learned something very relevant to this situation since my time began here. Sometimes you need to take the first step toward healing on your own. Only he can face his deepest fears. We are here alongside him, so he's not physically or emotionally alone, but I know it's important for him to do this on his own. And Sally is challenging him to do just that.

Minutes pass, then he swallows deeply. His low voice is surprisingly soft when he replies, "Yes."

Sally smiles, partly with relief, but mostly with pride. Her entire body seems to relax when she answers. "Michelle

Griffin was formally adopted over a year ago. She has two loving parents who adore her, and an extremely protective older brother three years her senior. She has a safe home, and a new life in a new city. She's doted on every minute of every day, and smiles just as often."

Oh my God. She's okay. Please hear those words, Lukas. Please hear them.

Lukas swipes a nervous hand through his hair while Sally speaks. It comes to rest on the nape of his neck just as she adds, "She's happy, Lukas. Because of you. Because of what you did for her. And her parents have asked me to thank you personally for saving their baby girl."

And upon hearing those last words, all defenses Lukas had in place disintegrate. He scoots forward in his chair, placing his bent elbows on his knees, and scrubs his face. His powerful body trembles uncontrollably, years of worry and relief slowly being released.

Genny, Adam, and I stand, moving next to him. Together, we place our hands on his shoulders, giving him strength. His body sags with our touch, calmed by our presence. Sally rises as well, taking the three strides necessary to stand in front of him, then crouches on her knees. Eventually, Lukas removes his hands from his face, and with red-rimmed, bleary eyes, whispers quietly, "Thank you."

Sally places her finger under his chin, nudging his head back gently. I fully expect him to refuse her touch, but surprisingly, he's okay with it. Her eyes hold his for a brief moment, then she smiles. "A passionate heart that demands action cannot be defined by such simplistic terms like 'black' and 'white,' or 'good' and 'bad.' It acts without fear of consequence because love drives its action, not intellect. It's wild and reckless and uninhibited, but it's that heart that garners the ability to change lives. To reroute someone's very existence. Someone like Michelle Griffin, for example."

She drops her hand. "Lay your guilt to rest, Lukas. You did what you needed to do to keep her safe. End of story. You changed Michelle's existence for the better. Your actions did not make you a bad person. They made you a hero." She narrows her eyes, and when she finally speaks again, her tone is demanding. "Accept that."

He nods his head in response.

Sally, clearly fluent in Lukas-speak, beams at him before standing and directing her grin at the rest of us. "I'm so proud of every single one of you. You're all growing by leaps and bounds, right in front of my eyes. Each of you is maturing into your own beautiful, caring soul, and I'm honored to be a part of your journeys."

She laughs quietly, then adds, "While I'm here to help you, it's you who are opening my eyes with your willingness to embrace change. So, thank you…Wildflowers."

She turns, effectively ending today's group session. Her customary yoga pants swishing and the brush of her swinging ponytail are the only sounds as she leaves the living room.

Shocked, we gape after her as she exits. Not once have we mentioned our being Wildflowers to anyone outside our group.

Wide-eyed, Adam turns to Genny. "Did she—"

Genny nods. "She did."

I giggle at their bewildered expressions and offer my two cents. "She probably hypnotized us at some point. We just don't remember it."

"That's kind of the point of hypnosis," a deep voice rumbles.

All eyes fall on Lukas, whose mouth is tipped up at the corners. I'm amazed at the youthful expression on his face. Vulnerability stares back at me through reddened eyes, a wry smile, and worry lines that have almost been completely erased. Although he's been more at ease lately, this is the first time I've ever seen him truly at peace. And the sight is, well, it's indescribable. It's the way Lukas deserves to be seen. The way he should've been seen since the moment he was born, yet all these years, his true form remained hidden behind hard lines of fury and reluctance.

But to see him now, in all his glory...

Witnessing Lukas completely uninhibited, free of whatever demons bound him in his darkness, well...it's true happiness.

I smile, cupping his cheek with my hand. I remain silent, but my eyes speak for me. *I'm so proud of you.*

He leans into my touch, then turns his head to place a small kiss on my palm in response.

I smile wider and so does he, as though we're sharing a secret, which in the presence of the other Wildflowers, is a completely ludicrous notion.

Together, Genny and Adam roll their eyes, but it's Adam who breaks the silence. "Are we going or what?"

"We're going," Lukas replies, his unwavering eyes never leaving mine.

Adam chuckles. Genny clasps her hands together, impatient. "Then let's go. We have to be back in two hours. And I want to bowl, bitches."

She points then swings her finger between Lukas and me. "You two can eye-fuck each other there. Here, you're just wasting precious time and getting nothing accomplished."

She winks.

Lukas chuckles.

Adam nods.

My cheeks flush crimson, and I frown when I realize all eyes are on me. "Then let's go," I announce. And then I nearly laugh, because this will be my first date with Lukas. Well, for me. Evidently he's been on many without my knowledge. The thought threatens to split my face in two.

Lukas stands. I watch his black V-neck stretch taut across his back, then his triceps flex when he drags his hands over his jean-clad thighs. I'm, mesmerized watching the waves of rippled muscles. He stops and looks over his shoulder. Seeing my expression, he smiles smugly, his eyes bright with amusement. I crinkle my nose at him. He throws his head back and laughs outright. Helpless against it, I fight my grin, and lose.

His heavy booted steps sound as he walks to where I stand. Smile wide, hair pointed crazily in every direction, he inquires, "See something interesting?"

I narrow my eyes, "Yeah. I'm wondering how you can afford an entire container of gel every time you style your hair. You must go through like ten bottles a week."

He gently drapes an arm over my shoulders. "Hair putty. A little bit goes a long way."

"Good to know," I remark, inhaling his smell before adding, "maybe I'll borrow some. For Halloween. When I'm the Bride of Frankenstein. Or Guy Fieri."

He presses his lips to the top my head, his warm chuckles tousling my hair. I grin as we fall into step with the others and head toward the front door.

Twenty minutes later, we're standing in the front of Bowling Barn. Eyeing the entrance, I shake my head at the odd name. Bowling in a barn? It makes absolutely no sense, but I go with it, because they have ten-dollar lanes today. All day, including shoes.

Badass Chloe, meet Bowling Chloe.

Seth arrives soon after we do, and I get a warm feeling when he and Adam greet each other with longing stares and a lengthy embrace. After we pay, we grab our rented shoes and take our seats at lane eleven.

I watch instead of participating, which is pretty much the norm for me. I'm a people watcher. I haven't even put on my shoes when Genny throws her first strike.

Just as I take off my tennis shoes, I hear laughing and murmurs from behind me. I cast a glance over my shoulder to see a group of men pointing and whispering, then turn to see Adam and Seth a few feet in front of me, currently hand in hand as they discuss the weights of the bowling balls.

Innocent enough, right?

But their interlaced fingers are enough to catch the men's curiosity.

"Well, aren't they cute. Two boys holdin' hands," a deep voice rumbles, followed by more laughter.

I shake my head, disgusted. Then I roll my neck, trying anything I can to ignore that such intolerance exists here and now, but unfortunately it does, and it's glaring.

Literally.

Fed up with their ignorance, I turn in my seat to face them, but I'm momentarily blinded by the amount of plaid flannel they're wearing. I almost lose focus, but thankfully I pull it together, suppressing the need to point out that just because it's the Bowling Barn, actual farming attire is not required.

I make eye contact with one of them, let's call him Farmer Ted, to the right. "I'm sorry."

He smiles. "For what, sweetheart?"

I swallow a surge of bile before replying sweetly, "You just missed your ride."

He looks around, counts his crew, then leans into my very personal space, confusing my statement for flirtation. "Did I? I think another one can be arranged." He arches an eyebrow, and I stave off nausea.

Double gross.

I feel rather than see Lukas take a seat next to me, no

doubt wondering what the hell I'm doing. Farmer Ted's gaze shifts, completely unaware of Lukas's threatening presence as he aims a scowl of disgust over my shoulder. I twist to follow his eyes and watch as Adam and Seth take their seats on the opposite side of the lane, clearly unaware of anything outside their love bubble.

Turning back to Farmer Ted, I narrow my eyes and clear my throat to regain his attention. "No, you definitely missed it. But if you go out to the back alley"—I point to the emergency exit to clarify—"I'm sure you'll find Doc waiting with a DeLorean, ready to transport you and your bigoted friends back to the 1950s, just in time to enjoy the lavender scare, you bigoted asshole."

Farmer Ted's mouth falls open. Since I'm sure he has no idea what the lavender scare was—thank God I was paying attention that day in history—I'm sure his reaction has to do with a woman actually speaking her mind instead of getting him a sandwich. Or it could have been the expletive.

Either way, I'm not done.

"You see"—I jerk a thumb over my shoulder, indicating our group—"we don't get out much. And I"—I jab my chest—"don't appreciate you attempting to ruin the tiny amount of freedom we've been given with your archaic mindset and homophobic tendencies. So, go jump in a DeLorean or find another lane. Either way, I need you to disappear. Now."

Ted clamps his mouth shut. Then he opens it again and sputters, "Bitch—"

That single word is all he manages before Lukas stands, rising to his full height, and turns to face Ted. His face is stone, his eyes are ice, and his tone is deadly. "Apologize."

I grin obnoxiously, watching Ted's head slowly drift backward as he takes in Lukas's massive form. It takes some time due to Lukas's height, but when they eventually lock eyes, Lukas crosses his arms over his chest and lifts a challenging brow. Ted blanches and drops his gaze to mine.

He clears his throat.

After a lengthy swallow, he finally manages a measly, "I'm sorry."

I halfheartedly accept his apology, pursing my lips, still not quite satisfied. I cock my head expectantly while Lukas remains steady and stoic next to me. After receiving a blank stare in response, Lukas demands, "Apologize to them, too."

Right about that time, Seth, Adam, and Genny migrate over to us, noticing our dispute. I watch Ted's eyes widen as they take in Genny with her black lips, pink hair, ripped tank top and cargo pants. She lifts her left combat boot up and slams it down next to me in my chair and leans in, moving her body protectively in front of mine.

"Is there a problem here?" Her hand dangles nonchalantly from her knee. She even takes a moment to examine her chipped, black nails before refocusing her attention on Ted's quickly paling face.

I don't think they have many Gennys out in farm country. Just cows. And pigs.

I scan him thoughtfully.

Definitely pigs.

His gaze travels over my head and I instinctively feel both Adam and Seth tense behind me. Ted drops his stare to what I know must be their joined hands, and as soon as his expression begins to tighten, I clear my throat again. Loudly.

Lukas silently backs up my threat by uncrossing his arms, his hands balling into fists as they fall to his side.

Ted lifts his eyes then mutters, "Sorry."

"Nah, it's cool." Adam's tone is jovial. "It wouldn't be a regular outing if at least one person didn't gawk at us as though we're lepers or something. So, yeah, thanks for helping us meet that quota so we can get on with our date." He chuckles and whispers something to Seth, then they turn and walk away, clearly done with Farmer Ted.

I frown, saddened that they're destined to deal with this shitty situation on a regular basis. Love is hard enough on its own. Adding in constant judgment and ridicule…I can't even imagine their hardship.

Lost in my thoughts, I watch as one of Ted's flannel-clad-bumpkin friends claps a hand on his shoulder and mutters something. Ted nods, and without further comment, they move to a lane at the opposite end of the Bowling Barn.

Genny shakes her head, "Always with the commotion. Is it too much to ask to have one drama-free excursion?"

"Looking at our track record, I'd have to say that's a negative," I reply, before rising and spinning around on my socked feet. When I complete the turn, I'm staring directly at Lukas's chest. Surprised, I look up to find him shaking his head and smiling widely.

"What?" I ask, stuffing one of my feet into a bowling shoe. Once it's in, I stomp it a couple times. I have no idea why, really. It's something I've always done.

"You."

My forehead crinkles as I put on the other shoe. "What about me?"

Lukas watches me, clearly amused, then reaches forward and tucks a section of hair behind my ear. I swallow, feeling the heat rising in my cheeks.

"You're loyal."

"You're fierce."

His hand drops to my arm, as does his stare. He grazes one of my scars with his fingers.

"You're brilliant."

I suppress a shudder, watching the intensity of his eyes as they track his movement. With no more scar left to trace, he tenderly grips my hand and locks eyes with me, his stare resolute.

You're mine.

I lift our hands, uncurl his fingers, and press a kiss to the center of his palm, answering silently.

And you're mine.

18

It's midnight and I can't sleep. Again.

I haven't really been able to lately, due to an insane amount of restless energy, and I'm pretty sure there's one person to blame: Lukas.

My mind reels and my thoughts border on obsession. His smile, his eyes, his lips, his touch—I'm drowning in him, and I do so willingly.

I inhale deeply and smile, adjusting the waistline of my pickle pajama pants en route to the kitchen. I tell myself it's for a glass of water, but in reality, the double chocolate chip cookies we made earlier tonight are calling my name.

Just as I round the corner, I find Mrs. Rodriguez sitting at the kitchen table.

My eyes widen right along with hers. She's so busted.

I put my hands on my hips and quirk and eyebrow. "Mrs.

Rodriguez," I say, grinning. "A Toblerone in the middle of the night?" I tsk. "Now what kind of example is that for the young, impressionable minds living underneath your roof?"

She narrows her eyes and breaks off a couple of triangular sections as a peace offering. Or a bribe.

Whatever, the gesture works.

Smiling wider because of my victory, I pull out the seat next to her, plop down, and greedily palm the two pieces the second they hit my hand.

"Whatcha doing?" I ask, taking my first bite. I savor the flavor, allowing the milk chocolate to melt on my tongue and rolling it along the roof of my mouth until I get to the best part: the nougat.

She grins, and I giggle. "Eating chocolate," she replies. I roll my eyes and she laughs. After another bite, she then says, "I'm also enjoying some quiet time with you."

This woman is why I'm where I am today.

Her kindness. Her unconditional acceptance. Her devoted presence. I'm sure she has no idea how much her words heal. As she pats my hand lovingly, I smile in thanks. "What are you doing up at this hour?" she asks.

"I couldn't sleep. I can't seem to turn my brain off long enough to get some shut-eye."

She looks from her candy bar to me, popping the last bit into her mouth, and settles back in her seat. "Penny for your thoughts?"

Um, no. Not even a million dollars, Mrs. Rodriguez.

I blush and shake my head, stuffing my mouth with the

remaining chocolate.

"Is it Lukas?"

Completely unprepared for *that*, I gasp, sending loads of saliva-infused chocolate down my esophagus. I sputter, covering my mouth as I cough, and through tear-filled eyes, watch as Mrs. Rodriguez calmly rises and gets a glass of water. The attack tapers off just as she slides the glass in front of me, and I lift it to my mouth to take a long gulp.

And another.

Then another.

Stalling at its finest.

Knowing Mrs. Rodriguez, how she's eyeing me with practiced patience, I'm certain I'll have to say something eventually. But I give stalling my all, drinking until not a drop is left.

Which is a really bad idea because now my stomach is all sloshy.

I set the glass on the table and meet her eyes. After wiping away some stray tears and clearing my throat, I finally manage to speak. "What would Lukas have to do with anything?"

My vocal cords are still riled from the coughing, causing my voice to shake. At least, that's what I try to convinced myself is happening.

Mrs. Rodriguez's eyebrows lift, her mouth dips, and she shrugs. "I don't know. Why would you have that reaction to my mentioning him?"

Yeesh. When did Mrs. Rodriguez become so sassy?

"I choked accidentally."

She chuckles, and when I say nothing else, she says, "He's changed over the past few months. And although I'd like to take credit, I think his positive transition has more to do with you than anything I might have done."

She's done everything for us, truly, but it sounds like she means something else. "What *did* you do?" I ask, folding my arms on the table.

She smiles then responds simply, "I chose him. I'm very thorough when choosing who to accept into my home. Sacred Heart is constantly sending applicants, but I don't select children at random."

My mouth drops open, confused. "I thought this *was* Sacred Heart."

Her giggle is spritely as she pats my arm. "No, my sweet girl. My home is a branch of Sacred Heart, one of many, in fact. Every branch has a specific purpose, a designated specialty, if you will. I take in teens closer to aging out of the system, in particular, ones who've experienced especially traumatic events or childhoods." She smiles sadly, and I cover her hand with mine as she continues. "I've done so for years, selecting particular youths who called out to me for one reason or another. I examine their profiles, their strengths and weakness, their personalities, then I move them as though they're pieces of a puzzle until I find the perfect fit. Genny and Adam were the first two in the group of four, then you, then finally Lukas."

I purse my lips, trying to comprehend what she's saying.

Chosen? But she's still talking. "I do this because you won't be within my care forever. You won't be in my home, or in the next room, or even down the street. Eventually you will move into the real world, and when I let you go, I need to know I'm releasing you with a solid foundation of people who will always be there for you. People capable of picking you up when you inevitably fall down. People who will be present throughout the remainder of your life. The world isn't easy, Chloe. But I sure as hell feel a lot better sending you into it with those three at your back."

"Mrs. Rodruigez!" I gasp. "Language!"

Together, we break into laughter.

And just when I thought I was off the hook, she comes back to her original topic. "I knew Lukas would find what he needed within your group. Acceptance, forgiveness, family. But what I didn't expect was for him to discover the experience of falling in love for the very first time."

I shake my head, but she cuts me off with her raised hand. "Chloe, you may not want to see it, or believe it, and that's fine. Take your time. But just know that because of you, that troubled boy is evolving into the confident man he was always meant to be. You may not be able to erase his past, but you sure can color his future."

I look at her stunned. "And you're okay with two people dating under your roof?" My entire face flushes with the question, but I'm so stupefied by all of this it just…slips out.

Mrs. Rodriguez exhales, careful with her words. "Not all will agree, but the way I see it, some loves cannot be denied.

Nor can they be controlled. Telling you that you can't see him, or vice versa, will do nothing but create fissures in the very foundation that I've worked so hard to cement. However, while your feelings are unavoidable, your actions are still very much within the realm of your control."

I know exactly where this has to be headed, and although I'm protesting in my mind, there is nothing I can do outside of it except keep listening. Mrs. Rodriguez's voice is stern, as it always is when she's setting down a house rule. "There will be no sexual activity between you and Lukas in this home."

And there it is.

"That is my one rule. And I trust you both to show me the same respect that I have shown you when it comes to this matter."

I nod, feeling chastised, and I haven't even done anything wrong.

She dips her head in acceptance, and I will my heart to slow its rapid beating in my chest. At this rate I'll never go to bed, so it's definitely time to switch topics.

"Have you always worked with Sacred Heart?" I ask.

"No. Not always. I started after my Eddie died. We were unable to have children, so when he rejoined the Lord, I was left in this house with nothing but my grief to keep me company. After wallowing for a year or two, I decided I wanted this house to be full of children until the day I died. So I made my decision and never looked back. Fifteen years later, I've impacted many, lost some along the way, but every group fills me with a sense of purpose. And when I see you children come into your own, find your confidence and bloom, well, I can't imagine doing anything else with my life."

I glance to the picture of Eddie Rodriguez hanging next to the clock and smile before meeting her eyes. They're warm and peaceful.

And then I realize. If Mrs. Rodriguez chose Genny, Adam, and Lukas, that means she also chose me. Even before she knew me personally, she chose me. An adult, not related to me by blood, wanted me.

Chose me.

There are so many questions I want to ask—the why, the how, the when—but they're largely irrelevant. It had already been done. *She chose me.*

"I'm so grateful for you, Mrs. Rodriguez." My eyes become moist, tears brimming along my lower lashes. "I can't imagine living without you."

Another sad smile crosses her face, and she stands, her arms extended. My feet move of their own volition, and before I know it, I'm buried in her chest, enveloped in a motherly embrace. She strokes my head lightly and murmurs into my hair. "Silly girl. I'm not going anywhere for a long while."

I squeeze tightly and grin contentedly, foolishly, comforted by what to me was the first and last lie Mrs. Rodriguez ever told.

FALL

19

Mrs. Rodriguez passed peacefully in her sleep not even two weeks later.

Sally found her early one morning, before we had even gotten out of bed. And as horrible as this sounds, I'm so thankful it wasn't one of us who found her body. I don't think any of us could've handled that.

The funeral was a blur. I don't remember much other than thinking that the only real mother I'd ever known is dead, surrounded by nothing but cold soil and burrowing insects. Standing by her graveside, I prayed for the first time in my life. I pleaded with God to give her eternal warmth and sunshine in the arms of her Eddie when she ascended into heaven.

There was a whirlwind of activity after that. Lawyers relayed that Mrs. Rodriguez had left the home and pretty much all of her other worldly possessions to Sacred Heart, with strict instructions that the children in her house at the time of her passing would finish their time in the home, if they so chose.

We did, adamant in our refusal to be separated.

So we stayed, Sally acting as our guardian in place of Mrs. Rodriguez until further arrangements could be made.

The director of Sacred Heart also graced us with her presence during this time. Mrs. Davies and her bouffant of blonde hair arrived without announcement and she barged into our home as if she owned it, which I guess, technically, she does. But still, her presence was uncomfortable and unwelcome, as was her unfortunate pantsuit.

We kept to our rooms while she surveyed our home, her annoying heels clicking across every square inch. We spoke as little as necessary when pelted with her gazillion questions. None of us trusted her enough to say more than two or three words to her.

Afterward, as we watched her drive away from the front porch, I asked Sally why she couldn't take over for Mrs. Rodriguez permanently, because it sure as hell felt right to me for her to just step in.

Her answer was simple. "It doesn't work like that, Chloe. As much as I would like to, I'm not equipped to care for you four on my own."

It sounded ridiculous to me. I mean, we're not four toddlers in need of constant care, diaper changes, and feedings every three or so hours. What equipment would she possibly need other than a functioning brain and a beating heart to just…be here for us?

I detest when adults just want us to accept whatever small, vague explanation they've decided to give us. So often they expect us never to question them, merely take them at their word because they said so.

Did I blame Sally for this? No, not entirely. Young, inexperienced, and bombarded with an onslaught of new responsibility, she was trying to find and keep her footing just as much as we are.

Was I disappointed in her? Absolutely. And the others were, too.

We all felt rejected, even though that probably wasn't her fault. We'd lost our lifeline, and Sally didn't want to pick up that slack. It might've been irrational of us, but we all distanced ourselves from her after that. She lost her access to the Wildflowers…and in turn, we lost her.

That was last week.

Since then, things have quieted down, and with not much to keep us occupied, my mind is eager to wander. I refuse to allow it to succumb to grief, so here I am, painting the fence we'd promised Mrs. Rodriguez would be finished by the end of summer.

I miss her presence terribly. She loved us unconditionally. She was our leader, our mentor.

And now, she's gone.

How do we go on without her?

Although fall is weeks away on the calendar, I feel

as though the season has come early for the Wildflowers. Everything is changing in preparation for winter, and there's an undertone of finality to it all that I can't seem to shake.

So, instead of focusing on the inevitable, I paint.

And paint.

And paint.

I perform the mindless activity every chance I get, because instead of a chore, it's become equal parts escape and obligation.

Genny helps sometimes, but I think its reminder of Mrs. Rodriguez pains her, so she tends to disappear pretty quickly after starting. She was the first recruit of this particular group, and was therefore given more time with Mrs. Rodriguez than the rest of us. Genny knew exactly how to get any particular reaction out of her. She was shown a special fondness, and I worry she's incapable of dealing with the loss of Mrs. Rodriguez.

This isn't the first person Genny has lost. Her parents, Gee-Gee, and now Mrs. Rodriguez... She's been quiet. So quiet. I truly can't imagine what she's thinking. I just know my heart is breaking for her.

I inhale sorrowfully on an upstroke.

Adam and Lukas help, too, but they also have other responsibilities upholding Mrs. Rodriguez's other wishes. Adam spends hours in the two acres surrounding our home, pruning plants and pulling weeds where he can, while Lukas seems to devote every single minute of his spare time to her truck. I think in a way, we're all trying to make peace, to pay homage to the woman who brought us all together, and I can't help but feel in doing so, we're losing touch with each other.

But this is what we need to do to survive the loss.

Just as the thought crosses my mind, something stirs behind me, and I look over my shoulder to spot Lukas walking through the field, his distance reminding me of how much of this land is actually ours. I smile, even though I don't quite feel it.

Several minutes pass until he's near enough to take a seat next to me, quietly picking up the brush I left for Genny, just in case. Together, we paint in silence.

We're three-quarters of the way finished when Lukas finally speaks. "How're you holding up?"

I shrug, unable to find my voice. My throat is blocked by anguish. It's agonizing—the pressure so immense, I know if I open my mouth it will escape in a sob.

So, I clench my teeth against it and continue with the task at hand.

Lukas exhales a long, deep breath, dragging his hand through his hair. It's unruly as usual, having grown much longer over the summer months, and the scruff lining his face tells me he hasn't bothered to shave in a few days.

He bends his legs and crosses his arms over his knees. I know he's watching me—I can feel his eyes—but I pretend not to notice, choosing instead to focus on my painting. Moments later, my paintbrush is plucked from my hand and chucked out of reach. *What the hell?* I watch it sail through the air, then glower in Lukas's direction.

His gaze isn't angry or condemning as I expected. It's sympathetic, filled with patience, but the brows framing his eyes press together in concern. "Talk to me."

The deep tenor of his voice warms me. Inside my chest, I feel that warmth kneading and prodding until finally the hardened mass of sorrow in me slides upward, fills my throat, and escapes.

"I was so happy."

My voice breaks on the last word, and the gallons of tears I'd refused to cry surge, streaming down my cheeks. Lukas opens his arms and I collapse into his body, sobbing as he envelops me.

His fingers run through my hair as he strokes my head and murmurs to me gently, and I clench his shirt between my fingers, anchoring myself to him as my grief consumes me. I hold on tight, replaying every moment I spent with Mrs. Rodriguez and wishing there were a million more.

Eventually, a strand of hair is tucked behind my ear, and I feel Lukas's lips on my forehead, my temple, my cheek. "You'll be happy again, Chloe. You need to let yourself grieve."

I sniffle. "I know. I don't want to let her go."

I can't. I can't let her go.

I don't know how to.

His arms tighten around me, and my head rises and falls as he breathes. "You never have to let her go. She lives on in our memories, and the memories of every other person she's been there for throughout her lifetime."

I nod, accepting his words, and take in the first real, full breath I've taken in days. "I'm scared," I mumble into his shirt.

"Of what?"

"The unknown." Having no idea who is coming into our house, who will be responsible for us now, scares me to death. I shiver. Lukas must feel it, because he begins rubbing my back in a large circular motion.

"We'll be fine. We have each other, right? I mean, we are the Wildflowers. Doesn't that mean anything to you anymore?"

He chuckles when I pinch his waist, and I can't fight back a grin of satisfaction. "Yeah, it means everything." I breathe in, then arch my neck to look him straight in the eyes. "You mean everything...to me."

His eyes flare with my admission, then slowly, his mouth quirks at the corner. He brings his hands to my cheeks, wiping away my tears before he presses his mouth gently over mine.

There's nothing more in the world that would make me happier than to belong to Lukas White, and have him belong to me. He deserves to have someone in this world that's his.

He leans away, noticing my smile, then I see his dimple as his teeth flash and he says, "There's my girl."

I can't help myself. I blush right there on the spot, and his grin widens. Then he jerks his head in the direction of the fence. "Ready to finish this bad boy?"

I nod, rising to my feet and brushing the grass off the

backside of my denim shorts.

Lukas watches, then offers, "I can do that for you."

I give him a cheeky grin before walking over to where my paintbrush landed when he flung it not too long ago. Familiar laughter fills my ears, and I pivot to find Adam and Genny approaching, brushes in hand.

I begin crying again at the sight of them, but they're happy tears this time.

Genny's face falls, and she stops where she stands. She takes one look at my tears, then glares at Lukas. "What'd you do, asshole?"

Lukas responds with a deep, vibrating laugh, nothing more.

Adam keeps walking, closing the distance between us and wrapping his arms around me, lifting me off the ground. "Missed you."

I smile into his neck, squeezing him just as tightly. "Missed *us*."

He sets me on my feet. His gleaming eyes crinkle at the corners as he bends, grabs my paintbrush from the ground, and holds it out to me. "Let's remedy that."

Four hours later, the fence is finally done, and we stand together, inspecting our work.

"She'd be proud," I remark, shielding my eyes from the setting sun.

"She'd be pissed." Genny points her brush at the plank in front of her. "She hates"—she stops, swallows, then continues—"hated paint drips."

She wipes the raised streak away with a stroke of her brush, the dried, hardened bristles etching lines into the fresh coat of paint. But she doesn't stop there. She continues painting, inscribing three large words across several planks in her unmistakable handwriting, then quietly turns and takes her place next to me.

YOU ARE LOVED.

The day after Mrs. Rodriguez and I shared our midnight Toblerone, I told them about how she had chosen us and why, which made her loss even more difficult to bear. In many respects, we had all been tossed away by those who should have loved us, except Genny. She recalled how lost she'd felt when Gee-Gee died, fearful no one would ever want her again. But she had been chosen, and I knew that had meant absolutely everything to her.

You are loved.

The words are nearly indistinguishable, but we see them, and will forever know they're there.

Shoulder to shoulder, we join hands, finding strength to do what we couldn't do apart. And a sense of peace wraps around us as we say our final goodbye.

20

After successfully surviving the first day of school, we gather together in the living room, completely deflated. A day that should have been filled with the excitement and anticipation of senior year was weighted down with sorrow. We spent it mourning. Missing things.

The encouraging notes from Mrs. Rodriguez tucked in our lunches.

The comforting smell of first-day-of-school cookies waiting for us when we arrived home.

The laughter in her eyes as we described our teachers and how much we already hated them.

In place of the warmth and comfort we're used to coming home to after a long school day, there is only a stillness. An absence.

And then there's Sally and her rattled state.

From our seats, we watch her—she's been granted temporary residence here as our interim guardian—furiously dash about trying to clean the house. That we've already thoroughly cleaned for her. Twice.

It's hard to not be insulted. Why ask someone to do something you're just going end up doing anyway?

I say nothing, though.

None of us do.

We just sit in our customary seats on the couch, strangely fascinated by the speed at which she's moving. It's kind of incredible, actually.

Instead of her routine yoga pants and a tank, she's wearing a simple, black tunic dress with matching heels that *click-click-click* against the floor while she scurries around like a deranged maid. Her hair is down, long tousled blonde strands whirling while she frantically glances around the living room for anything else that needs to be wiped down or straightened.

Our new guardians are due to arrive any moment, and clearly, Sally's losing her shit. I say "guardians" because now there are going to be two. A married couple.

It seems off when I think about it: a man living in the house. But considering that actually would resemble a child's typical familial scenario these days, I wonder how skewed my definition of family has actually become.

For me, Mrs. Rodriguez was the be-all and end-all. I needed nothing else, no one else. Throwing a man into the mix just means more unknowns, and it seems I really don't do well with unknowns.

But as I glance to the right, then the left, I see two boys beside me that have grown into astounding men. I reach out to them and grip their hands, tightly. Eyes still on Sally, they both take hold, without question, providing much-needed solidarity.

Genny, however, with her legs hooked over the arm of the couch and her Docs bouncing off its side, narrows her eyes, scrutinizing Sally's every move. Her head, perched on Adam's lap, shakes with tangible frustration. "What the hell? The house is fucking clean already."

A burst of laughter escapes my nose. Sally somehow manages to stop and wheels in our direction.

"Genesis! Language," she asserts.

Oh shit. We all bristle at the same time. The reprimand so often given by Mrs. Rodriguez is just not the same rolling off Sally's tongue, and my heart aches again. She, too, frowns in recognition of the difference then clears her throat. "I'm sorry. I'm just nervous. I need to make a good impression."

We all stare blankly back at her, not understanding. She inhales deeply, regains her calm, then explains. "I'm not guaranteed to stay in this home with you. And as much as I would like to think my time with you gives me precedence, nothing's for certain. I'm just trying to do what I can to make sure I stay through the remainder of your time here."

"Then why not accept the offer to take over when it was presented to you?"

Thank you, Lukas, for voicing the exact thought that has plagued my mind for weeks now!

She sighs, defeated, looking at the glossy wooden floors beneath her feet. When her eyes level with ours, they're brimming with tears. "I know you're all upset with me, and I understand why. You feel as though I've betrayed you, and honestly, I feel the same way. But Sacred Heart wouldn't allow it, and I can't say that I blame them. I'm only twenty-eight years old, which to you may seem old enough to be a fully-fledged adult, but it's not. I struggle to get my bills paid on time, I watch TV when I know I should be focusing on responsibilities, and I binge eat Chinese food every single chance I get."

After a despondent shake of her head, she continues. "I just…I'm barely able to take care of myself. Taking the four of you under my wing, well, I can't teach you all what I don't know. I think I've come to identify with you so strongly because I feel as though I'm growing with you. Is that right? Probably not, but that's where we are. And the God's honest truth is, I'm not the best person to fully care for you at this point in my life. I wish I was, but I'm not. I refuse to take on the crucial guidance of your lives when I'm uncertain of the direction of my own."

None of us respond. We simply observe her where she stands, hands on her hips, her candid admission having made her slightly nervous. And in this moment of openness, as she exposes her own weakness and insecurity, I realize how young she really is.

And by the hue of purplish-blue under her eyes, I also know her decision wasn't an easy one to make.

So, I decide to extend an olive branch on the Wildflowers' behalf. "Well, you look really pretty, Sally. You're going to make a great first impression."

Her mouth curves into a modest smile. "You think?"

Then Genny says, "Well, you've definitely made *an* impression. You've been racing around for hours like a crackhead on a cleaning binge in five-inch heels. So, color *me* impressed."

A burst of laughter explodes from my mouth, Adam releases my hand to cover his own, and Lukas chuckles silently beside me.

Sally goes wide-eyed and gasps, but the doorbell rings before she can respond. Her body stiffens with the sound. She closes her eyes and inhales deeply before opening them again. With a nervous smile, she looks at each one of us, giving us one last glimpse of Youthful Sally, then transforms into Professional Sally on her way to the door.

We, however, remain seated. Waiting.

As unfamiliar voices begin to drift into the living room, I look sideways at Lukas, swallowing a sudden surge of anxiety. He gives my hand an encouraging pump. When footsteps signal their impending approach, he twists to look over his shoulder. Squeezing his hand like a vise, I shift my body toward the sounds and wait.

Sally leads the pack, eyes narrowed in warning as she enters the living room, clearly noting our refusal to stand.

She jerks her head once, and four relenting sighs sound as we rise. The hairs on the back of my neck lift, and suddenly I'm hyperaware of a crucial point I'd missed in the fog of my grief: the two people entering this room have the ability to change the entire course of our lives.

I force myself to drop Lukas's hand, anticipating that they most likely won't be as accepting of our relationship as Mrs. Rodriguez. The mere thought of her pings my heart with sadness, but when I picture her warm smile, I take small comfort.

I trusted her, and it was the wisest decision I ever made. So, maybe I should extend these two the same courtesy. *And pray the end result is the same.*

I turn to face the moment I've been dreading for weeks.

My eyes land on an older couple, probably in their late fifties. She's wearing beige nylon pants and a white button-down with a blood-red sweater layered overtop, and black slip-on shoes with matching rubber soles that may or may not be from a product line of SAS footwear. She's decently dressed, but I can't shake the feeling that her grandmotherly appearance is manufactured. That being said, the man standing next to her clearly found any effort of disguising himself too taxing and is clad in a plain white T-shirt with what looks to be a coffee stain on the neck, loose brown corduroy pants, and tennis shoes that have seen better days.

Both have salt and pepper hair, but where hers is thick, gathered in a wiry bun, his has receded. The last few strands are greased over the top of his head and pale skin peeks through various sections of the comb over. She's noticeably taller than he is and approximately half his girth, but what really captures my attention isn't their attire or the shapes of their bodies. It's their eyes. They're black and beady and eerily similar. And the way they're surveying us is…creepy?

Their matching stares fix on me, then Lukas, then Adam, and their eyes widen slightly when they land on Genny. Not a big surprise there. She took her rebellious aesthetic to another level by dressing in black from head to toe. Black long-sleeved shirt, black jean shorts, black fishnet stockings, and of course, black combat boots that reach her knees. Add in her typical black lipstick and nails, and it's clear she's channeling goth instead of punk in honor of today's occasion.

Sally clears her throat, sweeping her hand in front of the couple. "Genesis, Adam, Chloe, Lukas, this is Mr. and Mrs. Duff. As you know, Sacred Heart has placed them in charge for the remainder of your time in this home." Her eyes bounce between the four of us as she adds, "You will show them the same respect and courtesy you afforded Mrs. Rodriguez."

Mrs. Duff waves a dismissive hand, curling her arm around her husband's. "Oh, there's no need for such a tone, Ms. Gillespie. I have no doubt that respect and courtesy will *not* be a problem in this house."

She smiles, but it doesn't reach her eyes. I mean, how can it? There's so much disdain in them—there's no room for anything else.

She observes us a few more seconds. "What an interesting cast of characters we have to work with this time around."

Mr. Duff chuckles, patting the hand draped over his forearm. "To say the least."

I frown at his snide comment, fighting the urge to reach for Lukas's hand. He must feel the same, because he shifts and presses his shoulder firmly against mine.

Mrs. Duff looks impassively at Sally. After a cursory once-over, she flashes her fraudulent smile and states evenly, "Well. Thank you, Ms. Gillespie, for the introductions. Your time in this home, however, will no longer be necessary."

Oh. Shit.

21

Standing beside Sally's car, an old boxy Volkswagen Jetta that predates our existence, possibly even hers, I wipe my cheeks free of tears and watch as she tosses the remainder of her office into the trunk. Her eyes mirror ours, watery and swollen in anticipation of our inevitable goodbye.

She slams the lid, and when she turns to face us, her chin trembles. Her bleary gaze meets each of ours before she releases a lengthy, resigned sigh.

"I'm so sorry. I had hoped nothing would change with their arrival." Her mouth tightens into a paper-thin line. "I will fight this. I will talk to every person I can at Sacred Heart and communicate my fears that more change at this point could be detrimental to your healing. I will do this until I have no voice. And when I can no longer speak, I will write everyone and anyone I can think of to get me back in here."

Her eyes flood with more tears, and as I watch her break down, I know she's coming to the same conclusion we've already drawn.

None of this would have happened if she'd just been able to take over.

Her eyes slam shut and her head falls into her hands. I take a step to comfort her, but I'm startled back into place when she flings her head back and looks to the sky. After inhaling deeply, she brushes the tears from her face, quickly regaining composure and resolve. "I did not prevent this, but I will do my damnedest to fix it."

She nods resolutely, and we do the same in acceptance of her words. It's all we can do.

Genny surprises me by stepping forward, then floors me when she wraps her arms around Sally in a warm embrace. Not once has she been inclined to hug someone outside our group. Not even Mrs. Rodriguez.

Sally's arms tighten around Genny's upper body, and her hand lovingly strokes her pink hair. We watch silently in awe, then together we move to where they stand, and we embrace them both as best we can.

From within the depths of our bunched bodies, Sally whispers, "Wait for me, hold on to each other, and never lose hope."

Then it's as if the pain can no longer be contained—we just kind of lose it. Eventually though, we force ourselves to release her and watch as Sally rounds her car and opens the door.

She leans inside, shuffles around a bit, and turns to face us with a pen clamped between her teeth. She glances around conspiratorially and hurriedly writes something on the back of what looks to be a business card. One by one, she distributes them to each of us. "This is my personal number. Strictly against Sacred Heart policy, but regardless, these are for you. Do not hesitate to call if you need anything, day or night."

We put the cards away swiftly, and when we look up, we're met with Sally's defeated stare. "I'm so, so sorry."

Adam blows out a breath, then answers, "Don't be sorry. Just come back."

Her head bobs, and after another long look at each of us, she climbs into her car.

As we watch her drive away, Lukas shakes his head. "I should have been doing maintenance on that piece of shit this summer instead of the truck."

I glance up at his narrowed, watchful eyes. "We needed the truck though."

"The truck was fixed a while back. I've just been tinkering under the hood to keep myself busy."

I crinkle my nose, fighting a giggle. The word "tinkering" from his mouth just seems all kinds of wrong. He must realize it, or hear my stifled laughter, because he looks at me and grins. I smile back wider when he runs his knuckle tenderly down my cheek. We watch until Sally turns the corner, and when we can no longer see her, we face the house.

Our home.

"Anyone else not want to go in there?" Genny asks.

"Definitely not."

"Hell to the no."

"Nope."

Genny whips her head to the side. "I think we need to visit our wildflowers."

"Definitely yes."

"Let's get the hell out of here."

"Yeah."

Much more motivated, we begin the hike to the truck. About halfway there, Lukas reaches in his pocket and mutters, "Damn. Keys are in the house."

Dejectedly and as one, we turn toward the front door, footfalls in sync. As soon as we're inside, Mrs. Duff greets us.

"Glad you're back. I need you kids to fetch our things from the car, take them into the main bedroom, then start on dinner. Early bedtimes are to be strictly observed in this house."

We all just kind of gawk at her until Genny raises her hand. When Mrs. Duff looks her way, she says, "We have somewhere we're obligated to be. We can do it after that."

Mrs. Duff raises her eyebrows, and she gives Genny a condescending grin. "Child, you are obligated to be where we tell you to be from now on. And where you will be is getting our things, taking them to the main bedroom, and then making our dinner."

Genny opens her mouth to argue, but Mrs. Duff leans

into her personal space, her tone as sharp and cold as ice. "You will be severely punished for disobedience. This is your one and only warning."

She breaks away from Genny, redirecting her statement to the rest of us. "Do not push us, or you won't like where you end up when you're pushed back. Trust me on that."

The look in her eyes? It's cold and bitter. I've known neglect, but this I've never seen.

I now fear I'll see it every time I close my eyes.

Pure evil stands in front of us, and it takes everything in me not to outwardly cower. On the inside though, I'm folding in on myself, crumpling like a piece of paper in an effort to make myself as small as I can. It's something I never thought I'd have to do again, yet I do it to get as far away from her as possible, even if it's only internally. I don't want her darkness anywhere near my soul.

Mr. Duff appears in the doorway of the kitchen, beer in one hand, the rest of a six-pack curled protectively under his other arm. "We havin' problems already, Tammy?"

Wow.

So, he clearly had no issue getting his beer from the car.

Lukas steps in front of me, his response even and cool. "No problem." Then to Mrs. Duff, *Tammy*, he states, "We get it. We've been warned."

Without another word, he brazenly turns his back to them and signals for our retreat with a dip of his head. I pivot woodenly, and along with the other three, we head out the door.

Once outside, we stare at each other until Lukas arrives.

He peers at the house, his teeth clenched. Seconds pass until he finally mutters, "Just like the fuckin' Harveys." When he twists back to us, his eyes are fierce. "Look, I've dealt with people like this before. They're predators. I can see it in their eyes. Just keep a low profile." He trains his stare on Genny. "Do not make waves." Then he looks between Adam and me. "Stay calm and never react when provoked. Ever. They will look for any reason to deliver whatever punishment they get off on giving."

My throat clamps shut at his assessment, because I know he's right. My heart kicks up into a panicked rhythm, and I watch as he glances over his shoulder before looking back at us. "Until I figure them out, stay together all the time, in twos at least. When possible, all of us travel in one pack. Safety in numbers."

And now I know the taste of fear.

I don't know if it's just the Duffs, or the fact that Lukas is declaring martial law on the Wildflowers, but there's an acrid fear settling in my stomach.

Lukas just meets my frightened eyes and states, "I will protect you. Just do as I say."

He lifts his gaze, and it's full of fire. "I will protect all of you."

His words are spoken with such ferocity and determination my racing heart completely breaks for him. Because standing in front of me is not Vulnerable Lukas, or the goofy, youthful, innocent version of him I've come to love.

The man in front of me is the hardened individual who entered this home, disconnected from feeling and fueled by anger and necessity.

He turns away from us and trudges to the Duff's car, flinging the door open and tossing their bags to the ground. Adam and Genny pass me on their way to help, but I can't seem to make my legs move. I'm gutted. Fate—*again*—has dealt Lukas a cruel and unjust hand. Just a few months after having finally found his freedom, he's trapped, forced to relive one of many nightmares he's worked so hard to escape.

I have no idea what our future holds with the Duffs. I wonder if maybe Lukas is overreacting, but all the same, he might be right in his need to act preemptively.

What I do know for certain is that the light within him, the one that has soothed and nourished each one of us, is now an inferno of lethal fury.

A fiery blaze, capable of both protecting and torching us all. Just as he feared.

22

The first month with the Duffs goes pretty smoothly. Well, as smoothly as it can, considering we hole up in our rooms after school, only to surface when being called upon to perform some unwarranted chore of their choosing. It feels as though they're testing how far they can push us until we finally lash out.

Somehow we manage to keep our cool, focusing on the tasks at hand. Not even Genny loses control, though her clenched jaw, narrowed eyes, balled fists, and extremely long exhalations do not escape me. They don't escape Mrs. Duff's notice either. I see her eyeing Genny often, just waiting for her to explode, but thankfully she's managed to rein in her temper, and even more astonishingly, she's muzzled that normally unfiltered mouth of hers. For now.

We haven't talked about it, but I can see she's frightened,

too. She knows her silence is the only way to get through this, and I hate seeing her so…stifled.

It's Tuesday, the sun bright and shining, but as I look out the window a sense of sadness creeps into my heart. I really hope our wildflowers don't think we abandoned them. I picture their jovial bobbing in the wind, but as I continue to stare, the images morph into that of them drooping hopelessly toward the ground, sorrow and longing weighing down their usually pliant stems. Our kinship, it seems, knows no bounds.

Yeah, we feel you.

I sigh glumly, my breath fogging up the glass. I press my palm over the patch of condensation and spread my fingers wide.

Soon, I promise them, and I pray it's one I can keep.

"Kids!" Mr. Duff shouts from the bottom of the stairs. "We have some more cleaning to do." His voice is gruff, most likely from the twenty packs of cigarettes he smokes every day, and his words slur together from the equal number of beers he continuously drinks.

Our grocery budget has been cut dramatically in order to support his habits. We haven't had a decent meal in weeks. If I have to eat another cracker, I'm liable to gouge my eye out with it instead.

Genny growls from her bed, tossing her worn paperback copy of *1984* to the floor. I turn to find her with both middle fingers furiously directed at the door, her mouth open wide in a frustrated, but thankfully silent, scream. I chuckle, allowing her to speak for me while toeing on my flip-flops and securing my hair in a messy ponytail. She's panting by the time she's through, her face bordering on maroon before she regains control and inhales deeply.

"This is bullshit," she remarks under her breath as she stands. "This house is cleaner than God." She stomps her boots on the rug beneath her feet, forcing the hems of her olive-green Dickie cargos to slide over the laced tops.

I angle my head, considering her statement. "Is God really clean? Wouldn't there logically be a scenario in which he was occasionally dirty?"

She aims an apology toward the ceiling before responding. "Haven't you ever heard the saying 'cleanliness is next to godliness'?"

After a hefty snort, I remark, "I think that's in reference to spiritual purity, not actual dust bunnies."

She shakes her head, as though dismissing my ignorance. "What do you know? You never even pray."

I jut my chin defiantly in her direction. "I prayed at Mrs. Rodriguez's funeral."

Her eyebrows shoot toward the heavens.

Nodding deliberately, I conclude, "So there."

Genny's relationship with God is one that never ceases to confound me. The same girl capable of weaving ordinary curse words into auditory works of art can be found every single night kneeling reverently by her bedside as she prays. It seems so contradictory, but then again, Genny's a living, breathing paradox. She often projects darkness, yet there's a vast, indescribable essence of life in her that is both captivating and contagious. She's so brilliantly flawed, but it's those imperfections that make her...flawless.

So much so, I know without a doubt not even God Himself would change a thing about her.

And to be completely honest, if we're made in His image as the Bible proclaims, I'm pretty sure God Himself has dropped a few of His own F-bombs while witnessing the senseless acts of stupidity so often demonstrated by humanity these days.

Our bedroom door swings open, revealing both Lukas and Adam in the doorway. How many days now have I seen the hardened looks on their faces? The ones that silently tell me they're just as angry as we are about being summoned downstairs.

Lukas locks eyes with me as I mosey toward the door, my flip-flops slapping with each step I take. He directs his intense gaze at my feet and his steely expression softens a smidge, the corners of his mouth lifting slightly. Adam smiles broadly at me, lifting his arm so I can snuggle into him. So, I do.

I grin, nestling into Adam while his arm folds across my shoulders, then meet Lukas's penetrating stare.

I know, I wordlessly convey. *I belong in your arms.*

He nods his head in agreement, but makes no move to hold me, and I understand why. He can't, not now, not with the Duffs' close proximity. Instead, he grazes my cheek lightly with his knuckle, silently acknowledging his longing with a touch.

When Lukas drops his hand, I shiver with the loss of his warmth, and Adam tenderly curls me into his frame. I tear my eyes away from Lukas to grin at Adam in thanks. He winks, giving my arm a sympathetic squeeze.

The sound of Genny's heavy boots against the floor breaks the moment, and we all swivel our heads in her direction.

She looks between Adam and Lukas. "You know you don't have to stay on our account."

Adam looks to the ceiling then responds, "Not this again."

His normally relaxed expression is stern and his tone resolute. "Yes, Genny, Lukas, and I are eighteen. Have been for a while now. And while we are well aware that we are free to leave this shithole, something you insist upon reminding us daily, we are not going to leave you and Chloe in their care. Alone. So, we're staying. Do we really need to have this conversation again?"

Genny's eyes flare, then narrow. "Well, we just did so I guess that answers your question." She releases a relenting sigh. "I hate that you're willingly subjecting yourselves to their bullshit. I feel guilty. And I don't like to feel guilty. It's icky."

She whines her last words, and I fight to suppress my giggle. Something tells me her "icky" will become "cranky" if she spots me laughing at her little temper tantrum.

"Kids!"

Cancel that.

Genny rolls her eyes, shouldering past Lukas and Adam with a growl. Her stomps down the stairs are heavy and defiant, and the steady beats echo around us as we follow her forged path.

As soon as we've cleared the last step, Mr. Duff and his greased comb over appear in front of us, halting our movement. Dressed in his typical stained white tee and saggy pants, he's holding an open can of beer in one hand, four toothbrushes in the other. My face tightens in confusion, but when he tilts his head back to take a greedy draw from the can, my expression morphs into pure revulsion.

His bleary eyes roam the entire length of Genny's body, and I grimace in further disgust. Clearly feeling the same way, Adam draws me closer into him then angles himself so I'm no longer in Mr. Duff's line of vision. Directly in front of me, Lukas's entire body tenses as he observes Mr. Duff's clear ogling. His shoulders bunch, and his biceps bulge as he clenches his fists. After a deep inhale, he slowly reaches forward to grip the hem of Genny's black tank top and tug her backward. She willingly complies, allowing Lukas to take her place.

Mr. Duff's transfixed gaze breaks from Genny and he narrows his eyes on Lukas's carefully molded expression. An expression I know masks the hatred simmering just below surface, wisely hidden for fear of our punishment. And something in me already understands the reason why.

Under the Duffs' reign, we will all be held accountable for each other's actions, and Lukas has taken it upon himself to be our sole representative in their twisted game.

With obvious effort, the muscles in Mr. Duff's face relax and his mouth curves into a smile.

Game on, it seems to say.

Lukas makes no discernable play in response to the challenge. My guess is he's offering a bored, blank stare. "Is there something you need?"

"Yeah." Mr. Duff thrusts the toothbrushes in Lukas's direction. "Floors need cleaning."

My appalled gaze locks on his extended hand. "With all the unexpected visitors that came by last week, we need to continue to look our best." His words are half-slurred, half-snarled. I grin inwardly, and Genny snorts softly beside me, having probably already drawn the same conclusion I have.

I know with absolute certainty that the influx of random visitors is due to the fierce efforts of Sally as she works behind the scenes to make sure we're being properly cared for. Social workers, case managers, and various Sacred Heart personnel have shown up on our doorstep unannounced, scrutinizing and quietly observing us in our environment while searching for clues of anything strange or remiss. With each surprise visit, Mrs. Duff expertly turns on the charm. Replacing her usual scowl with a saccharine smile, she eagerly provides them a tour of our home regaling them with her visions for our future and plans we know would never come to fruition, while Mr. Duff wisely locks himself in their bedroom, no doubt hiding the remnants of the prior night's alcohol binge.

Unfortunately, each and every person leaves the house with a smile on their face, clearly pleased with the level of care being provided. And of course they are, since we're never really granted a chance to speak without Mrs. Duff present.

But in all honesty, there's nothing we could say at this point about the Duffs, except that they're complete assholes who give off a seriously sinister vibe.

Being forced to clean the floors with toothbrushes has to be in violation of certain child labor laws. Right?

No, probably not.

This is nothing more than punishment in retaliation for Sally's actions. Punishment we willingly accept as we're comforted by the fact that she's out there doing what she can to ensure our safety.

Lukas remains stoic, stepping forward to relieve Mr. Duff of the toothbrushes before turning to face us. Silently, he distributes one to Adam and myself, which we reluctantly accept, then he extends one to Genny, who does not. Her expression is pinched and unforgiving as she stares coolly at Lukas's face, not even bothering to look at the toothbrush in front of her. Lukas stubbornly holds her gaze, equally defiant. Their eyes remain locked, the two seemingly at an impasse, until Lukas arches a brow and cocks his head to the side, silently reminding Genny of her unspoken promise to not react when provoked.

After a few tension-filled seconds, Genny purses her lips and narrows her eyes, but eventually relents and takes the toothbrush.

Mr. Duff laughs, the sound menacing as it echoes around us. "So the crazy-haired kid is the leader of this bunch. I thought it might be Pinkie over there, but based on how easily she surrendered, clearly I was wrong."

He has no idea what our names actually are.

And I fear Genny might shank him in his sleep for that statement.

As I watch him down the last of his beer and carelessly toss the can onto the floor, I consider joining her in the effort.

Mr. Duff gestures to where it falls, looking directly at Genny. "Pick it up."

His tone is patronizing, and his eyes are filled with such evil, I can't breathe. A muscle in Lukas's jaw pulses wildly as he carefully assesses the situation playing out in front of us. Genny, much braver than I, refuses to cower and meets Mr. Duff's stare with unadulterated loathing. Adam moves to step forward, but the glare of warning from Lukas stops him.

Horrified, I watch Lukas step to the side, purposely giving Genny necessary space to fulfill Mr. Duff's humiliating demand. Apology is displayed in his eyes when they meet mine, and I breathe a sigh of relief. He's not betraying us. This is just another unfortunate protective measure he's taking to keep us safe. And Genny, well…she really needs to pick up the stupid can so we can move on and get past this ridiculous situation without starting an outright brawl.

With her eyes still cemented on Mr. Duff, she clears her throat. Then, slowly, she crouches to the floor and whisks the can into her hand.

With a glare aimed in Mr. Duff's direction, she curls her fingers around it and squeezes like a vise, crushing it with her fingers. Mr. Duff grins victoriously, exposing rows of yellowing teeth.

My heart pounds in my chest as I watch their standoff, the air thick with tension. After a few anxiety-ridden seconds, Genny ends the stalemate by closing her eyes and taking a long, deep breath. She whirls on the heel of her boot, turning her back to Mr. Duff, and heads to the kitchen trashcan.

Lukas, Adam, and I stand in silence, our toothbrushes still gripped in our hands. Once Genny is no longer in the room, Mr. Duff aims his foul grin in our direction and gestures widely, indicating the wood floor beneath us. "Get to it. I want the grooves scrubbed clean. They're packed with dirt."

I don't have to look down to know he's lying through his rotten teeth. The floors couldn't be any cleaner than what they already are. He's just an asshole on a raging power trip.

Just then, Mrs. Duff breezes into the room with a bucket of cleaning solution and a smug smile. The rubber soles of her slip-ons squeak with every step she takes, providing further evidence that the floor is indeed...squeaky clean.

"Actually, we have our own visitor coming today, a welcomed one." She sets the bucket on the floor. "Bobby's coming today, Lonny."

When she looks at Mr. Duff, I can't figure out if my shiver is from her nasty grin or his. They're both maniacal. We exchange concerned glances but remain silent, waiting until Genny reappears to begin our torture session.

Twenty minutes in, my right arm is shaking, painful and sore as I force the use of muscles I never knew existed. Mr. Duff has since fallen into his recliner with no intention of getting up any time soon based on the twelve-pack next to him. He turns the television on, settling in for the long haul. I scowl, watching him down another beer, before transferring the toothbrush to my other hand in search of some relief.

I look at Lukas next to me, his expression stony as he focuses on scrubbing.

Clink!

The sound of aluminum hitting the floor draws my attention away from him. A can rolls across several planks of wood before coming to rest a couple of feet away from me.

"Take it to the trash."

I look up to see Mr. Duff staring at me, though I'm not one hundred percent sure he's seeing much of anything right now. Eyes glazed, he expels a rather gruesome belch from deep within the pit of his stomach. I grimace in disgust.

My eyes find Lukas's, who's no longer devoting his attention to the task at hand, instead observing my interaction with Mr. Duff. He narrows his eyes, assessing the situation, then gives me a slight nod of his head indicating to do as I'm told.

I push off the floor, my knees aching with the slow ascent, and I notice divots embedded in my skin as I rise.

Slowly, I make my way to the can and pick it up. As I pass Genny on my way to the kitchen, she murmurs under her breath, "Asshole."

My sentiments exactly.

And so it continues.

Every half hour or so, another can hits the floor, followed by Mr. Duff's demand to pick it up.

Two cans later, I force a cough, and once I have the other's attention, I touch the tip of my nose. Three grins form, and since Lukas is the last to catch on, he loses. A slight curve lifts the corner of his mouth before he accepts his punishment.

Genny loses once, as do I, and Lukas loses an astounding three times. Actually, I think he lost the rounds on purpose because those cans in particular landed the closest to Mr. Duff.

Although we manage to work a bit of laughter into this chore to offset the sad reality of it, it doesn't last long.

When Adam, who evidently possesses superhuman reflexes, loses for the first time, everything goes to absolute shit. As he bends to retrieve what seems to be the umpteenth can from the floor, Mr. Duff mumbles, "Faggot."

I suck in a breath at the unexpected expletive, watching the blood drain from Adam's handsome face.

There's no way...how could he possibly know?

Shortly after the Duffs moved in, Seth made the mistake

of showing up at the house unannounced. Thankfully, they weren't here. When we explained the horror of the Duffs, Adam politely suggested that Seth not come back. Though they've since been able to arrange some visits at our school, the time they have together isn't nearly enough.

Adam is slow to rise. Whether stunned into silence or fighting the urge to take his stand, Adam doesn't respond, ignoring the jibe.

The lack of reaction does not go over well with Mr. Duff.

As soon as Adam steps in the direction of the kitchen, Mr. Duff goes on, provoking him. "Your *boyfriend* stopped by this morning. Warned him not to step foot on this property again, or it would be you who paid the price. I went into great detail. It wasn't pretty. I don't think you'll be seeing him again."

I guess Seth didn't heed Adam's warning.

Adam's shoulders slump, all the liveliness normally brightening his features disappearing from his face. My heart splinters. He's sacrificing Seth to remain with us. The only comfort is that at least this time they both know the truth. Adam won't be here forever.

Still, Adam says nothing, struck silent by Mr. Duff's continued cruel intentions. His steps are slow, defeated, as he simply turns away and leaves the room. Upon his exit, Mr. Duff shouts over his shoulder, "You're a heathen, boy! Goin' straight to hell!" It's then that he finally gets the reaction he's been seeking.

But not from Adam.

Genny jumps to her feet, the tread of her boots squeaking against the floor before she launches herself in the direction of Mr. Duff's recliner. She doesn't make it far. Lukas is up in a millisecond, absorbing her impact when she rams straight into his chest. He stumbles a few steps, but manages to wrap a heavy arm around her midsection, maintaining his iron hold while she thrashes. Her face is contorted with absolute fury, her words are unintelligible as Lukas lifts her off the ground and swiftly hauls her from the room.

The sound of Mr. Duff's resulting laughter makes my skin crawl, and all I can think as I try desperately to mute it is this: none of us are *going* to hell.

We're already there.

23

The visitor is not actually a visitor at all.

Mr. Duff's brother, a skeevy man named Bobby, has become a full-time resident of our home over the past month. We refer to him by his first name because one Mr. Duff is more than enough. His appearance is similar to his brother's, same shade of greasy hair and just as many discolored teeth, but his eyes…it's unnerving. They very closely resemble not only Mr. Duff's, but Mrs. Duff's as well. In fact, with each passing day spent observing the three of them together, their movements and gestures so uncannily parallel, I become more and more convinced they're all related in some way.

That is definitely cause for concern, but I won't share my suspicions with my fellow Wildflowers. I don't want to set them off for fear of the consequences. We've been on edge having to live under the same roof with three unfamiliar sadists, virtually no food, and for the last week, absolutely no time spent outside these walls due to Thanksgiving break.

Thanksgiving.

What was once my favorite holiday to spend with Mrs. Rodriquez has now become a prison sentence spent narrowly avoiding people constantly trying to give themselves reasons to hurt us. Definitely no splurging on turkey and fixings this year. No laughter. No celebrating our thanks.

Especially when we can't find much to be thankful for...

For safety reasons, we've been staying in groups as Lukas instructed, which means Genny and I are currently side by side and folding laundry in the kitchen. I watch as Genny pulls a familiar skull shirt from the heap, the one she dressed me in the day of the hamburger incident with Leah Warner at school.

I even miss *her* at this point. Which shows how truly miserable I am.

I sigh as Genny creases the arms of the shirt. "It seems like an entire lifetime has passed since the break started."

"Yeah." Genny nods. "I never thought I'd say this, but I'm actually looking forward to going back. Being cooped up in this house is"—a shiver courses through her—"suffocating."

Mrs. Duff chooses that exact moment to breeze through the kitchen. She's clearly been listening to our conversation, because she stops in front of us to declare, "Going back to school will not be a possibility for the four of you. You are to be homeschooled for the remainder of your senior year."

Oh. Hell. No.

Does Sally know about this? It can't be right. It has to be wrong.

Face bright red, Genny grips the counter and inhales deeply as she fights to maintain control. She opens her mouth, closes it, then opens it again. "I'm sorry, what did you just say?"

Mrs. Duff smiles innocently, but the menace in her eyes betrays her. "You have all been withdrawn. You, my dears, won't be going anywhere."

My fingers curl, forming clenched fists, and my nails dig into the skin of my palm. I look to Genny—her face, bright red a few moments ago, is now borderline purple. I will her to keep calm, to restrain whatever blistering response is forming on her tongue. She doesn't need the unwanted attention she'll undoubtedly receive if she detonates right here in the kitchen.

She must receive my message, because after a staredown with Mrs. Duff, she releases a conceding breath. Avoiding the woman's eyes, she focuses on the shirt in front of her and silently resumes folding. I can practically see the steam escaping her ears.

Mrs. Duff says nothing else. She just turns and grabs a dishtowel from the sink before leaving us alone in the kitchen.

As soon as she's gone, Genny lifts her gaze. "I swear on all that is holy, I am two seconds from going nuclear on these people. I will gladly sacrifice myself in the explosion that rids them from this earth."

It's absurd, but I know she's not joking. She hanging on by a thread so thin a spoon could slice clean through it.

The fates, however, are not deterred by her anger. Just as I begin to tell her my thoughts on the ridiculous homeschool threat, the door to the kitchen flies open and slams against the wall. I startle, knocking the entire pile of newly folded T-shirts over, and I cringe as they fall into a jumbled mess on the table. And just as it always is with his brother, the stench of alcohol fills the air around us, preceding Bobby's entrance into the room. I feel like I'm going to be sick.

Genny and I lock eyes when he passes us, staggering to the fridge. We watch in stunned silence as he flings the door open, then props himself against its edge. The wrinkles in his dingy T-shirt disappear when he leans in, swaying on his feet while inspecting the contents. When he reaches forward, the shirt climbs above his waist, exposing torn underwear that crests the top of his sagging jeans.

Genny turns to me, her face pinched in revulsion. I bite my bottom lip to keep from laughing. Bobby turns with an unopened beer in hand and slowly leans to one side, much like the Tower of Pisa, before righting himself. His unfocused gaze travels the length of Genny's body, lingering on the short hem of her skirt before locking on her chest. A fresh wave of nausea washes over me.

With carefully measured steps—I know this because he doesn't stumble—he walks to Genny, setting his beer on the table. He looks down to her arms, transfixed, then reaches forward to skim the darkened scars dotting the crook of her elbow. A shudder crawls along my skin, but Genny somehow remains impassive. She watches his fingers and brazenly meets his eyes once he's through.

He licks his lips. "If you give me what I want, I can get you what you need."

His tone is suggestive, grimy, *revolting.*

Genny's throat bobs with a deep swallow, and I can't tell if it's from disgust or if she's actually tempted.

After a long, contemplative look, her lips curve into a flirtatious smile as she tucks a strand of pink hair behind her ear. Then with a slow hand, she reaches forward, the tips of her fingers grazing his upper thigh.

"Genny." *What the hell is she doing?*

She doesn't answer me. She leans into him, her hand moving up, up, up until she's an inch away from his crotch. His eyes roll into the back of his head and his mouth falls open.

Hoping to God I can erase this moment from my brain, I step forward to intervene, but I'm not fast enough. Her lips find his ear just as she venomously whispers, "You disgust me."

Then with lightning-fast accuracy, she grabs hold of him through his jeans, squeezes with all her strength, and as if that isn't enough, finishes with a 180-degree twist of her wrist.

Bobby's eyes fly open and he howls in deafening agony before crumbling into the fetal position, landing on the floor with a thud. We stand above him, Genny grinning wildly, shock plastered across my face as he writhes in pain. His eyes full of tears, he looks at Genny, spittle flying from his lips as he shouts, "You will know real pain when I'm done with you, bitch!"

Heavy footsteps sound all around us, drowning out Genny's laughter.

The first to enter are Mr. and Mrs. Duff, their faces transforming into identical horrified expressions when they spot Bobby on the floor. Lukas comes in close second. His eyes wildly search the kitchen, but when he finds us unharmed, they calm just a fraction. Adam is right behind him, practically running into Lukas's back.

Mrs. Duff falls to her knees. She crawls to where Bobby lies, placing his head in her lap and running her fingers through his oily hair, trying to comfort him. Another wave of nausea rolls through my stomach.

Mr. Duff, unaffected by his wife's display, has his eyes locked on Genny. They're pure evil, brimming with loathing, and sickeningly enough, joy at the promise of punishment to come. Lukas steps in front of her, blocking Mr. Duff's view. But Mr. Duff doesn't look away. His stare burns into Lukas, as though trying to sear through him to get to Genny.

"Get to your rooms. We'll deal with you later." Mrs. Duff's voice trembles with her whisper. The lowness of her tone seems more lethal than her husband's stare.

After a hesitant look between us, we do as instructed, filing out of the kitchen as quietly as possible. Once we're upstairs and out of harm's way, Lukas stops, causing all of us to do the same.

He pivots to face us, and his words spew out in a frenzied rush. "We have to get out of here. Like, *now*. These people are too dangerous."

We nod in absolute agreement, then Genny asks, "How the hell are we going to get out of here? Just break out?"

Lukas shakes his head, frustrated. "I don't know, but I'll figure something out. Just get in your room and lock the door. Pack a bag but do not leave yet under any circumstance. We'll come get you when we're ready."

"Okay," Genny and I state in unison.

Just as we turn to face the door, a firm grip is latched onto my arm. I twist at the waist to find Lukas's piercing stare. He releases his hold and lifts his hand to brush his knuckles tenderly along my cheek, his expression pained.

"I'll be okay," I whisper, trying to reassure him.

He searches my face then gives me a soft nod. "Stay together. Stay safe."

He leans, presses his lips to mine, and then he and Adam are gone. *God, how I've missed his lips.*

As soon as we're inside and the door is locked, Genny sighs and takes a seat on her bed. "I'm sorry, Chloe. I really am. I just couldn't take anymore."

"It's okay." I smile softly at her. "He deserved it. And honestly, I'm impressed you lasted this long."

Her grin is that of pure satisfaction. "I think I broke him."

Even though I want to laugh, I can't. I look at my friend and admit, "I'm scared."

Her smile lessens, and she reaches for my hand. I take hold as she states, "Me, too."

An hour later, we're packed and waiting, seated together on Genny's bed when we hear the sound of glass shattering down the hall. Then, a scuffle is followed by a strange rustling sound. Genny starts to rise, but I pull her back down.

"Don't," I warn with a shake of my head.

I grip her hand tightly, my entire body beginning to quake with fear. A squeaking sound draws our attention to the door, and we watch as the handle begins to turn. I clamp my hand over my mouth.

"It's locked," Genny quietly reminds me.

The handle jiggles, then Mrs. Duff probes, "Girls?"

We remain mute and deathly still. The door jostles, as though she's trying to push it open. Genny squeezes my hand.

After a few seconds, there is nothing but silence. It's eerie, like the calm before the storm.

My heart gallops unsteadily as we listen.

It's quiet.

Too quiet.

Then the door splinters and flies off its hinges. Mr. Duff and Bobby burst into our room, eyes wild with fury and purpose as they rush to where we're seated. Bobby wrenches Genny from the bed, her body launching into the air, then flips her around so her back is to his chest. Mr. Duff grips my upper arms and hauls me up, doing the same to me.

We're facing each other now, helplessly captive.

They're going to hurt us.

Please don't hurt us.

When their arms cross our necks, we just look at each other, squirming, fighting, tears rising in our eyes as we try to breathe.

There's no air.

The last thing I see is Genny crying out for me.

Then everything goes black.

WINTER

24

Wincing, I try to open my eyes, but my lids are too heavy and refuse to budge. The pain is excruciating. I lift my hands to cradle my head, but they only make it as far as my stomach before a wave of agony rolls through me, so intense it forces me to curl into myself. A bead of sweat rolls along my forehead, and my skin is warm to the touch, but I'm so cold. So cold.

I try to speak, to call for help, but the muscles in my jaw are clamped so tightly they begin to cramp. My mouth feels as though it's full of glue, my tongue thick and unmoving. I try to force my jaw open, to release the scream clawing inside my chest, but nothing comes out. With my failed attempt, a sense of helplessness washes over me, its bitterness chilling. I begin to shiver as a whimper works its way through my gritted teeth.

I'm so cold.

My heart beats in a panicked frenzy and I inhale deeply, trying to lock on to something, anything, I can make sense of. I focus on the rapid beats, searching for a sense of calm within the rhythm, yet I find nothing.

There is only hysteria, suffocating me.

And then it's as though I'm the sole viewer in a private movie theater, forced to watch as torturous moments are cinematically displayed in my own darkened mind.

It's a horror movie.

And the Wildflowers are the stars.

Genny, her back scraping the wall as she falls to the side when Bobby crawls off her. Her inner thighs, bruised and bloody, slamming together as she slowly descends to the floor.

Adam, his beautiful face beaten beyond recognition as he reaches for her, catching her head before it strikes the cement of the basement floor. His sobs echo all around me as he offers apologies to her that she can't possibly hear while tenderly cradling her head in his lap.

I open my mouth to shout and let them know I'm here. That I will help them. But nothing comes out.

A cry lurches from my chest, but finds no escape. It's lodged painfully in my throat as I become weightless, drifting out of my body, my closed eyes still forced to see. I reach for my friends, yet my crumpled body remains motionless as another painful memory slices through my mind.

A strong hand around my neck before I'm effortlessly

hauled into the air, then slammed against the concrete floor. All breath is expelled from my lungs on impact, and white-hot pain sears the inside of my head.

A heavy body lands on top of me. I'm trapped as pure evil straddles my waist. Warm, terrified tears slide down my face. I claw desperately—my nails tear at his shirt, his arms, his face.

Then suddenly, he's off me, and thick, clumsy fingers find the button of my jeans, both hands now working frantically as darkness begins to blur my vision.

I force my mouth open, try to take a breath, but before I have the chance to inhale, the back of my head is slammed against cement.

Stars explode behind my eyes and I struggle to stay conscious. My arms become too heavy and fall limp at my sides. I know what's about to happen. A strangled sob escapes my throat.

Find solace.

I begin to fade.

Search for that familiar place in your mind. Escape.

I go to where I do not exist.

Hide.

This is not happening.

I will never be found again.

Darkness begins to cocoon me, wrapping me safely in its arms, but not before I'm dealt one more painful blow. An inhuman, guttural roar is the last thing I hear before I completely disappear.

Lukas.

I'm thrust into our sick, twisted present. Back in my body, I'm no longer comforted by numbness.

There is nothing but unadulterated agony.

Lukas?

With pained effort, I finally pry my eyelids apart. I see Adam, who has Genny's seemingly lifeless form in his lap. His cries are muffled into her neck as he gently rocks her back and forth.

A creak sounds from above, and my widened eyes are torn from Adam and Genny—locked instead on the basement ceiling. I stifle a sob and listen as the sound of footsteps begins hesitantly, then gains and picks up speed. My cheek skims the concrete as I follow their path toward the basement door.

We need to get out of here.

Slowly, I roll over onto my stomach, fighting the urge to vomit—*it hurts, it hurts so much*—and with all the strength I can muster, I begin to press my weight off the floor, but when I hear the doorknob turn, I freeze.

The door is thrown open, and panic surges through my entire system, giving me the adrenaline rush I need to haul myself upright. Once on my feet, I teeter to the side and try to grip the wooden beam next to me for support, but my hands are trembling to the point that I can't hold on. My legs buckle beneath me, and I fall back to the floor. Just as I land, I hear a soft gasp, then a familiar voice.

"Oh my God."

I don't see Sally, because as soon as I hear her, the tears start, uncontrollable, blinding. My head falls into my hands and I can do nothing more than cry while listening to the quiet murmurs exchanged between her and Adam. After some shuffling, I hear what I assume are Adam's heavy footsteps carrying Genny safely away from our hell. Pregnant seconds pass before a gentle hand finds my cheek. I startle, my head jerking away from the hand and my eyes landing on Sally's tear-stained face. Her hair is messier than usual, haphazardly gathered into a ponytail, and she's wearing flannel pajamas, as though she came directly from bed.

My voice is hoarse. "Genny?"

Sally's eyes fill with more tears. "She's been drugged. Adam said they shot her full of heroin before…"

Sally's voice breaks and she shakes her head, unable to vocalize the horrendous tragedy. Her sorrowful eyes fall to my open jeans before rising to meet mine. "Were you…?"

I shake my head. "No, I think Lukas stopped him." *Lukas.* Frantically, my eyes dart around the room. "But where is he?"

Sally reaches out with both hands, hindering my search as she forces me to meet her eyes. "He's why I'm here. I know everything." Her gaze is apologetic and her voice thick. "He's gone, honey."

"Gone?" My throat has constricted to the point I can barely utter the word. I don't understand. How can he just leave us, leave me, after everything that happened?

Sally sweeps her thumbs along my cheeks, and nods,

regret laced through her tone. "Gone."

That single word is my undoing.

As realization sets in, my face crumples. Sally gathers me in her arms, pulling me close, whispering, "A love like yours is destined to come full circle. You *will* see him again. And when you do, no matter how far gone he may be, do not give up on him. You hold on to that love like a lifeline, because it will be. For the both of you."

I want to find hope in her words, to gain some sense of strength from their meaning, but there is nothing left inside me to anchor them.

I'm hollow.

Sally's face is blurry when she dips it back into my view. "Chloe, I need you to concentrate and memorize every word that comes out of my mouth. Can you do that for me, honey?"

I give her a slight nod in answer.

Her lips tighten before she exhales a calming breath, then announces, "Okay. Lukas and Adam left Sacred Heart of their own free will. Genny ran away with them, and you haven't seen them since. Got it?"

Another nod.

Sally's eyes are grave as she scatters my friends to the wind. "I'm sorry, Chloe. I know this is hard, but they can't be here when the fire department gets here."

I swallow the sobs clawing up my throat. "Fire depart—"

She silences me with a stern shake of her head. "The Duffs have been gone for a couple of days, and you haven't heard from them."

My brows furrow. "Where *are* they?"

Sally ignores my question, persistent as she continues weaving her story. "You called me last night because you were alone and frightened. We stayed up all night trying to track the Duffs down. I lit candles—we fell asleep but the smell of smoke woke us. We ran downstairs to find the kitchen and living room in flames, and we ran out of the house, which is when I called the fire department."

She eyes me for a few moments, allowing time for me to process it all.

But I can't.

"We're going to burn down Mrs. Rodriguez's house?"

"No, I'm going to burn down the Sacred Heart house," Sally says. "It's the only way, Chloe. We have to destroy any and all paper trails leading to Lukas, Genny, and Adam. All evidence that links them to being here on this night."

I shake my head, still trying to understand. "But shouldn't there be some sort of paperwork regarding them leaving?"

"Not if the Duffs were delayed in processing it, and not if it was consumed in the fire." Sally grips my shoulders firmly, her tired eyes livening with resolve. "This is the only story that covers all our bases. We need to convince the authorities that the Duffs were terrible caregivers, so that anything that doesn't add up is their fault."

My gaze drifts over her shoulder, to where Adam and Genny were moments ago. Bile fills my throat, and rage fills my heart.

Try seriously fucked-up assholes who deserved whatever happened to them.

I feel it in my bones, in my gut. *Lukas.*

"He's gone, honey."

And now I know why.

Sally must sense my sudden awareness because she says nothing more. She simply pulls me in for another embrace before whispering, "We need to get out of here." I inhale deeply and nod against the crook of her neck. After slipping one of my arms over her shoulder, she tugs me upright, and I lean on her for support as we make our way up the stairs.

But I'll never be free of the hell behind us.

I will forever remain its prisoner, forced to relive this nightmare, sent back to this concrete room every time I shut my eyes to sleep.

And I will be absolutely, utterly…alone.

25

We step outside right as the morning sun breaks the horizon. But I don't feel its warmth. I feel nothing but cold.

For me, there is no sun anymore.

He's gone.

Focusing on the ground, I shove my hands into the pockets of the coat Sally grabbed for me, then step off the porch. Leaving Sally, I head to where Adam stands, now cradling Genny against his chest. She's wrapped in a blanket, her pallid skin peeking through its folds, contrasted sharply by the colorful pink strands of hair blown across her face.

Just as I make my approach, Adam speaks. "Truck's gone."

I lift my gaze from the ground, my eyes darting to where the truck was parked. "Lukas."

If my memory is correct, Adam was conscious when

Lukas entered the basement. I could ask what happened, but why would I? I already know what I need to know.

He's gone.

Adam jerks his chin in affirmation before shifting Genny in his arms. In the sunlight, his wounds are far worse than I'd thought. One eye is completely swollen shut with a large purplish-black bruise forming beneath it. The other eye is nearly as bad, though he can manage to see through the thin slit between his lids. His nose, angled a bit to the side, has clearly been broken, and his lips are scabbed over from being split so many times.

Clearing my throat, I tuck a loose strand of hair behind my ear and reach hesitantly toward Genny and do the same to her. My thumb lingers on her cheek, and I hiccup a sob as I stroke her face gently, lovingly, before dropping my hand. She stirs at my touch, but her eyes remain closed.

Adam's glistening eyes meet mine in understanding. "I can't put her down. I don't want to let her go."

"I know. I can't... What will this do to her?"

His tears well up, rolling down his face. "They broke her."

Before I can respond, the screen door slams and Adam and I watch as Sally hastily exits the house. I look from her to the backpack looped over her shoulder.

The one Genny packed.

Sally notices my observation. "She's going to need a change of clothes. There were some already in here so I just grabbed it on my way out."

Her stare drops to Genny then lifts, focusing over Adam's shoulder. We turn in unison, watching as a familiar car begins to make its way up the drive.

"Seth," Adam breathes, then gives Sally a furious glare.

She shakes her head quickly, refusing his anger. "I had to, Adam. I'm sorry."

Adam's voice quakes. "I don't…he can't know any of this."

"Well, he does." She steps to him and curls her fingers around his forearm, giving him an encouraging squeeze. "And yet, he's here. For you."

A muscle in Adam's jaw jerks as he fixedly looks at the ground. Sally releases her grip and runs past him, throwing the back door of the car open just as Seth's car screeches to a stop.

Dust clouds stir up around her as she gestures frantically to the inside of the car. "Adam, we need to get you both looked at. Please, I know you're angry, but we need to hurry." She pauses then adds, "If not for you, do it for Genny."

I don't know if it's Seth's presence, or Sally's plea, or if Adam just couldn't take it anymore, but we're all forced to watch as the boy who has somehow managed to maintain such stoic strength over the past few hours completely shatters.

He curls his entire frame over Genny, clutching her protectively in his arms, and dips his head to where she lies, unmoving. Then, he weeps.

Completely broken.

I choke on my own sobs as I watch, helpless and heart-broken. "They broke her. They broke…"

Us.

And in this moment, I know exactly what Adam means, what he feels. Our group, our connection…it's severed.

They broke all of us.

Sally quickly leaves the side of the car to stand in front of Adam. When she reaches to release his grip on Genny, he tightens his hold. She redirects her movement, instead tenderly placing her hand on his head, and leans into him, whispering in his ear. Eventually, Adam nods and lifts his head. He looks tortured. He refuses to look at Seth as he passes Genny's drug-filled body into his waiting arms.

Sally turns slowly, and with measured steps, leads the way back to Seth's waiting car. She opens the back door for him to lay Genny down carefully, then gently sets the backpack inside before leaning in to check on her.

Adam refuses to look up from the ground.

Seth's expression is one of agony, his eyes brimming with tears as he takes a hesitant step in Adam's direction. He pauses, gauging Adam's reaction, before taking another.

And another.

And another.

And when there is no distance left between them, Seth gently curls his fingers around the base of Adam's neck, willing him forward into his arms. Adam bristles at the contact, refusing to allow it, going as far as to slam his palms flat against Seth's chest and shove. His eyes, finally lifted now, are wild and frenzied as he attempts another push, but Seth doesn't budge. He just grabs Adam's wrists and fiercely hauls Adam into his strong arms. Adam struggles against the hold, screaming in frustration, fingers clawing Seth's back. Seth says nothing, but tightens his hold, refusing to let go.

And I thought my heart couldn't break any more.

After a while, the screams turn to sobs, and I watch as Adam's frantic fingers still then curl into the back of Seth's shirt, white-knuckled as he clutches the fabric.

"I love you. I love you. I love you," Seth murmurs, holding Adam as he cries. "We'll get through this, together. Always."

The smell of smoke begins to fill the air, drawing our attention to the house. Thick tendrils of gray begin to rise into the sky, prompting Adam and Seth to break apart and Sally to speak.

"You need to get going." She wipes away her tears and inhales deeply. Reaching into her pocket, she draws out a piece of paper. Handing it to Seth, she adds, "Take them here. I have a friend waiting to see them both."

Seth nods briskly, then with Adam tucked into his side, leads him to the car. Crackling sounds from behind me, and I know without looking that the house is quickly becoming its intended inferno.

Sally redirects her attention to me after watching Adam climb in Seth's car. "Chloe, I need to tell you something—"

But before she can finish, my eyes fall on a sleek black Mercedes making its way up the drive, passing Seth as he speeds in the opposite direction. My glare rivals Adam's when I look back to Sally, knowing there's only one reason a one-hundred-thousand-dollar car would be approaching.

Bitter cold floods my body, my skin prickling in its wake.

"How?" I ask without bothering to look in her direction. "There hasn't been enough time."

"There has been, Chloe." Her tone is soft, concerned. "I think you're in shock."

She may be right, but that shock is quickly turning to rage as I watch the car coming closer. I tear my eyes away from it just to scowl at her.

As Sally takes in my reaction, her chin begins to tremble. "I had no other choice. I need to make sure you're safe when this is all over. Sacred Heart, this home at least, will no longer exist."

"You know just as well as I do how safe I'll be with *them*." Seething, I gesture to the now burning house. "Especially after everything that's happened."

Sally's throat works a hard swallow before she squares her shoulders. "I know you're angry with me, but it's our only option. Your safety—the safety of all of you—is my only priority right now. Just please, try to hang on and focus on how far you've come. What you've learned. And remember, it's not forever. You'll be eighteen soon enough, then you can leave."

"I have no place to go!" I scream, my voice breaking as the Mercedes rolls to a stop in the driveway. My nails dig into my palms. "Don't you see?! I have nothing! No one! Every bit of happiness and hope I've dared to hold on to is gone!" Ripped straight from my heart. My soul. "Why, Sally?! *Why?!*"

It takes everything in me not to claw off my skin. An indescribable mix of fury and guilt has leached into my heart, filling the gaping voids left by the loss of my friends. Fury at myself, and guilt, because even though I may never voice it, I can't deny there's a part of me that feels everything that happened tonight is my fault. That the possibility exists that if it hadn't been me in the kitchen with Genny, or if I had never come to this place, none of this would have happened and my friends would be okay. That I somehow contaminated them, bleeding myself into their existence and infecting them with whatever punishment God thinks I deserve.

And as I succumb to this silent admission, the darkness of dejection and absolute emptiness begins to swallow me. I don't fight it, but allow it to drown me as I turn from Sally to watch one shiny black dress shoe hit the gravel. My blood, my heart, my soul—I'm glacial. I feel myself wilting, starving for the warmth I once knew.

But there is no warmth.

No sun.

No sustenance.

Life no longer blooms inside me. There is only a frigid, suffocating cold that slowly encases me.

And when my eyes drift upward to the face of the man exiting the car, I realize what a stupid, stupid girl

I've allowed myself to become. The normalcy I've experienced over the past year has clouded my judgment and expectations.

Because standing in front of us is, of course, not my parents.

His stern face, dark suit, and impassive, cold expression. Even to him, I'm nothing more than an inconvenience. Gerard.

The butler.

I still mean nothing.

Nothing has changed.

His eyes flick from me to the house, narrowing slightly. Sally still stands in front of me, seemingly as dumbstruck at his presence and clearly warring within herself as to whom she should engage first.

Me, and my impending mental breakdown.

Or him, my guide to "safety."

A loud crash followed by a rush of embers makes the decision for her.

She gives me one last look, her expression laden with apology, before rushing to Gerard's side. As she frenetically begins her practiced story, his scrutinizing stare transfers to her, and he listens calmly, patiently, until she's through. He says nothing, just gives her a slight nod of his head, to which she releases a long, heavy breath before leaving and running to her car.

We watch in silence as she opens the door, leans inside, and gets her phone. It's already to her ear when she faces us, slamming the door shut behind her. Her tone is anxious and frantic as she speaks, giving the operator our address. She listens for a moment before nodding her head, and after a solemn "thank you," shoves the phone in her back pocket and moves to stand next to me.

Together we watch the walls of the house begin to cave in, smoke and embers filling the air, the smell of fire all around us. There are no words. There's nothing left to say.

I have absolutely nothing.

Soon, the burning house is replaced by images flashing before my eyes: Mrs. Rodriguez's many loving expressions, Lukas's blinding smile, Adam's hopeful eyes, Genny's infectious laughter.

My sun, my earth, my lifelines...all gone.

Nowhere left to root.

I accept my fate, because just like Adam, there's no fight left in me. There is only the frozen nothing crystallizing in my soul.

I barely hear the sound of sirens in the distance before I let myself shut down, sealing myself in my grave.

Feeling absolutely nothing but cold.

26

There is darkness all around me as I float, my feet never touching ground. This used to frighten me, but now I find comfort within its confines. I blissfully remain suspended, my arms and legs useless as they drift above my body. I don't even register their presence anymore.

I just float.

And float.

And float.

I've been here for months, yet something about tonight is different.

There's a sense of searching, of longing, of missing some vital piece of my existence. My heart aches for it, but I have no idea what it is I seek.

Dazedly, I turn my head, noticing a sliver of light infiltrating my darkness. Its rolling edges beckon me as it hovers, illuminating a corner of what I thought was an endless space. As though drawn by the sun, I twist my body, winding through the nothingness until the light is inches in front of my face. It begins to grow, glowing more brightly with each passing second. Curious, I tilt my head, inspecting the light as it summons me, as though it's a long-lost friend.

Heat radiates from its core, and I am helpless to do anything but reach for it. The corners of my mouth lift ever so slightly when I make contact, and a relieved shiver racks my entire body as my fingers begin to thaw. The light stretches for me, and I watch, awestruck, as its essence forms the shape of a silvery hand. I mimic the gesture, placing my palm flat against the palm that forms. Warm fingers lace with mine, the grip comforting as it gently tugs my drifting body. I revel in the feeling as I'm drawn with it, away from my blackness and into a neighboring space full of sunlight and warmth.

My feet land softly on the grass below me, no longer suspended in the cocoon of darkness. A light breeze whips around me, carrying with it a familiar floral scent. I inhale deeply and glance at my hand to see it's no longer joined with the other. My eyes drift downward, finding a sea of white wildflowers beside my bare feet. They too wave cheerfully, joyfully bounding in the breeze. Crouching down, I grin at them, my heart elated and pumping wildly as we become reacquainted. I reach for them, tenderly brushing my fingers along their petals and smiling wide when they bounce and stretch, eager.

You have been asleep for long enough. It's time to open your eyes.

I lift my gaze from the flowers to find an incorporeal figure in the distance. I can't make out much since it's translucent. It floats gracefully, stoically, above the grass, and although I can't make out its eyes, I know it's looking directly into my soul.

I rise tentatively and take a step, but it negates my movement, prohibiting me from lessening the distance between us.

Soft laughter fills the air. *You cannot reach me because I'm not really here.*

Echoes of the soft whisper swirl all around me, wrapping me in what feels like a light embrace. Confused, I look to the flowers still happily bouncing with our presence. They seem so real. This seems so real.

My gaze drifts back to the form as it seems to drift farther away. An overwhelming sense of sadness floods me and instinctively, I try to reach for it.

I watch helplessly as it ascends, a sense of longing squeezing my heart as the distance separates us, more and more.

Time to wake and roar, my little lioness.

Tears flood my eyes, surprising me. Something about the endearment jars my happiness with an indescribable, agonizing ache. It's curiously familiar, tugging on some part of my consciousness I can't seem to grasp.

I tilt my head back farther and watch the form fade,

warmth cascading down my cheeks. Words carried on a light, fluttering breeze are the last thing I hear before it disappears.

Do not mourn me. Revive me.

"No!" The scream rips from my soul as I reach for the figure. I begin to cry. Hot, searing pain slices through my body at the loss, my knees buckling, forcing me to the ground. My hands shoot out in front of me, and I sweep them wildly, seeking the solace of the wildflowers, but they're gone.

Sunlight and warmth no longer surround me. There's just endless suffocating darkness.

Sobs wrack my body, stealing my breath and crushing my heart with each bellowed cry. I have no idea how long I remain in the darkness, the same cruel darkness that's been swallowing me for months. I am utterly alone, accompanied only by loneliness and solitude as they hollow from the inside. I'm terrified the grief and loss will consume me.

Maybe it's that fear that drives me, or perhaps it's unwillingness to no longer exist in this place, but somehow, after the tears have dried and I can cry no more, I find the strength to stand. My legs are unsure beneath me, and like a newborn foal's, unsteady from lack of use.

My eyes, swollen and sore, take in the blackness around me, and suddenly I'm terrified with the knowledge of how truly lost I've become.

"How do I get out of this place?"

I told you.

I gasp, surprised to hear the melodic whisper as it swirls all around me.

Open your eyes.

Something sparks to life within me, filling my hollowed soul with a sense of promise. Because I'm finally able to understand. I may still be blinded in the darkness, but now, I finally see.

I will weather this storm and emerge, newly born as spring welcomes me.

Because winter will pass.

And I no longer fear the pain of what's to come.

27

I awaken in my bed to tear-soaked pillows and sweat-laden sheets. Looking blankly at the ceiling, I rub the wetness from my face, unsure why I'm crying. Another nightmare, I suppose.

Still, unlike every other morning I wake from my nightmares, there's a growing, burning sensation clogging my chest. It's a sadness that floods me, spurring more tears. I try to ignore it, to ward against the feeling, but the pain is too potent. It's pure acid corroding my defenses, tearing open fissures and seeping through. And I don't understand why. Why today? Why, after months of numbness, am I suddenly thrust into the agony of feeling?

It's been a daily struggle to keep thoughts of the Wildflowers at bay. If I don't think about the loss, the associated pain is prevented.

A weight settles around me, making my morning tasks slow and grueling. Getting out of bed proves extremely taxing. Brushing my teeth is like lifting a one-hundred-pound dumbbell. Even walking down the stairs takes too long.

I don't bother with breakfast.

A warm cup of coffee awaits me on the island, and I grip the handle before heading to the table, as I've done every morning since arriving here. And as always, I'm alone and in complete silence. I have no idea where my parents are and I don't care.

I haven't spoken a word since someone from Sacred Heart came by shortly after I was brought back here. And even though it was months ago, I remember it as though it was just yesterday.

"Hello, Chloe."

I stare blankly at the woman in front of me. Her gentle tone and concerned expression seem genuine, but I don't trust her.

"My name is Patricia and I'm the director of Sacred Heart. I've come to see how you're doing after everything that…happened."

Her eyes dart in the direction of my father, but like me, he remains silent. He holds her gaze for a brief second, then turns to me. He's angry. Bothered by her presence. And he blames it on me.

Of course it's my fault. It's my fault she's here. It's my fault my parents had to take me back. It's my fault I lost all of my friends, that I'm right back where I started. Alone, abandoned, inconsequential.

Patricia clears her throat, then looks back at me. "I read the medical report from the night of the fire. You were fully examined?"

I nod slightly, bringing my knees to my chest. I feel my father's glare when my feet rest on the leather of the chair, but I keep my eyes locked on Patricia.

"How did you receive the head injury?"

My heart rate spikes at her mention of that day. I don't want to answer any more questions. It was all I could do to hold it together then. I may not be as successful this time. I inhale deeply, but my voice trembles when I speak. "If you read the report, then you know I tripped and hit my head on the way out of the house."

She gently folds her hands in her lap before responding. "Yes, but I wanted to make sure you weren't injured otherwise." Another quick look at my father before she meets my eyes.

I don't have it in me to lie, so I don't. I was injured in ways no one could possibly understand. Except the Wildflowers.

She sighs, but her tone remains calm. "I'm very concerned, Chloe. I hope you can understand that. I need to know what happened so I can make sure it doesn't happen again. The Duffs...well, the report said they left you alone for days and we still can't locate them. I cannot get over what my gut is telling me, which is that something else was going on while you were in their care. While you were in our care. Is there anything you can tell me that would help me understand? Any idea of where they could be? Where the three other residents may have gone when they left?"

I grit my teeth in frustration and shake my head. My bare feet hit the floor and I stand, eyes locking on to hers. I need to know without a doubt she hears what I say. "This is what I will tell you. You should have stopped by to see how we were coping with the loss of Mrs. Rodriguez. You should have let Sally stay when she asked to be our caretaker, and you should have gone so far to ask us what we wanted. We deserved to have a voice."

My throat is constricted as I speak, but I get the last bit out before it starts to slam shut. "And you should have definitely told your inspectors to talk to the children alone while visiting the home, and not just rely on the information provided by those they're there to inspect."

Patricia shoots to her feet, offering me her hand in the process. "Chloe, I'm so sor—"

I step away from her, dismissing her attempt, then say, "There's nothing else you can do for me. The damage, as you already know, is done. Maybe you should focus on the other children you placed in the care of those monsters, the ones you didn't protect who are still suffering in silence. That's the only way you can help us now."

My father rises, but of course, says nothing to comfort me.

I look into Patricia's eyes a second longer, noting the tears rolling down her cheeks, then turn my back on her and leave the room.

Not one word spoken since then.

I've completely shut down so I don't have to remember. So I don't have to feel. But with that one memory, the ones I've been trying so hard to deny become inescapable.

Unimaginable pain and coldness.

Lukas's agonizing scream.

What did he see?

Adam's cries of torment.

He saw it all.

And Genny…

She…

My heart clenches every single time I think of her limp body in Adam's arms.

Where are they? How are they? *How is…she?*

I have no way of knowing.

The only point of contact would be Sally, but her phone number burned along with the house. Not that I would contact her, because that would mean I'd have to actually acknowledge everything that happened. And until this moment, I've been somewhat successful at avoiding that.

But as I sip my coffee, I'm frustrated I haven't heard from her. That she has made no effort to reach me, to check on my mental status, to talk me through the tragic events of that day.

I'm not her responsibility anymore. None of us are, I guess.

But it hurts.

She was right. She didn't have it together.

Newfound anger sweeps through me, heating my blood and warming my cheeks. It's odd to feel this emotion, any emotion, after so many months. But this morning, I welcome it.

My thoughts veer to Lukas, the most difficult to shake when it comes to evading my memories. His abrasive demeanor in the beginning versus the kind soul he was shielding inside. His tortured expression when he opened up about Michelle. His need to protect her.

His need to protect *us*.

Which he did.

Absently, I twist the plastic ring I still wear on my finger and trace the scars lining my arms, remembering his plea to never cover them.

"You have nothing to be ashamed of. These scars are a part of you that should never be denied. They're your battle scars, and they should be worn with pride. When I look at them, I don't see the mark of a frightened girl, but of a warrior. I see someone I strive to be."

He still left me.

What about his scars?

My heart aches. They may not be visible like mine, but after what happened, he undoubtedly bears some now. *What did he see?*

I think of Adam and his beautiful face marred with gaping cuts and swelling bruises. More scars, both inside and out. I hope Seth is with him, helping him heal.

And Genny. The girl who once wore her scars with pride. Who worked so hard to bring me back to life. Again and again I see her limp in Adam's arms...but mixed with that memory are all the times her fuck-you-all attitude inspired us, claimed us all. But I fear what the evil did to her that night.

Around and around my mind goes, thinking of Sally, Lukas, Adam, and Genny, each revolution crumbling my defenses.

By the time I finish, I ache all over and my heart hurts. I have no idea how long I've been sitting at this table, but my coffee cup is empty, and I have no memory of drinking it.

I inhale deeply and promise myself this is a one-time occurrence, a slight mishap in my plight to block any and all feeling. A moment of weakness only, nothing more.

Just as I place my palms on the table and begin to stand, I notice a lone envelope. I frown, confused at when the hell it appeared. It's addressed to me with no return address.

Weird.

Flipping it over, I examine the back to find it blank. Slowly, I slip my finger under the flap, inching it open, and peer inside. I extract the paper quickly and begin to unfold it when another piece of paper falls free. It flits to the table, this one smaller and lined, as though from a journal.

I observe it curiously before opening the last fold and flattening the paper against the table. The scrawl seems hurried, the message written with agitated strokes.

It's time to come home. Your Wildflowers will need you now more than ever.

My heart leaps into my throat at the mention of the Wildflowers, and I choke back a surprised sob as I continue to read.

Meet at 5103 Stillhouse Ave. as soon as you can. We'll be waiting. ~ Sally

Unexpected tears rise and blur my vision. I mean, I've been crying pretty much all morning, but these tears are different. They're driven by a sense of fear, not the sorrowful, weighty ache I've felt over the last few hours.

Heart racing, I reach for the other sheet of paper, and my hands tremble as I open it. Because something deep, deep within me already knows what I'll find.

I just didn't expect to hear it from her.

My Wildflowers,

This is a rare moment of clarity for me, a brief stint of calm before the storm ravages my mind again. Though I've fought many unwelcome battles, I fear this one will be my undoing. That I will go too far to quiet the voices. To stop the pain.

I don't want to die.

I do not want to die.

I need you to know this, to believe this.

Please, please, please do not think less of me for using again. This is the only way I know how to numb my agony, even if it's only for a few fleeting moments. I'm well aware that by doing so, I'm teetering a very dangerous edge. An edge from which I'm in constant danger of falling, yet I do it anyway.

That night, I was unwillingly plucked from my happiness, uprooted and replanted on this dark and desolate path as soon as the drug entered my veins. Yet through the haze, I remember everything. I know what was done to me. I feel it every moment I continue to breathe. It's his face I see every time I close my eyes, every morning when I wake, and right before I put another needle in my arm, even if it's only for a brief escape. In those moments, I welcome the nothingness, the erasure of the events that haunt me. Because if only for a short while, I'm no longer trapped in my own personal hell plagued by the face of evil, but back in our field with our wildflowers. Only during these times am I able to find peace, to be free of the memory, innocent and laughing with the only three people who dared to know me. To really know me.

I feel each of you overestimated my strength, because the truth is, I had none before meeting you. With each Wildflower, I was gifted more. It was you who gave me reason to be strong, but now without you near, that strength is waning. Quickly.

For now, I continue to fight, to run the only way I know how.

I do not want to die, but if you are receiving this letter, it means I ran too far, pushed too much, and for that, I cannot apologize enough.

As you know, my greatest fear is being forgotten. That my existence made no impact, that my life didn't matter. If this letter finds it's way to you, I must ask one thing…

As I have no remaining family, my body will be cremated, as dictated by the state.

Please spread my ashes in our field with our wildflowers. I know only there will I find the peace I've been searching for, and only there will my roots find the will to survive, unforgotten as I begin the next stage of my existence in the soil that gave birth to so much more than flowers.

It gave me you.

It gave me strength.

And it gave me purpose.

It's a selfish request, I know. But in this moment so full of despair, it's all I can ask.

Do not mourn me. Revive me.

—Genesis

It's an unavoidable wrecking ball, delivering a final, crushing blow.

The dam has finally broken, unleashing every ounce of agony I've suppressed. It claws through my soul, shredding me. I can't breathe. The pain…it's too much.

It hurts *too much*.

No!

No!

No!

I search frantically for the darkness, for my numbness, but there is none. *Where are you now when I need you?* Nothing. This amount of anguish…it's too overwhelming, stealing my breath. My fingers clench the paper with purpose, but I release it before I rip it to shreds.

Her words replay in my mind. Over and over again. Relentlessly.

The sorrow coursing through my body ignites into fiery rage. Red fills my blurry vision. With every ounce of strength I can muster, I swing my hand in front of my body, sending the crystalline vase in the center of the table flying. I watch as it connects with the side of the island and shatters. Water sprays into the air and the pristine arrangement of flowers scatters before landing on the floor.

There is only the sound of my rapid breathing as I inspect the damage. I watch, mesmerized as rivulets of water curl along the lip of the island, then as each droplet separates and plummets.

Seconds pass, and I tear my eyes away from the shattered glass, once again taking in the open letters on the table.

Your Wildflowers will need you now more than ever.

I wipe away my tears, then inhale a long, steady breath. Resolve settles in my heart, cementing the shattered pieces and fusing them back together. It's misshapen, a distorted shell of what it used to be, but determination fills me.

Revive me.

Like a seed taking root after being blown aimlessly by the wind, somehow her spirit plants itself within me, suffusing me with renewed vigor and awakening my senses, allowing me to take my first full breath in months.

A glimmer of reason flickers in my soul, bringing me

one step closer to living beyond my darkness. And I take that step, no matter how painful and torturous. I do it because there's no other choice.

Because in Genny's death, I find my reason. My purpose.

I refuse to let Genny's existence die with her. I will not allow her greatest fear to come to fruition.

I will make sure she lives on.

And I know how to do it.

28

It's funny how much I actually don't feel over the next hour.

I experience absolutely no fear when I charge up to my father's study and, using the combination I figured out years ago out of sheer boredom, extract the large sum of money he keeps inside.

There is no sense of dread when I pack my belongings into a duffle bag, lug it over my shoulder, and close the door on my childhood.

Not one ounce of remorse surfaces when I enter the garage and pick one of the several cars available. Though my first choice was my mother's Range Rover, because it's her favorite, something in my gut tells me to take my father's 1970 Chevelle. Not only is it a badass muscle car that's screaming to be driven, it's also the only one without a GPS installed.

I feel nothing watching Gerard throw open the door in my rearview, vaguely wondering if I've somehow gone numb again while pulling out of the garage. But that is quickly proven incorrect when something close to elation stirs in me as I roll down the window flip him the bird before peeling out of the drive.

It all seems so easy.

Until it's not.

The drive itself is probably the most difficult thing I've ever had to do. It's just me, alone, forced to face the reality that the Wildflowers lost one of our own as I sit in complete silence. I don't know if it's my own form of penance, or just the thirst to feel everything I can after all this time locking it away, but I allow nothing to soften the blow of the loss of Genny for two solid hours.

It's pure torture, but somehow, instinctively, I know it's necessary.

And when I finally park in front of the quaint house at 5103 Stillhouse Avenue, I'm overwhelmed by a sense of pride. I made it through my forced solitude, through the tears and wailing, through the anger and resentment. I made it. I felt every single emotion I could possibly feel as I made the drive.

And I survived.

A tingling sensation washes over me and goosebumps erupt over every inch of my skin. I inhale deeply, embracing this new warmth. It gives me the strength to make my way to what I'm guessing is Sally's house. Am I afraid of what

I'll find, of whom I'll find behind that door?

Absolutely.

Yet, I'm comforted in the knowledge that even though we may be broken, we are capable of being mended. And although we may never be the same, we will survive.

Together.

Because we are, and will always be, Genny's Wildflowers.

I lift my arm to knock, but before I'm able to make contact, the door flies open and I'm once again standing face to face with Sally. Her wide grin is contagious as she looks me over. Then she steps onto the porch and gently cups my cheeks, her relieved eyes locking with mine as she breathes, "You're here."

"I am," I reply, curling my fingers around hers and giving them a slight squeeze.

While the reason for my presence lingers heavily in the air, I allow myself this one moment of joy, because for the first time in months I feel the sensation I've been craving since I was forced to leave Sacred Heart behind.

I'm home.

Her smile drops slightly, and I sense her guilt as she holds my face in her hands, watching me intensely through her tears.

I didn't understand her decision to send me home at the time, but now I do. She did what she thought was best in an impossible situation, and I love her more than she will ever realize for doing what she needed to do to keep me safe.

Sally opens her mouth to speak, but I cut her off with

a dismissive jerk of my head. "No more apologies, Sally." With my grip still tightened around her fingers, I lean in and press my forehead against hers. "No more."

A sob escapes her, but she just nods as another form fills the doorway. His presence is so familiar, I don't even have to break eye contact with Sally to know who it is.

"It's about time, Number Three. We've been waiting." Though Adam's voice is cloaked with a sense of sorrow, I grin as I break my gaze from Sally's to meet his.

"Well, anything's better than waiting on 'Number Two' because that can be painful. And a quite possibly a health risk," I remark.

He grins in return, his bright blue eyes crinkling at the corners before he offers me open arms. And that's all it takes. I'm enveloped by him in seconds, saturated with a sense of belonging I've felt only within the Wildflowers' presence. As I hold on to him, I mentally note how long his blond hair has grown. It now grazes his shoulders, wild and free as the breeze carries it, just as it should be. Just as *he* should be. My fingers curl inward, and I cling to the soft fabric of his shirt, inhaling deeply while memories of our brief reprieve from suffering play out in my mind.

Adam and Genny by our pond, his head thrown back in laughter at something she said, her expression daring and mischievous.

Genny's arm slung around my shoulder in her usual protective manner, her combat boots pounding against the pavement as she strides with a confidence I aspired to.

Adam's and Lukas's quizzical expressions while Genny and I giggled at some private joke shared between the two of us.

It's a strange mix, the warmth of our reunion suffused with the bitterness of a marked absence. I shiver in Adam's arms as I murmur into his chest, "I can't believe she's gone."

My knees buckle and Adam tightens his grip, holding me securely while I cry. I feel the heat from his fingers as they sift through my hair and the warmth of his breath soothes me. "You still feel her though, right?"

I nod because I do. All around and inside me.

Adam releases me and lifts his hands to cup my face, thumbs sweeping away my tears as he softly states, "Then she's not really gone, is she?"

Earnest eyes bore into mine and I shake my head, a tiny grin forming with the recognition that even from beyond, Genny still binds us. We are her creation, her vision, her purpose. And somehow, even in death, she gifted each of us with whatever piece of her we found most impactful, cementing us together for the remainder of our lives. And though I may never truly comprehend what she bestowed to Adam, I'm certain she left me with a ferocity for life that could have only come from her. Which leaves me wondering what she left with...

"Where's Lukas?"

Adam's stare disengages from mine, sliding to Sally still standing behind us. A muscle in his jaw jumps, and he swallows slowly before looking at me again. He shakes his head, his tone clipped when he answers. "I don't think he's coming."

My brows furrow confusion. "What? Why?"

I feel Sally's hand on my shoulder and whirl around to face her. Her voice is gentle, but slow and hesitant, as though I'm a feral animal about to bolt. "Lukas has…" She pauses, clearly searching for the appropriate explanation. "Well, what happened that night, what he did…it's taken its toll. I've spoken to him, and he's really struggling, Chloe. He feels guilt for his actions, guilt for not being able to prevent what happened, guilt for Genny's death."

She looks to the floor then back at me, tears welling along her lashes. "He's changed."

I shake my head in refusal, ire igniting my blood and warming my cheeks. My teeth are clenched as I seethe, "We've all changed, Sally!" I throw my hands up in frustration. "Do you honestly believe any of us will ever be the same after what we experienced, after what we've seen?! After what we've lost?!"

My voice breaks, and although the obvious meaning behind the last words would be the loss of Genny, the loss of our very innocence cannot be denied, either. A part of each of us died that night, and I'm as certain as the anger pumping through my veins that the only way for us to be fully revived is to be together.

"Lukas does not get the monopoly on brokenness here. We're all damaged, we all feel guilty, and yet"—I gestured between the three of us—"we're here." Another shake of my head. "He owes her this."

We all stare at each other until the silence is broken.

"She's right."

My entire body jolts. Sally gasps. Adam's eyes widen in surprise when the deep, gravelly voice sounds from behind us.

"I owe her."

Slowly, I turn to see Lukas standing in the open doorway, a duffle bag thrown over his shoulder, his hardened gaze aimed in my direction. It's impossible to miss the meaning behind his words. He's only here for Genny. Because this time it's not about us. And surprisingly? I'm okay with that.

"Us" died that night, too.

I take in his wildly spiked hair, black thermal, faded jeans, and heavily booted feet. And though his outward appearance is strikingly familiar, it's his eyes that truly hold me. They're no longer warm, vulnerable, accessible. Staring back at me are pools of pure ice—cold and distant—filled with the same anger as they were the first day he came to Sacred Heart.

Sally was right. The Lukas I fell in love with is not here. He's stowed behind the protective exterior we worked so hard to demolish. A seemingly impenetrable wall composed of fury and self-hatred, one that I pray Genny bequeathed us the tools to dismantle when the time is right.

Lukas says no more—he simply stalks past us and through the living room, until he slams a door behind him.

My brows raise at the obvious familiarity Lukas possesses regarding Sally's house. I watch as she makes her way to the front door and quietly shuts it, shrugging meekly in the process.

She looks at me, my confused expression spurring her to explain. "He's been over here a couple of times since I contacted you all about Genny. I've been trying to help him cope in the short time since."

She sighs. "My sessions with him are clearly lacking."

Adam speaks up from behind me. "As in therapy sessions?"

When Sally nods, he chuckles to himself. "Isn't that like a conflict of interest or something?"

Sally's concerned expression softens with a wide, knowing smile. "Absolutely." She winks. "But then again, when have we ever really been ones to follow the rules?"

Adam wraps his arm around my shoulders, both of us breaking into quiet laughter at her response. Sally's always been an honorary member of the Wildflowers, but with that one simple statement, she's pretty much solidified her standing as one of us. In fact, Genny would be pleased to know her name, as it's a derivation of "Sarah," is also of biblical origin, so we aren't breaking any of her rules by bringing Sally into our fold.

Sally holds each of us with a determined stare. "Don't worry. We'll get there."

I smile and lean into Adam, my head resting on his shoulder as I concur. "We'll get him back. We've done it before."

Warmth rushes through me, and I know Genny is here

and in complete agreement.

I look at the ceiling and tears escape as I repeat it just for her. "We'll get him back, Genny. I'll make sure of it."

29

The smell of taco seasoning wafts through the air as I stir the simmering meat in front of me. I try to focus on the task, something I volunteered to do in order to keep my mind occupied, but my eyes rebel as I steal another glance over my shoulder, tracking the path Lukas forged over an hour ago. I halfway expect to be met with a sly half-grin offset by apologetic eyes.

But there is no sign of Lukas. There is no light. There is only seemingly infinite darkness ebbing from behind his closed bedroom door.

You would think after the first five hundred disappointments that I would eventually resign my efforts and give up hope. Yet, I can't seem to stop looking.

My eyes slide to Sally standing no more than two feet away, wordlessly shredding mounds of lettuce, then to

Adam who fills a bowl with cheese. And although he too remains silent, when his eyes lift to meet mine, they speak volumes.

Give him time.

My mouth tightens, and my eyes narrow. Adam dismisses my obvious frustration with a quick grin and a shake of his head before redirecting his attention to dispensing dollops of sour cream into another bowl.

Once everything's ready and the table is set, the three of us move to Sally's dining room and take our seats. Just as I begin to reach for an empty taco shell, Sally clears her throat, halting my movement.

"Shall we pray?"

On her last word, a door squeaks open behind us, and we all focus on the table as Lukas makes his way down the hall. Then, without so much as a word or even an angry glance, he slams his body into the fourth chair, and like the rest of us, his attention is directed at the taco makings on the table.

Palms facing the ceiling, Sally reaches for my hand still hovering above the taco shells. Once I slide mine into hers, she reaches toward Adam who does the same. I sit in silence, waiting, until Sally applies a freaking death grip to my hand, cutting off precious circulation while she not-so-subtly jerks her head in Lukas's direction.

I frown at her, but she widens her eyes in a silent threat before again squeezing my hand so hard, I seriously begin to worry for the welfare of my precious fingers.

In the midst of a sip of tea, Adam chokes on his laughter, amused watching the silent faceoff between Sally and myself. I glare at him with the same look I've been aiming at Sally, and once he stops chocking, Adam's lips curve into an off-kilter grin. Slowly, he sets the glass on the table and traitorously reaches his free hand for Lukas's, eyes on mine the entire time.

I look at the ceiling, inhale deeply, then reluctantly do the same. Lukas's hand trembles as it envelops mine, his heated touch at odds with the cold stare he's trained on the table. I make my face as blank as I can when he willingly grips Adam's hand as well, remembering Lukas's refusal to touch us in the beginning. *Does this mean he's not as lost as we'd thought?*

I store that knowledge for use at a later date.

Once we're all joined, Sally dips her head, closes her eyes, and begins to pray.

"Lord knows I'm not a very religious person, but in this moment, I'm both humbled and overwhelmed with the need to express my thanks for four very remarkable individuals who have impacted me in ways they may never comprehend. I know with absolute certainty they were brought into my life for a reason, and although they may feel I was the person responsible for guiding them as they navigated their hardships, they more than returned the favor by simply existing. Initially, there was so much unrecognized beauty within them, concealed behind the ugliness they each had to face. But through our time together, these four broke through the molds placed upon them, and they did so unapologetically."

Sally squeezes my hand, and I clench hers in return in preparation for what I know is to come next.

"One of those blessed people is not here with us tonight."

A tear tickles my skin as it races along the bridge of my nose, but I keep hold of the hands anchoring me while she continues.

"Tomorrow we will honor not only her request, but her memory as we spread her ashes with the wildflowers. We ask only that she takes root and flourishes with the same palpable spirit she possessed here on earth, so she may cultivate others in the same way she did these fierce souls she left behind." Sally pauses, sniffling, holding back her own tears. "Souls that may be damaged, but because of her, will undoubtedly find strength. I end this prayer now for those seated with me. I ask you to heal their wounds, to grant them peace, and to gift them the reinforcement of an ideal that Genny worked so hard to instill."

Sally inhales deeply and when she says exactly what Genny would say in this moment, I know without a doubt she has made the same indelible mark on Sally as on each of us. Her words are directed to the person seated at my left, because out of all of us, Lukas needs to hear them, now more than ever.

"There is no judgment within the Wildflowers—there is only acceptance. Come as you are and they will absorb your grief as our own. They will house it, they will own it, making it no longer your burden alone to bear."

As soon as the words leave Sally's mouth, Lukas's hand drops mine, and he springs to his feet, his seat scraping against the wood flooring before he stalks back to his room, without so much as a word.

Or even a taco.

Instinctively, I stand, but Sally releases her grip on our hands and offers, "I'm sorry. It was too much, too soon."

And suddenly I'm angry, not at Lukas, but *for* Sally. That she seems to be warring with the same guilt as Lukas, for circumstances that were completely beyond our control. My head whips in her direction. "No more *fucking* apologies, Sally. Stop it. He needs to hear—"

"Then we're all in agreement." Adam, who's risen with me, slams his hands on the table and leans in toward both of us. His eyes are gleaming with intensity. "He needed to hear it. We owe him the time to absorb what was said."

My breaths are quick and shallow as anger works its way through my system. I remain standing, willing my heart rate to slow, and watch as Sally silently acquiesces by taking her seat instead of running after Lukas. Adam, still standing and clearly done offering his advice, exhales long and deep, then reaches for the taco shells and grabs three. Once they're stuffed with meat, cheese, and lettuce, he drops into his seat and leans back, brows raised, eyes full of challenge and locked on me.

And although there is so much I want to say, my stomach speaks for me. A low rumble reverberates through my stomach, only to morph into a full-fledged, furious growl. Appalled, I glance down before looking at Adam. His mouth lifts at the corners and his eyes light with humor. My gaze shifts to find Sally's hand covering her mouth, clearly attempting to conceal her own laughter.

It doesn't work.

She giggles, then much to my surprise, releases the most heinous snort I've ever heard, which prompts her to laugh harder. Her eyes fill with tears and her entire body shakes, and no matter how hard I try to fight it, I can't.

I laugh right along with her, the tension of the last few moments dissolving instantly.

I needed this. Needed them.

Half an hour later, my stomach is finally stuffed, and thanks to a light-hearted discussion we shared over the meal, I'm feeling more relaxed than I've felt in months. I find out over dinner that Adam is living with Seth, both of them working for Seth's parents' landscaping business. I guess the time spent working on the yard this summer was the perfect training for his new career. Sally, on the other hand, has begun expanding her practice from Sacred Heart patients to others in this area. My heart swells with happiness for them both, and a tiny bit of hope for me, too.

Across from me, Adam tosses his napkin onto his plate and slides back into his seat, just as Sally sips the last of her tea.

We look at each other, knowing there are things that need to be said, but none of us are quite ready to descend into the darkness of the situation surrounding us. After a few minutes, it's Adam, always the trailblazer, who decides to bring us back to reality.

He glances in the direction of Lukas's harsh retreat, then shifts forward in his seat, speaking in a hushed tone. "I was next, you know."

Sally gasps beside me in clear understanding of his meaning, but I just stare back at him, confusion made evident by my blank expression.

He gives Sally a sad, small smile, before looking back at me. "In the basement, I was next, after Genny. They were going to rape me, too."

My hand flies to my mouth, and my throat constricts at the horror of his revelation.

Adam looks once again over his shoulder. "Lukas saved you, but he has no idea he also saved me. What he needs to understand is that even though Genny couldn't be saved, others were."

His eyes begin to glisten, and he clears his throat. "At the time, I couldn't process everything that happened that night. It was too much, too soon. So, I get where Lukas is coming from. The anger. The guilt. I think right now, for him, it's still too...raw. I can see it in his eyes. He's still there. Still lost in that night just as I was for quite some time. I was lucky. I had Seth to help guide me through that darkness—he was my lifeline."

Adam levels me with an unwavering stare. "When Lukas is ready, you will be his lifeline. You will guide him past the anger, past the remorse and shame, to finally grasp what's he's purposefully keeping himself from seeing: the fact that he protected us, and saved our lives." He tightens his grip. "And you will return the favor."

Sally's words that terrifying night rush into my mind.

"A love like yours is destined to come full circle. You will see him again. And when you do, no matter how far gone he may be, do not give up on him. You hold on to that love like a lifeline, because it will be. For the both of you."

I give Adam a smile in thanks, then look at Sally, who must be a mind reader because she grins and shoots me a knowing wink.

Then, I look down the desolate hall.

Do I possess the strength necessary to pull Lukas back into the light, where he deserves to be?

30

I'm enveloped in blackness when I open my eyes, but it's not cold. There's a sense of warmth that seems to fill the dark, a soothing ebb and flow that courses through me and all around me, calming my churning mind.

I look upward, expecting to find the ceiling of Sally's guest bedroom, but there is nothing. I wiggle my toes, seeking the cotton sheets that surrounded me when I fell asleep, but I feel nothing but air. It's disorienting really, as I expect to be lying down, yet in this place I seem to float, to hover above infinite nothingness, buoyant in my weightlessness.

I'm not afraid. I feel serene and at peace, at home in this blank environment. And within it, I find a familiarity I can't describe. It's as though I've been here before, equipped with an understanding that remains just beyond my reach.

My eyes search for something to focus on, and just when I'm convinced there's nothing, small ripples of light begin to take shape, interrupting the stillness encasing me. The wavy lines, small at first, begin to elongate and grow in intensity. It's odd, I think, that the increasing brightness doesn't affect my vision. I don't feel the need to squint or shield my eyes from the luminosity. I simply watch them grow and morph until the lines become one, forming the outline of a person approaching me from inside the darkness.

Light laughter echoes all around me, its touch as soft as a feather against my skin. I grin widely when the presence comes to a standstill in front of me. The pink shading gives her away.

"Genny…" I breathe. Elation fills my heart.

"Surprise. It's me." More laughter ensues. "I always said that if I was a ghost, I'd haunt you from beyond, just for fun."

A chuckle escapes me. "Well, you are rather incorporeal." I narrow my eyes, trying to focus. "I can see you, but I can't."

"Here, let me see what I can do."

I watch, completely in awe as the blur in front of me morphs into the very distinctive form of Genny. The same smattering of freckles along the bridge of her nose, green eyes bright with mischief, and that familiar smile. As though stolen directly from my memories, she even dons her Sex Pistols T-shirt (sans grease stains) and the same short plaid skirt I've seen her wear so often. I glance at her Docs and my heart nearly implodes at the sight.

"Ta-da!" She bends forward into a deep bow, still smiling when she rises.

As though removing a layer of dust, she sweeps her hands along the pleats of the skirt then looks back at me. "Much to my disappointment, however, I am not a ghost. I'm a winged guardian from above." She points to the heavens.

My eyes pop. "You're an angel?"

"In the flesh. Or not. Whatever." She reaches forward and takes my hand into hers, grinning back at me. "Who would've thunk it? A foul-mouthed former addict and teenager, skating right through those infamous pearly gates."

I respond without hesitation. "Me. I couldn't imagine you being anything less."

Genny gifts me a thankful smile, one that turns rueful when she adds, "Sometimes I think I'd prefer to be a ghost. This angel shit is a lot of responsibility."

I giggle, the fact that I'm talking to Genny still a bit surreal. I'm sure this is nothing but a dream, but still, I'm overwhelmed with joy. "So," I begin, "I'm taking it you finally met *your* Jesus?"

Genny nods happily, wide grin spreading across her face. "I was right. He definitely overlooks a lot of shit."

My grin matches hers as I prompt, "And God. Have you met Him?"

"Him?" Genny snorts. "Of course those responsible for biblical translation would assign God a masculine connotation. I mean, of course the all-knowing, all-powerful, creator must be a man, right?" She rolls her eyes. "Sure, it's great for the male superiority complex, but it's not true. God isn't male. God just is."

I nod, impressed by her wisdom.

She narrows her eyes, her expression thoughtful. "Although if I had to choose between one or the other I would say female. I mean, come on, everyone knows men can't multitask for shit. And multitasking would have to be the numero-uno requirement for the position."

She winks, and we break into laughter, the familiar chorus stirring up some of my favorite memories. I brace for impending heartache, but none follows. There is only pure happiness as I stand here with my friend.

Genny extends her arm, and I hook mine around it, just as I used to. We begin to walk, though our feet never seem to touch any sort of surface. After a while, she exhales and says, "I called in another favor. It's rare you know—you should feel very special that we are able to have this conversation. There are rules."

I feel her eyes on me and sense the mischief radiating from her gaze. I whip my head in her direction, with an insatiable sense of curiosity I ask, "Can you share some of them? With me?"

She laughs. "I sure can. Because one of the rules is you can't remember anything. You may feel as though something is tugging at your memory, but you won't really be able to make sense out of it."

I frown at her. "Well, that sucks."

"It really does. You have no idea."

I curb my disappointment and quickly ask, "Another one?"

"Well." She pauses before continuing. "I have to keep my advice somewhat cryptic. I can't just tell you what to do outright, because the decisions you make need to be yours."

"What if I make the wrong decision?"

Genny curls her hand over my arm. "You may. You may not. You may completely veer off your path. But if you do, you'll need a little guidance to get back on course. Which is where I come in."

"But how the heck is that supposed to work if I can't remember anything?"

"Right?" Genny laughs. "It makes no sense, but it works."

She stops walking, and I turn to face her. She takes both my hands in hers, her tone soft yet stoic as she explains. "You know those 'gut feelings'? The waves of intuition you get when you're faced with certain decisions that you can choose to follow or ignore?"

My eyebrows skyrocket with her revelation and she returns the gesture with a slow nod. "Well, that'll be me from now on."

I'm still trying to wrap my head around this notion when she tugs me forward. Our hands remain joined as we continue along whatever path Genny has chosen. We walk in silence, Genny allowing me time to process her words, her presence. It's a lot to take in, but I know she's telling the truth.

Which means her time with me in this place has been granted out of necessity. So instead of asking her more pointless questions, I ask her the one I think she's been counting on me asking. "Do you have a message you need to deliver? To me?"

Genny squeezes my hand, halting my forward movement. When I turn to her, a soft, sad smile graces her face.

"Indeed, I do." She clears her throat, taking a deep, long breath before continuing. "Spring is near, Chloe. The winter that fell on each of you was harsh, and it was not without casualty, but it has served its purpose. The slate is clean and rebirths are imminent. The time will come when each of you will instinctively yearn to blossom again. But the ground into which you've sunk your roots may still be impacted, cold, and unyielding." Her eyes are insistent with her plea. "You must keep trying. Keep pushing. Because as you find the strength to reemerge, you will soften the soil around you, making it possible for others to follow. In particular, a person who would have otherwise remained trapped, fruitless, and idle beneath the earth, unable to breathe and therefore, unable to bloom."

Lukas.

I nod my understanding. "He needs me."

"You all need each other," Genny says. "Each of you serves a specific purpose within the realm of the Wildflowers. Roles that change as you continue to grow. As I stated before, you, have always been the fresh bloom, but now it's your blossoming that will ensure the resilience of the group. Adam is the soil in which you will continue to find an anchor and derive your strength, and Lukas…well, Lukas will always be your light. He will nurture you, and in doing so, he finds his purpose—you give him a reason to shine. Together, the three of you will do amazing things."

There's so much weight in Genny's plea I begin to nibble my bottom lip, cold slivers of self-doubt leaching into my mind and stealing my joy.

Genny places both hands on my shoulders and grips them gently. "You can do this, Chloe. You've always had more strength than you've given yourself credit for. It's time for you to become the lioness you're destined to be."

She winks, then looks upward before bringing her eyes back to mine. "It seems our time is up."

No. I'm not ready yet. I'm struck with tangible sadness. *I need more time.* The side of her mouth lifts in an apologetic half-smile before she looks upward once again.

"Can I ask you one more question?" I shout as she begins to fade.

Genny floats in front of me, obscured in a blurry haze like she was before. "Shoot."

A sob claws at my throat, and my voice breaks as I inquire, "Are you happy?"

A burst of light explodes from Genny and as soon as it hits me, I'm sheathed in warmth, the ache in my heart no longer throbbing. I hear her voice all around me.

"I am the happiest I've ever been, outside of my time with the three of you."

Heat embraces me, and although she is no longer physically here, I lift my arms and hug her back, smiling as I revel in what she wordlessly relays to me.

Peace.

And then she's gone.

31

It's the morning after my arrival at Sally's and after a surprisingly peaceful night of sleep, I'm standing with my hip against the counter, watching Sally scramble eggs. I'm still in my pajamas—cotton shorts covered in cherries and a matching red tank—with my hair piled not so neatly on my head.

"How did it happen?" I try to ask nonchalantly, taking a sip of coffee.

Sally's spatula stills, and though I mentioned no name or circumstance, I know she understands the meaning of my question. Yes, it's morbid, but after the whirlwind of drama last night, I never had a chance to ask. And I need to know. I need to gain some sort of closure regarding the loss of my friend.

Adam strolls into the kitchen with a severe case of bedhead, his blond hair tousled as he sleepily pours himself a cup of coffee. He turns in my direction, his white V-neck clinging to his chest and his flannel pajama pants sweeping the floor as he makes his way to stand beside me. I grin at him, then reach over in an attempt to finger brush his hair, but he swats my hand away, laughing.

Shaking my head, I watch Sally, now plating the eggs, and repeat, "How did it happen, Sally?"

Adam chokes on his coffee, probably aware of what I'm asking and most likely shocked by my brusqueness. I ignore him. My eyes are locked on Sally as she braces her hands against the counter, leans into them, and sighs.

"I don't know, honestly." Her voice trembles with her admission. She inhales deeply and turns to face us, eyes glistening. "The address I gave Seth is that of a very close friend of mine, a doctor. After discharging Adam into Seth's care, she agreed to take Genny in and monitor her until everything calmed down. I took care of everything with the fire department and police, who thankfully ruled the fire accidental based on the corroboration of our stories. Thank you for that, Chloe." She looks at me. "I know it wasn't easy."

I shrug and offer her a smile, which she reciprocates. "Genny was out of it for the next day or so, which was to be expected. One afternoon, my friend left to pick up some things from the store, and by the time she arrived back home, Genny was just...gone."

Sally shakes her head. "We headed into some pretty rough neighborhoods looking for her, even some well-known drug houses, asking if anyone had seen her, but the answer was always the same. No one had seen her. She completely disappeared." A tear rolls down her cheek as she fights to maintain her composure. "We kept searching, even in other cities, but we couldn't find her. About a month later, I received a call from a police officer in Johnson City. He'd found Genny's body in a hotel room. While they identified several needles strewn around the room, they also found her backpack. When they searched it, they found my business card along with some clothes and other items, including Genny's letter, which was why they contacted me." She looks gravely at me then Adam. "She died of heart failure due to the amount of heroin in her system. I had to identify her body."

I gasp and cover my mouth, swallowing the sob I want so desperately to release. Adam wraps his arm around my shoulder and pulls me closer, setting his chin on the top of my head as Sally continues. "She was correct in that she would be cremated. I requested her ashes be transferred to me so we may carry out her wishes." She shrugs in conclusion. "Then I contacted each of you. Phone calls to Adam and Lukas, and the letter to you because I wasn't sure if your parents would let you speak with me."

Then she says no more because I rush forward and wrap my arms around her tiny frame, silently thanking her for all she's had to go through to bring us back together again. She grips me just as tightly, breaking her hold only to reach for Adam. Together we embrace, clinging to each other as we mourn, each of our collective tears serving to honor Genny's memory.

Half an hour later, with watery eyes and runny noses, we're seated at the table and finishing breakfast. Sally sets her coffee cup down, looking between Adam and me before she speaks. "I looked into the Duffs. It took some digging, I didn't find much regarding their activities in other homes, but I did discover something…" Her expression is pinched as she contemplates the next word. "Disturbing."

I know what she's going to say before it even leaves her mouth. My suspicions confirmed, I finish for her. "They were siblings. All of them."

Sally's eyebrows lift in surprise and I shrug. "I figured as much. They were too much alike. Identical eyes. Expressions. Gestures. Cut from the same vile cloth." I look to Adam in apology. "I should have said something."

Adam gives me a soft smile then reaches across the table to take my hand. "You're not the only one. I think we all knew, but none of us wanted to voice the truth. Not even to ourselves."

I refuse to taint the reverence of what we've been brought here to do with the disgust of their memory. My eyes focus on the shining plate in the center of the table. It's glaring in its emptiness, and I find myself extremely irked by this.

Releasing Sally and Adam's hands, I clear my throat and ask, "So, you've been working with Lukas?"

She breaks eye contact to look at her own plate. "Trying to work with Lukas, yes."

After giving a light nod, she meets my eyes. "He'd taken

a job about an hour away in Angleton, working construction. He told me before he left, so it wasn't too hard to track him down. I remember finding it odd that he was free to go anywhere he pleased, yet he chose to remain so close."

Adam leans forward, elbows on the table as he listens intently to Sally's recollection. "Anyway, after I told him, I expected him to lose control, hit something, break down and cry, scream at the top of his lungs, something. But there was absolutely no reaction. He was completely devoid of emotion, which really worried me. I urged him to speak with me, to talk about that night, his feelings about what happened to Genny, anything at all, so I could get a read on him. He refused, but I gave him my address anyway, just in case."

She laughs to herself, and I can't tell if the sound is laced with humor or dejection. "Two days later, Lukas showed up on my doorstep, disheveled and clearly sleep-deprived. So I invited him in. He sat in my kitchen, watching me scrounge up some sandwiches, completely silent the entire time. Once we were through eating, we moved to my living room and just stared at each other for over an hour. I was trying to give him time to find the courage to speak, but he never said a word." She shrugs. "This has been going on for about a week, almost every single night. Sometimes he shows up late and stays in my study, which he's seemingly claimed as his room." After a look down the hall, Sally returns her attention to us. "I don't know. As I said before, my sessions with him are very clearly lacking."

Something deep within me snaps. I look again at the

untouched plate. My face heats, anger and frustration igniting something within me I never realized existed. I get up, completely done with Lukas and his manufactured walls. We're all in pain, we're all hurting, and it's time for him to face reality instead of whatever deluded environment he's been hiding inside of these past few months.

"Well, I happen to think he's had enough time."

I ignore the shouts of protest and stomp down the hall. My strides are heavy and purposeful, driving me straight to the door of Lukas's ridiculous hidey-hole. Not bothering to knock, I throw it open, barely catching a glimpse of his unbuttoned jeans and his bare chest before it's all hastily covered with a black long-sleeved thermal.

I step inside and slam the door, my breaths coming in short, successive pants. "Ready to talk?"

Lukas's eyes widen in surprise then narrow on me. His jaw clenches. "No." He turns his back on me to shove some clothes into a duffle, which pisses me off even more.

"Like, for now? Or ever?"

When I receive no reply, I march right over to the couch and knock the bag onto the floor with one sweep of my arm. Still clutching what looks to be sweatpants, he glares at me. His eyes are cold and vacant, menacing.

I quirk an eyebrow in spite of the fury emanating from him. It rolls off him in waves, his entire body quaking with it. Yet his hardened expression doesn't frighten me. I've become well accustomed to Intimidating Lukas, but I also remember the gentle man I know he can be.

"That's unacceptable," I seethe, hands on my hips.

A muscle ticks in his jaw before he looks away and bends over, whipping the bag off the floor. I don't hesitate. I knock it out of his hand, watching as it lands with a thud.

His head whips angrily to the side, glaring in my direction over his shoulder. "You really don't want to mess with me right now."

Even though his tone is one of warning, I'm disregarding it. I don't speak. I stare back at him, eyes narrowed, mouth pinched.

Our stares remain locked in a silent standoff for several seconds, and I make damn sure I'm not the one to break eye contact. I know I've won when he disengages to shove the sweatpants still in his hand inside the bag on the floor. He stands, back still facing me, and takes a few steps to grab a couple of T-shirts off the arm of the couch. Immediately I lean forward, yank them from his closed hand, and toss them back on top of the leather. A deep, guttural growl escapes him before he turns to face me. "What the fuck do you want from me?"

His hair is spiked wildly, as though he's been running his fingers through it all morning, and his eyes are no longer cold, but fiery, raging. Good. At least he's still capable of feeling something.

Adam and Sally both suggested I give him time, but I clearly no longer accept that course of action. There's a feeling deep in my gut that tells me time is the last thing he needs, a voice inside my mind that whispers to me.

Keep pushing.

So, that's what I do.

"I want you to talk about what happened that night."

His head swivels to the right, his jaw still clenched as he aims his eyes at the floor. "Not gonna happen."

I chuckle to myself humorlessly. "It's going to happen, whether you like it or not, Lukas."

When he doesn't respond, I feel a wave of fury in me. I step to him and throw my open hands directly against his chest, causing him to stumble backward. Surprise flashes in his eyes before he make his expression blank, reinforcing his walls as he rights his body. He still refuses to say a word.

I close the distance between us in two strides and lift my arms to shove him again, but he catches my wrists before I'm able to make contact. He yanks me forward, and I collide with his chest before he warns, "You don't want to do that again."

I scoff, our heated breaths mingling as I state, "Oh, I *so* do."

Though his fingers are curled tight around my wrists, I muster all the strength in my possession and push forward, knocking into him again. His grip tightens, and he matches my movement, forcing me backward until my back hits a wall. And that's when I feel it. His composure is cracking.

He leans close, body trembling as he hisses, "You think your pure, precious existence can handle the filth of my truth?"

I roll my eyes, unaffected. I know too well what he's

trying to do, but pushing me away won't work, because there's something I've finally figured out about myself after all this time.

I've longed to be seen. For others to appreciate me, to accept me. But it's now obvious to me that I wasted so much of my life *wanting* to be noticed, instead of *demanding* it. I know now more than ever how short life can be, and I will no longer be cast aside as the timid, fearful girl I once was. I refuse to live in the shadows any longer.

So I meet his furious gaze, emboldened and unafraid. "Try me."

After a long, hard look, Lukas releases my wrists and turns on his heel, gripping the back of his neck. He exhales loudly, but his tone is softer than I expect when he speaks.

"I should have never split us up. Safety in numbers, right?" He scoffs to himself. "I will never understand why I sent you two to your room alone. I don't think I'll ever be able to forgive myself for that misjudgment. I mean, we outnumbered them." He releases another heavy sigh, his head low. "But I did. Adam and I were trying to figure out how the fuck to get out of there when Lonny and Bobby barged into the room. Bobby grabbed Adam, and I tried to pull him away, but I couldn't get a grip on him. I was so focused on freeing Adam, I never saw the lamp coming. He knocked me out. When I came to, I was alone. Adam was gone."

He turns to me, his expression no longer hardened but tormented. And although I long to comfort him, I remain where I stand, fearful to break this extremely fragile moment.

"I hauled ass downstairs, only to find Mrs. Duff in the kitchen. The minute she saw me, she ran toward the basement door. She just stood in front of it, blocking every attempt I made to try to open it. I couldn't figure out why, until I heard you scream. I lost all rational thought the moment I heard that. I barreled right through her to get at the door. She tumbled down the stairs right in front of me, and died." His guilt is so tangible it coats the air, making it impossible to breathe.

"Luk—"

"No," he says, his lip curled. "You wanted me to talk. You will hear all I have to say."

I clamp my mouth shut, narrowing my eyes. He doesn't notice. His eyes are unseeing. *He's there.* "It all happened so fast after that, yet everything seemed like it was in slow motion. I jumped over her, but skidded to a stop when I realized what was happening. The first thing my eyes landed on was Bobby climbing off Genny, and that sight…fuck, that will haunt me for the rest of my life. Because it was then that I knew what had happened. What he did to her. What I should have protected her from." Another shake of his head. "I heard a commotion and looked behind me to find that other fucker on top of you, and that was it. I lost all control. There was only wrath."

His eyes now focused, they lock onto mine. "I was so blinded by my rage, Chloe."

I swallow my sorrow, desperate to comfort him. *He saw too much.*

"I lost control just like I knew I would, and I lost all of you in the process."

I watch, completely helpless as tears brim then fall from his lashes. "I'm a monster, Chloe. I'm not 'good,' or 'light,' or anything you believed me to be. Darkness, which has always seemed to shadow me, now consumes me. I'm nothing more than a black hole. I destroy everything in my path."

Inhaling deeply, I swallow my own tears. "Lukas, please listen to me." I take a hesitant step in his direction. "You're not a monster. You are not darkness. Consider the lives you saved. The ones you protected."

Lukas's responding laugh is bitter and sardonic. "I couldn't protect Michelle. I sure as hell didn't protect Genny."

"Yes, we lost Genny." I take another step, which Lukas counters. "But you saved me. You saved Adam, too. Did you know that? What they were planning to do to him?"

A wave of shock flashes across his features before he carefully blanks his expression. "Lukas," I plead. "You cannot continue to assume the sole responsibility of preventing things beyond your control."

I dare to take another step, and again he takes a step back. "Do you blame me for what happened to Genny? Do you hate me for not being able to stop it?"

Lukas's dark brows dip in confusion. "No."

Two more steps forward. Two steps away. "Well then, you must blame Adam. I mean, he was there while it happened—he should've done something to help, right?"

"No. There was no way he could have done anything in his condition."

"Exactly." I take my last step, and Lukas's back hits the wall behind him. "So, as we were all clearly incapacitated in one way or another, I'm failing to grasp why you blame yourself, and not us as well."

My body is completely flush with his by the time I finish speaking, and I welcome his challenge, because I'm more than ready for it.

His expression is stone. "Because I could ha—"

"No, you couldn't!" I shout, my face mere inches from his. "None of us could! That's the point, Lukas. *We* are the Wildflowers. *We* are one. So, if you blame yourself, then you blame all of us. Or none of us at all."

Lukas says nothing, but he doesn't need to. I already know I've delivered a necessary blow to his defenses. With that knowledge, I back away. My voice is a whisper. "You know darkness follows you because you invite it, and it consumes you only because you allow it. But I refuse to believe there is no light left within you. I will never give up hope that one day you will burn as brightly as you're meant to, because that's my choice, and that's what I choose to believe."

With that I turn and head for the door. It's not until my hand finds the handle that Lukas speaks, his voice soft.

"What have you always been able to see that I can't?"

I open the door, answering simply and with complete honesty.

"You."

32

A beautiful collage of corals and pinks illuminates the horizon as the sun begins to set. The temperature, which was manageable when we first arrived, continues to drop along with the sun. I shiver inside my jacket, my hands inside my sleeves, fingers curled and clenching the fabric in an effort to prevent the chill from seeping inside.

The field in front of us is barren, brown, and bereft, not a spot of color in sight. Right now, it may seem as though it's just untended soil, but I know better. Soon, it will be brought to life once again, as it always is. It will sprout fresh spears of green as it's reborn, and not too long after, wildflowers will begin to pepper the blades of grass with every color imaginable.

I glance to the place where our wildflowers will reside, imagining them beginning to rouse beneath the soil, their roots stretching and unfurling as though waking from a much-needed slumber. Peaceful and rested as they begin to make their way to the surface above them, ready to reacquaint themselves with the world. I smile in anticipation, eager to see them again. I'm overwrought with joy in the knowledge that Genny will soon find root among them, forever housed within their liveliness and contentment.

Sally follows Adam as he directs her to the soil directly above our wildflowers, both of them relaxed as they laugh casually with one another. Sally's long blonde hair is down for a change, brushing the middle of her faded leather jacket as she walks, and her dark jeans are tucked into a pair of cowboy boots a shade lighter than the wooden box she holds securely in her hands. My eyes linger on the box for a few beats, and although there's definitely a looming sense of sorrow, its weight is offset by a sense of peace I didn't expect to feel today. I inhale deeply, allowing it to wash over me, and as I watch Sally and Adam talk and laugh, I'm guessing they feel it, too.

Next my eyes find Lukas, who was the first to arrive at Genny's final resting place, subdued and silent as he watches us approach. Earlier today, I braved the curious glances of Sally and Adam as I exited his room, but I said nothing, and they didn't ask. They didn't need to. When he made his way to the kitchen, slamming cabinet doors and numerous other items while making a plate for breakfast, it was pretty clear I'd done something to rile him up.

I left everything in that room—I'd said all I had to say.

It's up to him now.

Lukas doesn't meet my eyes when I stand next to him. Call me stubborn, call me insane, but something drives me in this moment to get as close to him as he'll allow. I refuse to give him the space he so desperately seeks just so he can disappear into an unfeeling abyss. Genny would expect no less, and I choose to honor her memory by ensuring Lukas is just as present as we are when we lay her to rest. I know he must miss her and my heart breaks for him because of that. But it's time...time for him to know he's not alone.

I smother a grin when a frustrated growl escapes him, satisfied that my mere presence incites such a reaction. Standing directly across from me, Adam's eyes meet mine. He looks from me to Lukas, then back at me, his lips quirking ever so slightly. Only then do I give my smile free rein, allowing it to spread across my face in a brief moment of shared solidarity before looking down at the ground.

Sally clears her throat, ready to commence the service. I sober immediately and redirect my attention to the wooden box in her hands. And although I still feel a sense of ease, of peace, it's impossible to deny the sorrow within my heart.

"We are gathered here today to honor the memory of Genesis Monroe, a girl who, in the few years I was blessed to know her, never failed to somehow wrench a smile from me during even the most trying times." Sally lifts her head, her eyes glistening as she gives each of us a small smile. A tear runs down my cheek and I quickly wipe it away, then offer her an encouraging smile in return. She nods her thanks then continues. "She may be gone, but even in death, she's incapable of being forgotten."

Sally flips open the lid to the box, directing her next words at its contents. "I hope you understand the indelible mark you seared into those you left behind, because I see it so clearly all around me. Residual traits soldered in the souls of those gathered in this place to bid you your final goodbye. Because of you, they've been transformed. You challenged them to be the people you knew they could be. And for that, I have no doubt, they will be forever grateful. As am I."

She inhales deeply, taking another moment to collect her emotions. "You called yourself the beginning, the creator, as your name implied, but you were so much more than that. You were the catalyst for the change they didn't realize they'd been aimlessly searching for, until they met you. Until you were all brought together."

One amazing woman did that. Brought us together. Knowing we'd need each other, and need her. It's only been five months since Mrs. Rodriguez died, and my heart hasn't really recovered. She allowed *us* to happen. Allowed the Wildflowers their place, their freedom. I still miss her. Part of me wants to add how it was that Mrs. Rodriguez brought us together. How she saw in Genny what Sally sees now, and how she knew what a crucial part Genny would play in all our lives.

But that's not for now. Not for this moment. I struggle through the deep breath I take, looking toward heaven, knowing Mrs. Rodriguez must be there with Genny.

Loving us from beyond.

Sally reaches inside and scoops a portion of Genny's ashes into her hand, then passes the box to Adam before crouching to the ground. We watch in silence as she squeezes her hand into a tight fist, as though giving a parting embrace, before she slowly uncurls her fingers and gently distributes the ashes along the ground near her feet. "We lay you to rest today with your wildflowers so that you may forever reside within the realm of hope and peace you so often sought with their presence. And we do so fully confident that you will find root with them, equipping them with the same sense of purpose you unwittingly did with each of us."

Warmth rolls through me, its joyful waves surging and bathing my heart with its essence. I smile in spite of my tears, watching Sally as she rises to her feet and indicates with a nod to Adam that it's his turn to speak.

His eyes shine with unshed tears as he gazes at the urn in his hands. "My Genny…" He swallows, his voice thick with unspoken emotions. "It's hard to describe the absolute torture of losing someone who is so deeply engrained in your heart, in your soul, that you don't really know where they end and you begin. It's as though you've been stripped from my body, ripping wide open the wounds your existence once served to heal. You were the first to believe in me after I was expelled from my family for just being myself, and it was in you I found the strength to continue being me, without apology. You gave me full understanding and unconditional love. A love even death is powerless to erase."

After wiping away his tears, Adam gently scoops some of the ashes into his cupped hand, then passes the box to me. We all watch in choked silence as he kneels on the ground, scattering the ashes. "You may no longer be with us physically, but I know you will continue to bloom. Not only here with our wildflowers, but also in our hearts with every beautiful memory you've left behind. May you find peace in the fact that you will never come to know your greatest fear…because you will *never* be forgotten."

Adam rises to his feet, his mournful eyes locked on mine. I deny the tightness in my throat, seeking courage in Adam's piercing gaze. I shut my eyes and nod, inhaling deeply before looking at the box in my hands. And as I gaze at its contents, a harsh realization finally sets in. My friend, my confidant, my savior in all actuality, has been reduced to nothing more than a handful of ashes capable of fitting into something the size of a shoebox. My throat constricts painfully with the thought. I'm not simply saddened for me, for my loss. I'm mournful for the many who will never know her. For those who won't experience her stubborn sense of loyalty and justice. I'm sad for those whose lives will never be touched by her grandiose joy and mischievous laughter, and for the lonely, misfit souls with whom Genny would have undoubtedly connected just so they would know they're not alone.

As she did for each of us, her Wildflowers.

And she succeeded in her mission, leaving us no longer tattered and broken, but fierce warriors who will find the strength, the compassion, to sustain her legacy.

I glance at Lukas, who's still staring forward, jaw tense. My brows furrow with my frown. One of us, it seems, may be more hesitant than the others.

Hands shaking, I redirect my attention to the remainder of Genny held within my grasp and swallow my sorrow once more before beginning. "Genny…" My chin trembles uncontrollably and my throat is so tight that the words are agonizing to speak. *How do I possibly say the hardest words of my life?*

I breathe in deeply and steel myself against the pain as I remind myself this isn't really goodbye. This is my insurance that she will not only live on in my heart, but long after it quits beating.

"I don't know what to say that hasn't already been said. It kinda sucks following those two."

I lift my head and grin at Sally and Adam through my tears. Their faces are blurred, but I can still make out their smiles. My eyes linger on them, gathering the calm I need to continue. "But what I have to add that hasn't already been said is this: my plan for your future."

I imagine her standing in front of me, and I deliver my promise. "As Adam said, your greatest fear was being forgotten. And yes, your fear was unwarranted because we will remember you, every aspect of you, until the day we die and probably even after that. But what I envision for you goes so far beyond our memories and our lives. You have impacted the four of us standing here in so many incredible ways, and I want to continue extending your reach to those other Wildflowers out there in need of somewhere to take root and grow, just like us. A place to foster hope and encouragement so that they, too, may thrive within the families they deserve. A loving and accepting home just as Mrs. Rodriguez provided for us, which will be named… Genesis."

I look at Sally. I sense her strength as she finds her purpose, no longer fearful of responsibility, but fully owning what's to come. What she's capable of.

My gaze slides to Adam, and I'm unsurprised to find a pride-filled smile gracing his beautiful face. I grin back at his unspoken seal of approval.

I then turn my eyes to Lukas, whose expression has softened. I don't know if he'll continue on this path with us, but I hope he dares to try. I know it won't be easy for him to face his demons on his journey toward forgiveness, but all he has to do is find the courage to take the first step. We'll be with him the rest of the way, and I hope he knows that.

I give him a small, encouraging smile in hopes of relaying that assurance, then continue speaking to Genny. "I have no idea how, but I vow that I will get this done, and I will do it in your honor." Looking at the sky, I add, "We will not mourn you. We will revive you."

I reach into the box and gather some of her ashes, and as I do, warmth envelops me. I feel relief filling my chest. I feel joy and elation. *She approves. I know it deep in my heart. She approves.*

A smile eases across my face as I crouch to the ground,

scattering her ashes on those strewn by Sally and Adam. I watch them settle, peace sealing the sorrowful rift in my heart. With my hand pressed to the ground, I whisper, "You are infinite, my friend."

I pat the earth gently, then rise, the box in hand as I turn to face Lukas. Making my way to where he stands, I extend my arms and offer him the remainder of Genny's ashes, locking my gaze with his. He peers back at me, hesitation and uncertainty dimming his expression before he takes the box. He begins to step past me, but he stops when I place my hand on his forearm.

I squeeze reassuringly, leaning into him as I speak. "She's here, you know."

His brows dip to form an unconvinced expression. I keep going. "Tell her what you won't tell us. Be honest, speak from your heart, and give her the time she needs to respond. I have a feeling she has something she needs to say to you." I release my grip on him and step closer to Sally and Adam.

Before he met us, Lukas spent a lot of time alone. In his own head. Somehow we understood early on that for him to speak, he needed to work through things internally first. I have wondered if at times we indulged that habit, and perhaps this morning revealed some of that frustration.

Now he needs his quiet—his time—to choose his words carefully. We turn and slowly walk away from him, entrusting him once again into Genny's crazy and loving hands.

As we're walking back to Sally's car, Adam walks up next to me, playfully bumping my shoulder with his. "I'm so on board with your idea."

"Really?"

"Absolutely. I can't think of a better, more selfless way to honor them both. I'm so proud of you."

Adam curls his arm around my shoulders and pulls me in. After placing a tender kiss on the top of my head, he turns us so we're facing Lukas again. Just a few steps behind, Sally catches up and turns in the same direction.

We watch as Lukas sinks to the ground, his baritone murmurs carried on the wind.

"Do you think he'll be okay?" Adam asks.

I shrug. "Only if he wants to be."

Sally sighs next to me.

Several minutes pass as he continues to talk to Genny, and when there's nothing left to say, he stills and waits. It doesn't take long. In fact, I know the exact moment it happens. His body relaxes and his shoulders slump forward, as though the weight of his guilt has been taken from him.

We watch as he leans forward and begins to dig a hole in the earth. When he's through, he gingerly pours the remainder of Genny's ashes inside and replaces the dirt, ensuring she's protected and able to find root. He packs the soil with cupped hands, then braces his weight on them as he seals her into her grave.

The moment between them is incredibly intimate, one I'm thankful he allowed us to witness, and one I know I will never forget. Because with that one protective gesture, I know the light within him hasn't been smothered by his darkness, but reignited by the fierce bond of a love not even death can sever.

The memory floats through my mind, the words Genny spoke during the Wildflowers ceremony soft, feathery murmurs.

"But even in death they remain connected, thriving within the comfort only they can provide each other, until spring brings them to life once again."

I look again to the sky, hoping she hears my heart as it softly whispers its reply.

Thank you.

SPRING

33

I'm eighteen today.

It's been three weeks and two days since we spread Genny's ashes with our wildflowers, and I've been counting the days since, anxiously awaiting my freedom. Thanks to Sally's kind hospitality, I've remained in her home, hopefully far off my father's radar.

But today's the day this little birdy spreads her wings and learns to fly.

I haven't mentioned that it's my birthday because, well…I need this day to be about me, my rebirth as I claim my life as my own. Only then will I find reason to celebrate.

First thing's first, I need a job. And my own apartment.

Next will be my GED.

With Sally's help, I've been slowly working through my anger at how the Duffs derailed my life. How I was stripped of finishing my last semester of high school. It seems like such a small aspect of our loss in the scheme of things, but it is something else they took. And according to Sally, it's right for me to feel angry. So, I do. At them. But I will not be beaten by them. They will not win.

After my GED, hopefully I'll get to go to college.

But before I get ahead of myself, I need to tackle the first two items on my list.

Which is why I'm currently seated at Sally's breakfast table, scouring the want ads. I've just finished circling a potential server position at a local diner when raised voices get my attention.

Well, one raised voice, actually. A familiar, deep baritone followed by Sally's soothing tone. A door slams, and my eyebrows raise at the sound of heavy footsteps making their way down the hall.

Lukas storms into the kitchen, barely glancing my way before he hastily grabs a glass from the cupboard and fills it with water. He takes a sip and, after a lengthy look out the window in front of him, finally turns to face me. His eyes are furious, his face stern, his hair completely wild.

Nibbling the end of my pen, I grin at him.

He narrows his eyes.

My grin widens into a smile.

A muscle tenses in his jaw.

We remain in this silent standoff until he heaves a heavy, annoyed sigh, then heads right back into Sally's office. I redirect my smile at the paper and chuckle to myself.

Some days are more difficult than others. I get that. I've been there.

He's trying at least, and I have no doubt that with Sally's help, he'll find a way to get past his demons.

I look at the circled ad. I snatch the paper from the table and carry it with me to Sally's phone, a landline, which reminds me I really need to get a cell phone.

Just as I reach for the receiver, it rings, scaring the hell out of me. I calm my racing heart before finally picking it up on the third ring.

"Hello?"

"Hey, gorgeous." *Adam.* "Any big plans this afternoon?"

"Actually, yes," I answer. "I'm daring to venture from Sally's into the real, actual world today."

A theatrical gasp is Adam's only response.

I smile into the receiver. "I'm thinking about applying for a job at the diner. I think they're hiring."

There's no mistaking the pride in Adam's voice. "They are hiring. Seth and I ate there for breakfast—there's a flyer in the window."

I clap softly but excitedly at the confirmation.

Adam laughs. "Well, I was just checking, but I see you're doing just fine without me."

It's my turn to laugh. "Come over tonight. I miss you. And bring Seth."

Twenty minutes later, I'm dressed in the nicest thing I managed to pack. Skinny jeans, a light blue button-up shirt, and brown riding boots. My hair is down, curled and tousled at the ends, and I've put on makeup for the first time in months. My light brown eyes are framed with mascara and my lips are glossed a pale shade of pink.

It feels odd, but good. I smile at myself before clicking off the bathroom light.

I tread lightly down the hallway, stopping in front of Sally's office door. Gently and hopefully unheard, I press my hand against the wood to send Lukas some positive vibes. After relaying all the positivity I have, I continue my trek, heading to the garage where the Chevelle has remained safely stowed since my arrival. I hit the button to open the garage door and notice Mrs. Rodriguez's truck parked along the curb. I grin at the fact that Lukas has kept it. It has served us well.

In no time, I'm parked at the diner, a sudden onslaught of nerves clawing their way up my throat. I wipe my clammy palms on my thighs and inhale deeply before looking at myself in the rearview mirror.

You can do this.

You will *do this.*

I will fly today.

The bell jingles above the door as I tentatively enter the diner, unsure of what to do or who to speak with. I peek at the window, grateful when I see the "Help Wanted" flyer just as Adam mentioned. A relieved breath escapes me, and I run my hands through my hair one last time in preparation before approaching the hostess station.

While patiently waiting, I take in the patrons seated

in various booths and tables. Families laughing together while they eat, businessmen in suits planning to conquer the world after chowing down on burgers and fries, some kids rounding a table playing a highly annoying game of duck-duck-goose…

And Leah Allen tucked into a corner booth on the other side of the restaurant.

I know I should look away before she sees me. My eyes, however, remain glued to where she's seated, alone with none of her usual entourage. I frown in confusion, giving her just enough time to feel my eyes on her and look up from her book.

When she sees my face, recognition flashes across her perfect features, immediately followed by surprise. Dumbfounded, I watch her mouth form a small, sheepish smile as she lifts her hand in a timid wave.

Shocked as shit, my brows jump up to my hairline.

What the hell am I supposed to do now?

Wave back?

Before I have time to formulate an answer, a middle-aged woman who looks like Flo from *Alice* approaches the stand, drawing my attention away from Leah. She's dressed in a simple white polo and khaki pants, with a tiny black apron circling her waist. She smiles sweetly while chomping steadily on approximately twelve slices of Juicy Fruit.

"Can I help you, honey?"

The slight hint of a southern twang in her voice makes me smile.

"Yes, I...uh, I'm actually here to apply for the server position."

She beams. "That's great. I'll go get Maggie. She'll be so happy to see a pretty young face. This place needs a little livening up."

She gestures toward the bar stools lined beneath the counter. "Take a seat. Maggie will be right with ya."

She winks before heading to the kitchen.

The legs of the stool scrape along the floor as I climb onto it. And I say "climb" because the thing is practically as tall as I am.

I'm not seated long before someone enters the open space next to me. I plaster on my best smile and turn to face the person I presume to be Maggie.

Except it's not Maggie. It's Leah.

My eyes widen in surprise.

Still smiling, Leah flashes her palms in an appeasing gesture then softly says, "Hey, Chloe."

"Hey," I remark, looking around for Flo or this Maggie person to rescue me, but sadly I see no one.

I clear my throat, nervously tucking a strand of hair behind my ear. "Can I help you?" My tone is cold, spiteful even, and when I see hurt flash through her pretty brown eyes, I immediately regret it.

I sigh and offer an apologetic smile. "Sorry. Old habits and all."

Leah shakes her head, her sleek black hair falling into her face. It's then I realize she's no longer wearing her high ponytail and unnecessarily huge bow, or her usual gratuitous cheerleader uniform. She's wearing normal-people clothes—a simple oversized T-shirt, yoga pants, and a pair of kick-ass fluorescent-green Nikes.

She nervously tugs at the hem of her shirt. "Weird, right?"

I can sense her apprehension, her subtle need for approval. Something so familiar to me that it's impossible not to recognize it.

"Nah." I grin at her. "It suits you."

Her entire body relaxes and she gestures to the open seat next to me. "May I?"

I glance toward the kitchen, no Maggie in sight. Not that I'd know what she looks like, but the only person I see walking the floor is Flo.

I nod. "Sure."

She gracefully slides onto the bar stool, and I fight the urge to roll my eyes. Typical.

Once she's seated, Leah's words seem to burst out of her mouth. "I'm so sorry for the way I treated you and your friends. I wasn't very nice."

I hide my shock at both the speed of her words and the directness of her apology. "No, you weren't. You were awful, actually."

She breaks her gaze from mine, looking at the mirror lining the wall in front of us. Her next words are spoken so softly, they're nearly inaudible. "I was jealous."

I crank my head in her direction, but she maintains her

forward stare. "Of you. Of your relationships. The four of you were so close—there wasn't anything you wouldn't do for each other. And every day I witnessed it, I became more infuriated, because it was a constant reminder of what I'd never have." She looks at me and her expression is filled with such regret, my heart breaks for her. "To be loved unconditionally is the greatest gift a person can receive. There's a sense of comfort, of ease, in knowing you are truly accepted for who you are, and more importantly, for who you aren't. I never experienced that. Not with my parents, and definitely not with those I had to bully into being my 'friends.'"

Leah shrugs sadly. "It was wrong of me. And for that, I apologize."

I stare back at her, dumbstruck. "It's okay," I croak through my astonishment.

She giggles lightly then offers, "You know that day you saw me in the parking lot with my dad?"

I nod, remembering how harshly he jerked her around before forcing her into his car.

"That day you changed my life. I want you to know that."

My expression must be skeptical because she rushes to explain. "After all I'd done to you, the hell I put you through, I saw you step forward to try to protect me. *Me.*" She laughs to herself, as though still in disbelief that it happened. "I realized then why your friends loved you so damn much, and in that moment, you became the person I aspired to be. Someone who possesses enough heart to see past someone's ugliness and make them feel like they matter, even if they don't deserve it."

A tear seeps from her eye, and she quickly wipes it away. "You have no idea how much I needed to feel that. It gave me...hope."

As we look into each other's eyes, a sense of understanding passes between us. I reach forward and squeeze her hand. "Well, you're welcome." I grin before adding, "And thank you, Leah. This conversation was not nearly as horrific as I'd thought it'd be."

Her eyes widen in shock, then simultaneously we burst into laughter.

After it dies off, she squeezes my hand in return. "I was sorry to hear about what happened to your home. And..." she stalls before finishing, "Genny."

"How did you—"

"Well, the fire was all over the news. And regarding Genny." She shakes her head in disgust. "What my mother lacks in maternal instinct, she's more than makes up for by gossiping." She sighs heavily. "It must be rough for you, losing someone so close."

Rough. Rough is the understatement of the year, but Leah Allen might not have loved like I've loved, so she might not know that yet. "Yeah, but she's still here. I feel her, watching over us."

Leah's eyes dart frantically around the diner. "God, I hope not. I'll be struck dead by lightning at any moment if that's the case. She hated me so much."

I laugh. I can't help it. "She hated the person you were.

But the girl sitting next to me? I think she would've liked this Leah very much."

Leah's cheeks turn pink. "You think so?"

"I know so," I say just at the kitchen doors swing open. An older lady with kind eyes and a warm smile waves in my direction. Her short, teased hair is an odd shade of purple, but I kinda dig it on her. Figuring this is Maggie, I wave back and return my attention to Leah.

"I have to go." I jerk my thumb over my shoulder. "Interview."

"That's great. So you're staying?" Her brown eyes gleam with excitement.

"For now, yeah."

She gives me a wide grin, placing her check on the counter before she begins digging through her purse. "Shoot."

She rummages deeper, oblivious to the pen that's just magically been thrust in her general vicinity. Her head jerks up, and she smiles in thanks at Maggie before taking it and jotting her number on the back of the check.

Maggie smiles, eyes on me. "I'll give you ladies a moment to finish up."

"Thank you," I say. Maggie turns away just as Leah finishes.

She gives it to me, almost reluctantly. "My phone number, in case you'd like to get together some time." Her expression falls. "Shit. I need this to pay."

I take the check from her. "I've got it. That's what

friends do, right?"

Her flushed cheeks barely register before I'm enveloped in an alarmingly strong embrace. "Thank you. For everything, Chloe."

When she releases me, her eyes are filled with tears. She gives my shoulders another tender squeeze before whipping around and heading out the front door.

The bell jingles with her exit, and all I can think of as I watch her go is even though she had no idea it was my birthday, she just gave me two gifts I'll never forget: the humbling experience of true forgiveness, and an unlikely friendship that I have a feeling will last a lifetime.

To be loved unconditionally is incredible, but to forgive feels pretty amazing, too.

34

I'm still in a daze when I notice Maggie motioning for me to sit with her in an unoccupied booth. Leah's check in hand, I carefully slide off the barstool, thankful when my feet hit the floor without incident. I fold the paper and shove it in my pocket as I walk toward Maggie.

When I take my seat across from her, she smiles. It reminds me of how Mrs. Rodriguez used to smile at us, and I relax a little. *I like her. A lot.* "Forgiveness is breath for the soul," she says sagely.

Suddenly nerve-stricken, I clear my throat before answering. "Yeah, that was a bit…unexpected. Sorry if it took time from your day. I know you must be busy."

Maggie laughs lightly. "My dear, the only thing that wastes time, as far as I'm concerned, are unnecessary apologies." She folds her hands on top of the table, still meeting my eyes with hers. "Now, I hear you're here to apply for the server position."

After my quick nod, she inquires, "Past experience?"

My lips purse to the side. "No, ma'am."

"No experience as a server? Or any job at all?"

Oh crap. I swallow, stalling for time. "Um…"

Maggie's brows lift ever so slightly, "No experience."

"That would be an accurate assessment, yes."

Her lips quirk ever so slightly in response.

I drag my hands along my thighs then place them on the table, folded together like hers. "But you have to start somewhere, right?"

Her sharpened gaze assesses me, and quite possibly, my soul as well. It's unnerving, but I hold her stare, determined to display no weakness under her scrutiny. Genny would be proud.

After a few seconds, she gives me a satisfied grin. Rays of light shine through the window, striking her at just the right angle and highlighting just how purple her hair really is. It's mesmerizing in a strange sort of way.

"How old are you, child? Seventeen? Eighteen?"

I tear my gaze away from her hair to meet her eyes, and I smile. Proudly. "My name is Chloe, and I'm eighteen, ma'am. Today."

"Chloe." Maggie nods expectantly. "Yes. I see it. You're hungry for freedom. There's a staunch determination in your eyes, yet they're still flecked with the uncertainty that often comes with being eighteen." The creases framing her eyes deepen with her reassuring smile. "Don't you worry, my dear. Those flecks will diminish with age and experience. Unfortunately, age is inevitable." She gives me a wry smile and arches an eyebrow. "The experience you can gain here, that is, if you're still interested."

My heart begins to race and I smile so wide my cheeks ache. I try to hold in the excited whoop clogging my throat. "Yes," I squeak. "I'm definitely interested."

Her smile widens. "Well then, you're hired. If you don't mind coming in on Saturday, we can get all the paperwork filled out and get you on the schedule to train."

"I'll be here." *Oh my God! I just got a job!*

Maggie plants her hands on the table, using them for support as she eases out of the booth. I follow suit, a massive grin still on my face. When we're both standing, I extend my hand.

As soon as she takes it, I glance at our joined hands, reluctantly realizing what I must do. As much as I hate to risk losing a job I haven't even started yet, I don't feel it's fair to show up to work without her knowing. With her hand still gripping mine, I look her in the eyes and start rolling up my sleeve. "I hope this isn't a problem, but I understand if it is."

Her gaze breaks from mine to catch on my scar, now clearly displayed. Her mouth drops open at the sight, and I tentatively offer, "There's one on my other arm, too." I shrug my shoulders when she looks back at me. "I just felt you needed to know, based on the uniform. Short sleeves and all."

Surprisingly, her expression isn't one of horror or judgment. Maggie releases my hand, then gently curls her fingers around the base of my scar. "Not a problem at all. It's easy to recognize someone who's battled their fair share of demons. We are kindred spirits in that war. I know you better than you think, Chloe. And the job is still yours."

"Thank you." I release a steady breath of relief. "You have no idea how much I needed this."

Her warm hand slides over mine. "Oh, my child, but I do." She winks and gestures to front door. "I'll walk you out. I'm sure you must have big plans for your birthday."

Instantly reminded of at least one plan I'd made, I whip Leah's check from my pocket. "I need to pay for this."

Maggie looks from the paper to me, then waves a dismissive hand.

I shake my head, "No, I *need* to pay for this."

She angles her head, her expression contemplative before it relaxes into one of acquiescence. "Cash register's by the door."

Check in one hand, the other fishes around in my back pocket, seeking the credit card I've saved for this very occasion. His card. The one I borrowed for this specific purpose.

Because once it's swiped, my father will know exactly where I am. It's the first step I need to take to make my stand and claim my life as my own. I refuse to remain shackled by my fear of being unloved, unwanted.

I love myself, and I'm choosing me.

I hand the card to Maggie with absolutely no hesitation,

eagerness setting in as I watch her swipe it. When the transaction is through, she looks up at me, hands me back the card along with the check containing Leah's number, and flashes me a perceptive grin I'm quickly getting used to seeing. "Happy birthday."

Taking the card and piece of paper from her grasp, I confirm, "See you Saturday?"

Maggie nods once. "Looking forward to it."

Once I'm outside, a warm breeze blows lightly, reminding me spring is near. However, as my heart blossoms with hope and excitement, it seems my personal spring is already upon me. With my sleeves rolled to my elbows, I look at my scars with a renewed sense of acceptance and pride.

Another winter has come and gone, and I survived.

Not only that, I'm stronger for it. And though our winter was not without casualties, I can feel Genny's not-so subtle push to embrace life and challenge myself to be the best person I can be with each new day I'm granted.

I promise, I think to myself, climbing into my car. *I will make you proud, my friend.*

Putting the car in drive, I state into the open air, "Thanks for not striking Leah down with lightning, by the way. Although the look on her face when she mentioned that was quite hilarious, and a bit satisfying, I must admit."

I grin when I almost hear the faintest bit of laughter echoing around me.

The remainder of the ride is silent, though I'm still reveling in the peace of Genny's presence when I pull into

Sally's driveway. As I do, my brows furrow, surprised to see Lukas's truck still parked along the curb. For the past few weeks, he's typically headed off to wherever the hell he goes after Sally's sessions.

Today, however, he seems to be waiting for me.

Based on the glower on Lukas's face, a sense of foreboding sets in, and what I felt of Genny's presence abruptly vanishes.

I take a long, deep breath before stepping out of the car.

Lukas watches me intently as I make my way to where he stands. His muscled arms dangle over the porch railing, his fingers intertwined. I note immediately the tense set of his shoulders and the tortured look in his eyes. Slowing my steps, I tread carefully, as though approaching a cornered animal.

His gaze drops to my exposed arms, and as though he's taking solace in the familiar, his expression softens slightly. But it's not until I'm right in front of him that he dares to meet my eyes. When he does, he swallows hard, his gravelly voice etched with pain. "I'm so tired, Chloe."

I nod, trying to reassure him without overstepping my bounds. "I know."

And I do. His skin is ashen, and purplish-blue shadows tinge the skin beneath his beautiful eyes.

"Every time I come here, I think, today's the day I'll make a breakthrough. Today's the day I find the courage to move on like you and Adam. Today's the day I prove how strong I am. But that day never fucking comes for me."

Lukas shakes his head, his eyes reddening, burning with unshed tears. "With every try, every reach, I find nothing left to grab hold of to help pull me from this void. I'm met with nothing but miles of emptiness in every direction."

He looks forward and braces his full weight on his elbows. Without a second thought, I duck beneath his bridged arms and slide myself between them, forcing him to take a step back when I rise. His arms remain on each side of me, effectively caging me with just inches separating us. He watches me with a bewildered expression, and though I fully expect him to put some distance between us, he doesn't.

When his eyes find mine, I lock on to his anguish, hoping to steal away some of it. "Then hold on to me, Lukas. I'm strong enough for both of us."

His breath catches, and I see a war in his eyes—a boy torn between wanting to let me in and wanting to shut me out completely.

Just as I see his familiar mask begin to slide into place, I remark harshly, "Don't do that. Don't insult me by trying to shield me from what you think I can't handle."

He says nothing, instead looking down at our feet. I wait patiently for his response, and it takes several minutes before he finds the courage to meet my eyes. And when he finally does, tears run down his cheeks as he searches my face, and I watch, transfixed, as reverence and awe soften his features.

"I won't let you go," I whisper. "Trust me."

Still silent, he lifts his arm from the railing to trail his thumb lightly along my cheek then down my neck. *Oh God,*

I've missed his touch. How have I gone months without this? I swallow, overcome with the sensation, and only then does he break his stare from mine. He watches the movement of my throat and timidly bends to place his forehead in the crook of my neck. I pull him forward and as soon as he makes contact, I wrap my arms as tightly around him as I can. His fingers curl into the back of my shirt and his entire body begins to quake.

Even though I may be strong, I'm no match for his weight.

His knees give way and together we sink to the porch, our arms around one another. I pull him to me, cradling him while murmuring soothing words with each sob. I recognize his anguish. I know the feeling of having your heart flayed wide open with nothing to deaden the pain. But I also know self-inflicted torment is a festering cancer that will continue to consume as it grows, hollowing you out completely and leaving you with no heart, no soul, unless you excise it. It's a torturous process, but one that's necessary to heal.

His voice is rough, strangely contrasted by the softness of his lips brushing my neck as he murmurs, "She forgives me."

My brows furrow in confusion, but I remain silent, waiting.

"Genny. She forgives me."

I grip him tighter as my throat clamps shut, making speech almost impossible. "She told you that?"

Strands of his hair tickle my cheek with his nod. A sad smile graces my face, and I take a moment to run my fingers through his hair then bringing him closer I whisper, "Of course she does."

My thumb tenderly strokes the base of his skull as I continue. "But, Lukas, what you need to realize, to accept, is there's nothing that needs to be forgiven. Every single one of us was there that night, and each of us suffered the effects of a senseless evil we will never understand. Our pain is the same. Yours is no more than ours. Yet you try to take on every ounce of it as though it's yours alone to bear." I grip the sides of his face, forcing him to meet my eyes. Tears well up, burning as they surface, causing his handsome features to blur together. "But there are three people who are more than ready to relieve you of some of that pain. Three people who...love you."

My traitorous cheeks go pink with the admission, but I blunder on. "All you have to do is find the courage to release it and let us take it from you, because that's what friends do for each other, Lukas. At least, that's what Wildflowers do. You want your breakthrough? Well, there it is. That's how you get it."

His gaze breaks from mine to roam my face, and when I place my hands gently on his shoulders, his muscles slacken beneath my touch. With vulnerability I haven't seen him demonstrate in months, he asks, "You really think you can handle the darkest parts of me?"

I wave a dismissive hand. "You don't scare me."

He arches a dark brow and his mouth quirks ever so slightly at the sides. "Is that so?"

"The only thing that scares me about you is living a life without you in it."

Lukas's expression morphs into one I don't recognize. There's a brief flash of shock, before it relaxes into one of complete surrender. He lifts his hand to gently stroke my cheek, then leans in to rest his forehead against mine.

"Then take it. It's yours."

I nod resolutely and do as promised, inhaling deeply and absorbing his pain as it's released. Lukas has unknowingly given me the perfect gift, and it's all I could have ever asked for on my birthday.

Him.

His absolute trust.

35

I look at Lukas seated across from me at Sally's breakfast table, unable to help myself. I grin at him, nibbling the edge of my pen, which I've been using to circle potential apartments in the paper, and he gives me a lopsided smile. His eyes are no longer dimmed with guilt but luminous with hope. My heart flutters wildly at the sight.

Today's his Saturday session with Sally, one after which—much to the surprise of both Sally and Adam—he decided to stick around and hang with us for a while. And if Sally's satisfied smile while washing dishes is any indication, I'd say their meeting went pretty well.

While they were in session, I met with Maggie, as planned. I'm happy to report I'm on the schedule to start training during Monday's lunch shift.

So, yeah, today's been a good day for both of us it seems.

I grin wider at Lukas, pleased with our progress.

Soft laughter sounds next to me, and I turn to look at Adam and Seth. I watch their gazes slide between Lukas and me before they share a knowing grin. Adam leans back in his chair, tosses his napkin on the table, then announces, "If you two wouldn't mind, could you ease up on the sexual tension? Just a little? It's making it impossible for the rest of us to breathe in here."

Sally giggles, Lukas chuckles, and, completely mortified, I throw my napkin at Adam's face, which he deflects masterfully. "You did not just say that."

"I did." Adam shrugs, no apology whatsoever in his mischievous eyes.

Just as I begin to stammer my objection, he takes advantage of my inability to form a coherent sentence to continue. "The first time around it was cute. But I refuse to watch you circle around what's painfully obvious while giving each other love-struck glances and dopey grins you think we don't see...for a *second* time. Get to it already."

Seth looks from me to Adam, then offers a simple suggestion. "Well, in their defense, you don't have to watch, you know."

With Adam's pitiful excuse for a glare aimed in Seth's direction, it's my turn to giggle.

"I love you, Seth," I croon.

Seth ignores the insulted expression on Adam's face. "You're not the only one."

He plants a tender kiss on Adam's mouth, and I watch

his previously offended expression soften. *They're so cute,* I think as grins form between their joined lips.

I feel so much happiness for them both, and as I do, I brave another glance at Lukas. His eyes are burning, focused on me, and there's not an ounce of hesitation or fear in them. "There'll be much less circling this time," he says with certainty.

My face heats. I guess with everything that's happened, I've denied myself the hope that Lukas would come back to me as more than a friend.

Adam looks at the ceiling and mutters to himself, obviously relieved. "Well, thank God for that."

I open my mouth to say something witty, but when I inhale, all thought escapes my brain.

"Is that…strawberry cake?"

My nostrils flare, confirming, then I look to Sally in surprise. She shrugs meekly then explains, "We forgot your birthday."

"Sally," I begin, but she cuts me off.

"No, we did, and we must remedy it immediately."

"So, that's why you stayed?"

Lukas shakes his head. "I stayed because I wanted to be near you." He looks at Sally and adds, "The cake is just a bonus."

She grins back at him on her way to the oven. After poking its contents with a fork and deeming it ready, she removes the cake and places it on the counter. Then she turns to me. "It needs to cool. Perfect time for presents."

I remain seated, watching in awe as they scatter to gather gifts they'd cleverly hidden. Sally bends to retrieve hers from underneath the couch, Adam and Seth pull a rectangular box from Sally's bookcase, and Lukas pulls a smaller square box from his jacket hanging on the coatrack in Sally's entryway.

One by one, they're placed on the table. I probably look like a dork, but I cannot contain my excitement. I've never received gifts like this before. Something so simple. So special.

As everyone stands before me with expectant expressions, I choose to open Sally's first. It's soft and wrapped in vibrant paper with presents and bows in every color imaginable printed on its surface. On top is a bright pink envelope.

I slide my finger beneath the flap and extract the card, giving Sally an inquisitive glance when I see the image on the front. It's the cutest Siamese kitten I've ever seen, holding a cupcake, the words "Happy Birthday" etched into the paper. Sally grins back at me, then indicates with a jerk of her chin to open it.

Inside, it reads, *Another birthday? Are you kitten me?*

I laugh softly before reading her inscription. My curiosity increases when I see she's written nothing more than the name and address of someone I don't recognize.

Mr. Jacob Newman

1043 Westlake Drive

"This is why I forgot your birthday. I was so focused on finding this man, I couldn't think of anything else until

I located him." She looks at Adam. "It was Adam who reminded me."

My eyes find Adam's, sorrowful as he explains, "I just realized it yesterday. I have no idea what made me remember, but I'd say someone looking out for you decided to remind me." He offers me an apologetic smile. "I'm so sorry, Chloe."

I shake my head. "It's not a big deal. Actually, my birthday was…well, it gave me several unexpected gifts that I will treasure for the rest of my life."

I look at Lukas, who gives me a knowing, extremely sexy dimpled grin. I give him a secretive smile in return.

Adam sighs in exasperation, which makes me giggle.

Sally clears her throat, bringing me back to the mysterious address. "So," she drawls, smiling wide. "I know you spoke of the possibility of building a new home in Genny's honor, and I just happen to know the perfect location. The name there is the landowner's name, and that's his address. I've reached out to him, and he's very open to hearing your proposal."

I meet her gaze, daring to hope.

She nods, grin widening. "Your field, wildflowers and all."

"Oh my God!" I exclaim, launching out of my seat. I rush to her, practically knocking her over with my embrace. "Sally, this is too much!"

She squeezes me tightly before releasing me, her hands falling to my shoulders. "I'm going to see about taking out a loan tomorrow."

"No need," I respond immediately. "I have the money to build."

Her brows dip together as her head jerks in surprise. "How do you have enough money to finance something like this?"

I look around, several prodding eyes awaiting my answer. "You forget, my father has more money than God." I shrug with absolutely no repentance. "So, I decided to relieve him of some of it."

Met with blank stares, I finish with, "So to speak."

I really wish Genny were here.

Sally's expression morphs into one of concern. "Is your father aware of this?"

"I'm sure he is now." I laugh, a bit surprised when no one else laughs. Spinning in a slow circle, I address each of their worried faces. "Trust me. I can handle him, and when I do, it will be for me. My declaration of independence is long overdue. Trust me. He owes me so much more than money he can do without."

Still concerned, Sally gives me a long, appraising look. Then, she nods, "Well, we're here if you need us."

"I know you are." I smile back at her and return to my seat. "But this is something I need to do on my own."

After another glance at the card, my eyes once again meet hers. "Thank you."

She graciously accepts my thanks before pointing to her other present. "I hope you like it." Her smile wanes a bit, and struck by her sudden onset of anxiety, I eye her present warily. But then I begin to unwrap it.

Her card was only the introduction to the true meaning behind her gift. As tiny scraps of wrapping paper fall to the floor, I gasp.

I see nothing but gray kittens.

In every position imaginable.

Pawing balls of yarn.

Gingerly, I pull the familiar cardigan from the paper and hold it up. Adam draws in a breath. I lean forward, lips trembling as I bury my face in the fabric and inhale deeply, filling my nose with Genny's scent.

Her god-awful kitten cardigan that she loved so damn much.

A single tear rolls down my cheek as I shoot a wobbly smile in Sally's direction. Lowering my hands to the table, my voice is thick as I whisper, "It's purrrrrfect."

Sally's stare, full of tenderness, lingers on the cardigan before she looks at me. "They found it in her backpack. As soon as I saw it, I knew she would want it to be yours." She smiles sadly. "Just a feeling."

I reach for her hand, gripping it tightly in mine. "Thank you."

"You're welcome," she replies, voice unsteady.

I release her hand to clear the tears from my face. After a deep breath, I set Genny's cardigan on the table, making sure it's still within reach, and I smile at Adam and Seth as I open their gift.

"It's not much," Adam says with a shrug. "But I think

you'll like it."

I tear wildly through the blue and green paper. When I'm done, I see a white box with a picture of a cell phone on top.

My mouth falls open and my eyes shoot up their direction.

Adam takes hold of Seth's hand, both of them unable to hide their pleasure at my reaction. "Don't get too excited. It's Seth's old one, but we figured you could use it."

Seth gestures at the box. "It's all charged up and ready to go. We put you on our plan to get you started." He smiles. It's no wonder Adam loves him so much. "Our numbers are already programmed on it. Mine, Adam's, Sally's, and"—he clears his throat to stifle a chuckle—"Lukas's, of course."

Wow. I really am only one without a cell phone. Typical.

"Guys, I can't accept this."

"You can," Adam says. "And you will."

I giggle, still a bit dumbfounded, yet grateful, for the gesture. I remind myself to add Leah's number in, then turn to face Lukas. His smile is contagious as he observes our interaction, and he looks…confident. I love that. He holds in his hand a small box, wrapped with nothing more than a bow. An exquisitely tied little bow.

My eyebrows lift in surprise. "Did you tie that yourself?"

"There's still so much you have to learn about me." He lifts his arm to draw my body into his. I comply, sinking into his hold as he places tender lips on the crown of my head.

I smother a ridiculously giddy grin against his shirt, take

a step back, and state, "Oh, I plan on it."

His grin widening, he hands me the box. Slowly, I tug the ribbon free and remove the lid before looking inside. *Oh my God.*

Looped on a silver chain, a circular gem of gold topaz sits perfectly in the center. Silver points curving every which way extend from where the stone is encased to compose the exquisite image displayed in front of me.

It's the most beautiful sun I've ever seen.

My eyes lift to meet Lukas's. His smile is beautiful. My sun is back.

Completely overwhelmed, all I can do is grin. *It's better than crying, which is what I'm close to doing.*

He reaches forward and flips the charm over. There's an engraving on the back.

I shine for you.

"Lukas," I whisper.

His fingers trace lightly over the etched words as he speaks. "I bought this for you months ago. I thought about you every single day we were apart."

I see him glance quickly at Sally, who gives him a reassuring nod before he looks back at me. "I tried not to, but every day, there you were. Just as stubborn in my thoughts as you are standing here in front of me." His eyes lock onto mine. "In the darkest of days, I allowed myself this one exception. This tiny bit of hope. Because as I bought it, all I could think was maybe, just maybe, the day would come when I would no longer be broken, but whole again.

As soon as that day comes, I will find her and be the man she's always known I could be." He stalls, tries to find the words. "But I was wrong."

I frown at him and begin to shake my head, but as I open my mouth to disagree, he silences me by pressing a warm finger to my lips.

"I was wrong because it's impossible for me to be whole without you. You give me courage to face what haunts me, and because of you, *with* you, I will conquer those fears. You give me reason to shine and this"—he turns the stone upright—"is my promise."

When he lowers his hand, I respond quietly, "Lukas, you already are. You have always been." Overwrought with emotion and without reservation, I rise on my tiptoes and brush my mouth tenderly against his.

I hear a sigh from behind me, followed by, "Yeah, I see what you're saying. It's impossible not to watch."

I grin against Lukas's mouth as my heels hit the floor.

"Thank you," I whisper, gently plucking the necklace from the box. "Put it on for me?"

Lukas removes it from between my pinched fingers and I turn my back to him, lifting my hair. The necklace, in all its beauty, dangles in front of my face just before it descends, falling perfectly against the top of my chest. Warm fingers graze my neck affectionately, and he leans in to whisper in my ear. "Another piece of jewelry to add to your collection."

I glance at the yellow plastic ring he gave me and chuckle, clasping my hand around the sun, its weight comforting.

My eyes find Sally's, directly across from me. They're beaming with pride. I smile at her before exhaling a long, deep breath.

"Thank you, everyone. For everything. I'm overwhelmed."

Soft laughter fills the room, as well as sniffles. After a long moment, Sally clasps her hands and announces, "Time for cake!"

While she heads into the kitchen, I look at the presents on the table. I pick up the card she gave me to scan the address again.

Lukas's soft, deep voice sends shudders down spine. "Are you going to meet with him soon?"

I nod, still looking at the card. In my periphery, his hand comes into view, and I watch his fingers as they trace the scar on my arm. The movement is so reverent and familiar.

His arm circles my waist, and he leans in close to whisper, "I'll go with you then. Tomorrow."

I suppress another shiver when his lips graze my cheek. Clearly having caught on to my reaction, he smiles against my skin. "Happy birthday, Chloe."

With his hand settled on my waist, I intertwine my fingers with his and nestle into his arms as I observe those around me. Sally, her wooden spoon in hand, swatting at both Adam and Seth in mock anger after their attempt to eat the strawberry frosting. Their surprised expressions and grins before breaking into laughter. I smile contentedly, then tear my gaze away to look at Lukas, loving his wide smile as he, too, watches. Then I glance at my scars, my forever reminders of a decision made in haste to end a life I thought wasn't worth it.

Yet, as I take in the love and laughter surrounding me, I can't help but realize how truly important my life is. If I'd given up my life as I knew it then, I wouldn't have met these people I've come to call my family. People who unknowingly gave me the strength and courage I needed to come to this very conclusion.

I lean forward, taking hold of Genny's cardigan, and I hug it to my chest as I relax into Lukas. I feel her presence as she envelops me, and I know without a doubt everything she stood for will be carried by those she touched during her time on this earth.

Lukas's arm tightens around me, and I turn my head to rest it against his chest. I take comfort listening to the soothing beats of his heart, feeling mine in my own chest, answering his.

I am so thankful to be alive.

36

1043 Westlake Drive. I no longer need Sally's card, because the address is seared into my brain.

I thought of it the entire day yesterday, it appeared multiple times during my dreams last night, and it was the first thing I thought of when waking up at the crack of dawn this morning.

I'm extremely eager to embark on this new adventure, this new course in all our lives, as we give back to those as lost as we once were. I peer out the front window, and feel a rush of excitement when I see Lukas's truck pulling into Sally's driveway.

Finally.

I've been up for hours already.

I narrow my eyes and tap my imaginary watch when he waves at me from the front seat. He laughs, not nearly as impatient as I am to hit the road.

After signaling for him to stay where he is, I sprint to the kitchen and pour two travel cups full of coffee—his first, my third—and once the lids are on, I make a mad dash out the front door. The breeze is warmer than I expect, and I take a very, very brief moment to enjoy the sun's rays and inhale the smell of the fresh blossoms before resuming my swift strides toward the truck.

He leans lazily against the passenger side door and seeing him in all his glory, my feet stall, causing me to stumble. Coffee sluices from the holes in the lids, causing hot liquid to dribble over my fingers.

"Shit." But I refuse to let go, even though my instincts scream for me to drop the damn things.

Lukas chuckles under his breath, taking the cups from my grasp. "Problems walking this morning?"

I glare at him. "I've been up for hours. What took you so long?"

A coy smile forms on his lips. "Chloe, showing up at a stranger's house any earlier than ten o'clock is rude."

My scowl turns into a frown as I consider his words, when he concludes, "Even ten is pushing it."

I growl under my breath and reach for the passenger side door, flinging it open, only for him to slam it shut.

His grin magnifies at my frustration as he leans in and whispers, "Good morning."

And there goes my anger when his lips touch my temple. *How does he always do that? The man who previously pent up all his storms somehow just calms mine.*

"Good morning," I reply. After a heart flutter and a suppressed grin, I squint at him. "Sorry. I'm just really excited."

"I can see that," he says, placing the coffees on the hood of his truck. With his hands now free, he cups my cheeks and bends down, tentatively touching his mouth to mine. I sigh, my entire body relaxing. He grins and deepens the kiss. Before I know it, my back is flush against the door and his body is pressed against mine.

Still. I grip his Henley and pull him closer. A deep rumble from his chest sounds before he slows, giving me sweet, long, leisurely kisses. Far too soon, he finishes with a quick peck to my lips. With his forehead rested against mine, we stare into each other's eyes and breathe shallow breaths.

His voice is gruff as he repeats, "Good morning."

Euphoric, I giggle. "Yes, it is."

His smile returns and he reaches for the door handle, pulling me into the safety of his chest while opening the door. Once I'm tucked inside, he rounds the front of his truck, snagging the coffees along the way.

I watch as he folds into the driver's seat, mesmerized by the newfound self-assuredness in his movements. When he turns to hand me my coffee, he catches me ogling him, his mouth curving into a lopsided grin. I don't turn away, choosing instead to brazenly hold his stare. His dark brows rise in surprise, then his grin widens, and he brings his mouth to mine. With another longing look and a gentle trace of his fingers along my cheek, he straightens and turns the ignition.

The minute the engine roars to life, I take a much-needed sip of my coffee. My recent bout of energy is on a steady decline, most likely as a result of the loss of adrenaline.

"Where're we headed?" Lukas shifts into reverse, looking to me for further instruction.

"1043 Westlake Drive," I respond.

After a quick nod from Lukas, we're off.

Two minutes into the drive, I kick my feet out in front of me, fully intent on relaxing. But when they strike something hard I glance down at the floor, spying a toolbox that I somehow missed before.

I point to it, "So, you've been doing construction."

When he nods, I add, "Middleton is an hour away. That must be quite a drive every day."

A line forms between his brows. "Not every day. I only make the trip here to meet with Sally. I have a place there."

I've become so used to seeing him, I forgot that Sally mentioned his moving. My heart plummets with the realization. "Do you plan on staying there?"

His gaze falls from the stretch of highway before us, landing on the ever-present light-up ring adorning my index finger. I'm immediately transported to our time in the market, when he first opened up to me.

"To me, 'mine' alludes to holding on to something forever, and I never really stayed in a place long enough to find something worth keeping."

And when he lifts his stare, his eyes convey what he doesn't say.

You're mine.

He looks back out at the road. "I want to make sure it's safe to come back first. That there's nothing to tie me to what happened. I won't return unless I know with absolute certainty I won't be forced to leave you again."

I nod, making a mental note to ask Sally about this as soon as we get back.

Sensing my thoughts, he reaches for my hand. "We'll be okay."

I squeeze his hand, then turn on the radio.

When "Summer of '69" blares from the speakers, I bounce in my seat, unable to conceal my excitement. I turn up the volume, shouting above the music, "I love this song!"

"You're a Bryan Adams fan?"

"Hell yeah," I respond. "I found a stash of my parents' old cassette tapes, indicating at some point in their lives they may have actually been human. Who knew?" I wave my hand, clearing their existence from my mind. "I remember lying in the study, listening to *Reckless* on repeat. This one was my favorite, but "Heaven" was a close second."

He laughs, shaking his head. "An eighties girl at heart. I should've known."

I shoot him a glare. "Don't knock the eighties. Madonna, Prince, Michael Jackson, Cyndi Lauper. Don't even get me started on the hair bands."

More laughter escapes him as I say absently, "They were my only friends."

Lukas sobers. I crinkle my nose when I glance over at

him, embarrassed at the admission. "Pitiful, I know."

But, in his returned gaze, I see no pity. Just acceptance of a past that cannot be undone. I watch the corner of his mouth tilt upward. "So, your favorite Bryan Adams song is one about sex. Interesting."

"No. It's one about the best days of his life. In 1969."

Lukas throws back his head in full-on laughter. Once he's done—the obnoxious jerk—he turns to me and suggests, "You should use that new phone of yours and look up that song. Bryan Adams was nine in 1969." A few more chuckles, then he adds, "Sixty-nine is a metaphor for sex."

I smirk at him, incredulous. "Well, we'll just see."

I snag my new phone from my jacket pocket. After typing in the search words, I read the first article, my eyes gradually widening the more I read. I stuff the phone back where it came from and vow to never pick the thing up again.

Because I've learned my entire life has been a lie!

Even though I'm devastated by this newfound knowledge, I refuse to give Lukas the satisfaction of being right. So I try to evade him. "You know, for someone so quick to judge my early listening choices, you sure seem to know a lot about eighties music. Just sayin'."

He laughs, though thankfully to himself this time, as we pull into a driveway. All thoughts of Bryan Adams and his sexual metaphors fly from my brain, replaced by the very important task at hand. I'm in awe—and fear—of the incredible significance this big change hinging on a single meeting with this one man.

Yes, I'm aware that if we don't get the land we can build elsewhere. But to be able to put a home to help others on the land that brought us so many beautiful memories, the land that now contains the ashes of our best friend, well… everything would come full circle. A poignant and meaningful beginning of a new journey where our old one ended.

We stop and Lukas puts the truck in park, looking over at me as he cuts the engine. He searches my face, and sees the anxiety in my eyes. He grips my hand in his, the warmth of his skin settling over mine.

"You can do this."

I nod and force as much oxygen into my lungs as possible, eyeing the house in front of me.

It's adorable.

Flowerboxes line the front windowsills, and fresh blooms are beginning to sprout from the well-tended ground beneath. The shutters are painted a light green, which oddly sits well against the limestone house.

I open the door and slowly slide out of the truck until my feet hit the pavement. Lukas is by my side in seconds. His expression is pensive, his face hardened, as he assesses the house in front of us.

I take hold of his hand, chancing one more look at his brooding stare before saying, "Do *not* scare these people."

He scoffs, feigning insult.

I raise my eyebrows in warning.

He grins.

"Perfect. Stay just like that."

His shoulders shake as we approach the door. It takes me three attempts to work up the courage to actually knock. Once done, we both back away from the door as though it might explode. I have no idea why.

Muffled footsteps approach, and I grip Lukas's hand so tightly, I fear I may be breaking it. He remains silent through the relentless assault on his fingers.

Instead of exploding, the door swings wide open, and I'm met with a charming smile and warm eyes framed with lines from years of laughter.

The man looks at me then Lukas, completely unsurprised by our presence at his door. "Chloe and Lukas, I presume."

Together we nod, and he extends his hand in greeting. "I'm James Newman. It's nice to meet both of you. We've been expecting your arrival."

After shaking our hands, he swings his arm wide, gesturing for us to come in. We follow him into the house, and as we do, I greedily inhale the scent of cinnamon and apples.

Apple pie?

The delicious fragrance wafts in the air around us while I take in the antique furniture arranged throughout the home. The pieces are quaint but styled with modern accessories to make them current, creating a very inviting environment.

It feels like a home.

We take a seat on their couch just as James shouts, "Margaret, the kids are here!"

Between the flowers outside and her incredible

decorating ability, I think I might adore this woman I have yet to meet.

Or at least that's my assumption.

An elated squeal sounds just before his wife peeks around the corner, and when I catch a glimpse of the familiar shade of purple, my eyes widen.

Maggie!

My entire body tenses. Lukas stiffens next to me. I turn to face him, giving him a small grin and a subtle shake of my head.

"Oh my goodness." She clasps her hands together in glee. "James, this is Chloe, the lovely girl I was telling you about. The one I just hired."

Maggie wipes her hands on her apron as she enters the room. Long, white streaks appear on the fabric as she does, and when I see a dash of flour covering the tip of her nose, I suppress a giggle. Her hair is up in a messy bun, purplish tendrils falling and framing her face, and her eyes, they're full of joy as they take in Lukas and me, as if we have just made her day.

Relief washes over me, and I relax. "Maggie. It's good to see you." And it is.

I stand as she approaches, and she embraces me with nothing short of a Herculean grip. Lukas stands with me, and as soon as I'm released, she wraps her arms warmly around him, too. He looks at me over her shoulder, clearly uncomfortable with her open display of affection.

It's cute and fun to watch, so I let him suffer.

James looks at me, sensing Lukas's awkwardness. His mouth quirks slightly when he spots my grin. "Margaret, let the poor boy go."

She giggles, actually giggles, before responding, "I don't think I can."

I try my hardest, but the laughter manages to bubble out of me. I do, however, cover my mouth when Lukas glares at me.

Eventually, Maggie relaxes her hold, though she doesn't let him go entirely. She holds his stare with hers, most likely searching his soul as she did with me. When she's completed her assessment, she palms his cheek, nodding once before addressing me. "He's a keeper."

Lukas finds my eyes, his expression pleading. This time, I don't even bother to hide my laughter when I respond, "Yeah. He is."

After offering me a knowing smile, Maggie settles herself into one of the armchairs while James takes his seat in another. I sit and James asks, "So, you're interested in building on our land?"

"Yes, sir." I nod, clearing my throat. Sally told me that he knows we lived together in a group home and that she was our counselor. "You see, four of us found kinship with a patch of wildflowers on your land. I know it seems ridiculous, but your flowers gave us hope. We identified with them so much that we called our group the Wildflowers in their honor. They were the epitome of strength for us, continuing to bloom for as long as they could, regardless of what the environment around them demanded. Just as we were inspired to do."

Meeting both of their curious stares, I further explain. "Because of our time spent together here, the beautiful memories we all shared, your property has come to mean a great deal to us. We would very much like to use it to construct a home to guide those struggling to find their place in this world, just like us."

Maggie's eyes are perceptive and she absorbs every word I say. I go on. "One of us lost our way recently. An invaluable life lost. And we feel…"

Grief hits me. I look at Lukas, unable to find the words for a moment before taking a slow breath and trying again. "We feel it's our duty to change others' lives just as she did for us, and we can think of no better way to honor her than to build this home on the land that brought us together."

Lukas's eyes find mine, and I nod at him. I look away just in time to see James and Maggie looking at each other, engaged in wordless conversation. Once they're through, Maggie looks at me, eyes tapering at the sides when she smiles.

"You're part of the four."

She folds her hands in her lap, settling into her seat. "Mary Rodriguez was one of my favorite customers. Had a hankering for sweets. Couldn't get enough of my chocolate cream pies."

A soft laugh escapes me, remembering the time Genny discovered the stash of Toblerones hidden in Mrs. Rodriguez's study. Maggie pauses, content in allowing me time to revisit the memory. "Mary adored the four of you. She spoke of you every single time she came to the diner, going on and on about how together, you were destined to change the world."

A sad smile forms on her lips and she reaches forward, taking my hand into hers. "It must have been difficult to lose her. And then when her house, your home, burned down, what a tragedy."

Not really, I want to say.

The words are on the tip of my tongue, and I clench my teeth to ensure they don't escape. Maggie eyes my reaction thoughtfully, and I swallow my brewing anxiety. I don't dare look at Lukas. I just hold her stare, watching as she loses herself in thought.

Damn it.

Her brows lift ever so slightly before she transfers her astute gaze to Lukas. "Well, it's a shame. The fire destroyed everything inside. Nothing but ashes remained by the time they managed to get it under control. Right, honey?"

She looks at James who nods in return. "Case was closed months ago. Ruled accidental."

Maggie returns her stare to me, casually explaining, "Even though James is retired, being the former fire chief, he still gets regular updates."

But her words barely register because my mind is lost in a sudden epiphany.

Remembering Sally's previous mention of the ruling, and knowing that Lukas didn't hear that conversation, I glance in his direction. His expression remains stoic, but I can see it. Relief. It's then that I become fully aware of the reasoning behind Lukas's hesitancy to come back.

I stifle a gasp.

"Nothing but ashes remained by the time they managed to get it under control."

As much as I want to throw my arms around Lukas, I remain seated, forcing my eyes away from his to meet Maggie's. And with one look, I see it. A mixture of sorrow and anguish swirling in those grey irises.

Even though she might not understand exactly what happened after Mrs. Rodriguez died, she knows that we did what was necessary to escape the horrors that occurred afterward. And with that one statement, she's just set Lukas's mind at ease, freeing him from the fear he's felt this entire time.

Maggie pats my leg gently. She watches me come back to reality. Then, she continues to blow my already very much blown mind. "You were forced to leave, but you came back because of what happened to your friend."

Timidly, I clear my throat. I've never felt more exposed as I do under her stare. "Yes, ma'am. Her name was Genesis."

She smiles softly at the mention of Genny's name. "And now you all want to build another home, a home like Mary's, in memoriam for both her and Genesis." I can only give her another nod in reply, then watch in amazement as a smile of utter pride crosses her face. She reaches over to me, taking my hand into hers.

"Perfect."

Taking hold of my other hand, she gives them both a comforting squeeze. "How I wish Mary was here to witness how truly magnificent you've become. No longer the fearful children she took into her home, but bold adults who dare to use the pain of their pasts to benefit others' futures."

She glances between Lukas and me. "You both need to know this: you're not only everything she'd hoped you would become. You're so much more."

Lukas's expression melts into a shy grin on hearing her words. She smiles at him then turns to me, tightening her grip on my hands. She whispers, "I'm sorry for the loss of your friend. Losing someone so close to your heart is one of the most difficult experiences a person can face."

She glances at James and when he gives her a small nod, she returns her attention to me. "As much as we wish we could, we can't erase your heartache. We can only hope to help you heal. We would very much like to do that by offering you the use of our land so you can carry out your plans."

I control the urge to scream out of excitement, choosing to exhibit a large, beaming smile instead.

Maggie mirrors my enthusiasm, her expression one of pure delight. "You have our full permission to build your home, and with each plank and beam, may you find solace in knowing the impact Mary and Genesis had on each of you will live on. A home built upon the soil of love and acceptance is the greatest gift you can provide any child. Plant the seeds, help them grow, and once they've fully blossomed, may the winds gently whisk them from the earth and deposit them so they may take root anew where they're needed most."

A knot forms in my throat just as her grip tightens around my hand. "With every seed that flourishes while in your home, you will spawn change, just as you were intended to do."

Her kindness is too much. After what she's seen, after what she knows, to welcome Lukas and me with open arms, well...A sob works its way into my throat, and I extend my arms in Maggie's direction. As soon as she envelops me, I nestle into the crook of her neck, allowing her reassuring words to comfort me.

The winds of change.

A phrase I thought I understood a year ago now has so much more meaning. My delicate existence was housed safely, then transported from a harsh reality into clean, fresh soil so I could be replanted where I am needed. And now, here I am, growing stronger, fiercer, and more determined than I'd ever imagined myself capable of being.

As I look at Lukas over Maggie's shoulder, I know the winds of change carried him, too. Because he is stronger, fiercer, more determined, and he's finally where he's meant to be.

I think of the insecure young girl a year ago who wanted to acquire a superpower. Although she realized she had her empathy and used it to the best of her ability, she was unable to fully comprehend how powerful it would help her become.

As I enter adulthood, I have been granted greater responsibility.

I am no longer just Empathy.

I am now Change incarnate.

37

"Just coffee for me," Sally says, taking a sip from her freshly poured mug.

I shake my head grinning widely, knowing she'll leave me no less than a ten-dollar tip with that single cup. Having already gotten Adam and Seth's orders for BLTs and Lukas's double cheeseburger, I drop my pencil in the front pocket of my apron.

Hands on my hips, I announce to the table, "You know the drill. Food'll be out shortly."

Adam looks at me, appalled. "Charming. Please tell me you don't serve all your customers with that attitude. That cannot be good for tips and you now have a monthly phone bill to pay."

I roll my eyes and laugh softly. "Nope. That was only for you guys. My VIPs." Leaning over, I give Lukas a quick peck on the cheek.

Just as I rise, he says, "And *that* better be only for me."

I grin.

He does not.

I whirl around and head to the kitchen. Nothing like a bit of a mystery to keep a relationship interesting.

Once I've placed their orders, I turn, scanning my tables for any necessary refills. Flo, or Wanda as she prefers to be called, comes up next to me. Refilling a pitcher of iced tea, she indicates with a jerk of her chin, "New customer, honey. Table seventeen."

I say nothing, just look back at her blankly, because firstly, I'm still confused by how well she effectively communicates with wads of bubblegum in her mouth, and secondly, it's only my third solo shift, so I'm not completely familiar with the numbering of the tables.

Wanda, noticing my silence, giggles, the sound reminiscent of the bell above the door. Still grinning, she points over my shoulder. "Back corner booth."

"Thanks," I answer under my breath. "I don't know why I can't seem to get the numbers down."

"It's because the numbering system makes no flipping sense. But don't worry"—she winks reassuringly—"you'll catch on."

My frustration eases and I give her a thankful smile in return. Tugging my pad from my apron, I inhale deeply, only to lose all breath when I turn to see *him* sitting at the table. He's perfectly dressed in a tailored three-piece suit, and not a hair is out of place.

I've been expecting him—hell, I baited him here—but I don't think I'll ever be adequately prepared for my father. The sight of him suffocates me.

My past insecurities flare up around him, the need to appear perfect for his approval an old and unbreakable habit. Unconsciously, I smooth the front of my apron, but as I begin to run my palms over my hair, laughter rings out from across the restaurant.

I look over to see Lukas and Adam giving each other a high five while Sally narrows her eyes in feigned frustration. The sight, so familiar and comforting, serves as a reminder of those I choose to call my family.

And with another glance at my father, I'm instantly reminded of those I don't.

My legs are heavy, but I force their strides in his direction, steeling myself with every single breath I take along the way. He doesn't even bother to look at me when I approach the booth. As soon as I'm standing in front of him, his tone is level and calculated. "You stole from me."

Since he's clearly not planning on ordering, I calmly place the pad back into my apron. "Well, you stole from me, so consider us even."

I place my palm flat against the table and lean in, daring him to meet my determined stare. Surprisingly, he does, and I'm shocked at what I find. There's absolutely no life in the eyes looking back at me.

No love.

No laughter.

No soul.

His answering tone is just as empty.

"What, may I ask, have I stolen from you? You have nothing worth taking."

His cold words are like lances of ice. I may be strong, but I'm not unfeeling. Yet, as I continue staring into the cold oblivion looking back at me, I'm extremely grateful for that fact. My feelings are a part of me, and the capability to openly acknowledge my pain is just one of the many things that sets me apart from him.

I smile with absolutely no humor, leaning even farther forward and whisper through clenched teeth, "You stole my childhood. You both did."

No reaction whatsoever. Not that I expected one. Not that I care. This is *my* moment, *my* time to express *my* thoughts.

So, I relax my weight onto my hand, effectively backing an inch or two away from him before I say what I've wanted to say for so long. "Because of you, I will never know the meaning of being a 'daddy's girl' or understand a mother's love. I will never experience adoration in my parents' eyes, seeing them *seeing* me as though I'm the most precious thing they ever created. I will never know the experience of being held in your arms, finding comfort in your strength, or hers."

I shake my head, sickened by the man in front of me. My expression is one of disgust when I repeat the words that have haunted me for years. "You didn't ask for me."

Humorless laughter passes through my lips. "Well, guess what? I sure as hell didn't ask for you, either."

With absolutely no hesitation, I thrust my scarred arms in his face. "But I'm the one who paid the price of your neglect."

His expression remains unflinching, as hard as stone. "It's impossible to neglect something that does not exist, and you simply did not for me. I know it's not what you want to hear, but it's the truth. I do not have the capacity for such things as love. I never have. I never will."

Something inside me just snaps. The cord I've unknowingly been dangling from my entire life, the need to feel some sort of connection with my father, is completely and irrevocably severed. Every bit of anger I've harbored for so many years seeps into my blood, and his words ignite my fury.

"Why?!" I shout, no less than two inches from his perfectly polished face. "Why did I not exist for you?! Why was it so easy for you to ignore me instead of love me?! Why was I never enough?!"

There is a commotion behind me, most likely Lukas shooting up from the table, but I'm too lost in my emotion to turn away from my father.

"Why did you bring me into this world?! And why did you bother to save me when I attempted to leave it?! Why?! Why?! *Why?!*" I scream at the top of my lungs, hammering the table with every gut-wrenching question.

I feel lighter with each question I ask, as if I'm purging

them from my soul. The sound of glass shattering finally captures my attention, and I break my furious stare from my father's soulless eyes to look over my shoulder. Sally is rising from her seat, hands covering her mouth while tears fill her eyes. Lukas is wild and frenzied as he tries to break free from Adam and Seth's iron-tight holds. They strain to keep Lukas held, but with one look at Adam's calm expression, I know he's preventing Lukas's interference for one reason only.

This is a stand I need to take on my own.

And I'm incredibly grateful to him for recognizing the significance of the next few minutes of my life.

Slowly, I turn back to my father, gaining composure with each shallow breath I take. Tears I hadn't even realized were there roll down my cheeks, and I sweep them away with the tips of my fingers. My father's eyes, having traveled to the table of heathens more than ready to go to battle if necessary, steadily trace their path back to me.

As soon as we lock stares, I continue. "But you did save me. Not just that night, but in the days that followed. Because when you sent me away, only then was I gifted the knowledge of what it's like to have a real family and the true meaning of home. Of unyielding love and support. Everything I craved from both of you but never received."

Indignant, I scoff. "And you say I stole from *you*."

My father takes a moment to observe the chaos around us. "Chlo—"

"No." I shake my head vehemently. "You don't get the privilege of addressing me by my name, like you know me.

Not anymore."

When I lean into him again, my tone is menacing. "I didn't steal a damn thing from you. I took what was owed to me."

He narrows his eyes before he speaks, but as always his tone is careful, contrived. "I beg to differ, because as I see it, I owe you nothing. Your mother knew I didn't want a child, yet she took what she wanted. Regardless, I housed you. I gave you food. I put clothes on your back. What more could you have wanted?"

I'm struck by the question. Well, maybe not the question itself, but the unassuming tone with which it's delivered. He truly doesn't understand.

Brows drawn, I tilt my head and examine my father, but this time instead of allowing my anger to dictate what I see, I actually look at him. And suddenly, I feel so sad.

Not for me, because I have a family and know love, but for him. He's never experienced either of those things. And he never will.

With my heart in my throat, I answer his question the only way I know how. Honestly. "I only wanted love and affection from you." A small sad smile forms on my lips. "But I understand now. I *see* you now. You never received those things, so you don't know how to give them."

No longer stoic, his eyes widen in surprise and confusion. I watch him for a beat. I inhale deeply, satisfied to see him come to this realization himself. Then, I remove his credit card from my back pocket and toss it on the table.

"Yes, I took money from you, but it's money you don't even need. Money that could make a difference for others. In fact, it's money I have already invested in doing just that." My voice is soft, but not timid or afraid. "I have never asked for anything, but I will ask you for this. Leave me, leave the money, and let's call it even. If I don't exist for you, then what does it matter? You will never see me again if you just walk out that door. I promise you. Just give me this."

With nothing else to say, I turn my back on him as I make my way to my friends. Maggie, the newest addition to the crew at table thirty-five—thank you very much—has her hand locked in a viselike grip around Lukas's forearm. With Adam and Seth no longer restraining him, I have a feeling she was the one who managed to get him under control.

As soon as my friends surround me, I turn back to my father and cross my arms over my chest while patiently waiting for him to leave. Behind me, I can feel the heat of Lukas's anger, and I uncross my arms to reach back for him. Relief surges when he relents and relaxes, his hands sliding easily into mine.

"It's fine, Lukas. There's nothing more that needs to be said between us."

And there's not.

I expel a long breath, cocooned safely within the center of my army.

Lukas, Adam, Seth, Sally, Maggie, and yes, even Genny. I feel her presence. Her warmth. It's impossible not to.

Every single one of them stands with me, a wall of

support and strength.

Several seconds pass before he plucks the credit card from the table and slides it into his front pocket. Then, with the entire restaurant watching, he slowly rises to his full height, poised to the point of perfection as he buttons his suit jacket and adjusts his tie. But regardless of the indifference he's trying to portray, I still *see* him and what he's so committed to hiding. My words turning over and over in his head as he leaves his table, strides casually past us, and out the front door, right out of my life without a glance back.

Pride fills my veins and a satisfied grin splits my face when I turn to face my friends. Adam is the first to embrace me, nearly suffocating me. "I'm so proud of you, Chloe. She would be, too."

I grin, touched by his words. After a few seconds, he releases me, and I move to accept hugs from the remainder of the bunch.

Sally wraps her arms around me, and I can't help but smile with pure contentment. She may have started young and inexperienced, but she's grown just as much as we have over the course of the past year. Loving, compassionate, supportive. I would have no one other than her in charge of the soon-to-be Genesis House.

After Sally comes Seth, his eyes filled with a mix of wariness and pride. "Remind me to never piss you off."

I giggle and squeeze him tighter, truly thankful for his presence in our lives.

Then there's Maggie, who after quite possibly the

longest embrace says, "Well, that dreadful man is no longer welcome in my establishment."

I laugh, but sober when her palms finds my cheeks. Her gaze looks deeply into me, but I'm no longer worried about what she'll see. I place my hands on top of hers and when I do, she smiles. "Freedom feels good, doesn't it?"

I nod my response as her thumbs tenderly wipe away the remainder of my tears. "My child, Mary always used to say you are a force to be reckoned with. I'd have to say I agree with her." She laughs lightly, her eyes drifting upward as Lukas moves to stand behind me. Her smile widens before she drops her hands, her tone maternal as she directs her next statement to him. "You do right by her, young man."

Lukas's response is instantaneous. "Yes, ma'am." His fingers curl gently over my shoulders, squeezing lightly. I watch as Maggie heads over to Adam, standing up on her tiptoes to give him a tender embrace. She met him during my first shift and fell in love with him immediately. As I knew she would.

She pats his cheek lovingly, then does the same to Seth.

Looks like Maggie just inherited herself another family in our mixed lot.

Still smiling, I turn, wrapping my arms around Lukas's waist and settling my chin on his chest. Looking up at him, I announce, "Well, at least the door has finally closed on that very unfortunate chapter of my life."

"That it has," he mumbles, his furious stare drifting to the door.

"Hey, down here," I whisper.

At my words, his scowl disappears as he looks at me. And then he smiles that smile. I find it impossible not to be enamored by the beauty of that smile.

He folds his arms around my shoulders, wrapping me in the safety of his arms. "Ready to start another one?"

I scrunch my nose. "With you?"

"Yeah, with me." His smile deepens.

I look into his eyes, eyes that now shine as brightly as the sun. Just as they should. I smile widely, rise to brush my mouth against his in answer.

His strong arms pull me closer and his warmth envelops me.

Nurtures me.

Sustains me.

My heart revives, and I sink into all he has to offer, reveling in the powerful feeling of finally, *finally*, reaching my full bloom.

SUMMER

EPILOGUE

Tomorrow is the long awaited day when we break ground on the Genesis House, and our excitement is at an all-time high. Adam and Sally walk where the house will be built, pointing out possible layout suggestions. Meanwhile, Lukas and I are hand in hand, enjoying the calm surroundings at the property's periphery. Flowers have sprouted everywhere imaginable in the field. Purple, orange, and yellow petals speckled among the green grass, their stems bowing and bending with the light summer breeze.

Looking up at the sky, sunshine warms my cheeks and I inhale the familiar sweet scent of the flowers as we walk. I can't imagine feeling more peaceful than I am in this moment.

"So, I'm going to be dating a college girl?" Lukas asks.

I grin at the sun, before squinting at him as I reply.

"Hopefully, if I pass my GED."

He chuckles to himself. "You've been studying non-stop, holed up in that apartment of yours. I think it's pretty safe to say you'll pass."

"Well, I'd better."

It's kind of a necessity to have a GED in order to attend local community college and get a degree in social work. That way, I can actually work at the Genesis House, instead of only volunteering my time. There isn't any other place I want to be.

Lukas grins at my response. Releasing his hand, I throw an arm around his waist just as his drapes his over my shoulder. As we walk, he glances at the rubber ring still around my index finger, then at the necklace I never take off.

"You know, I think I should add a little something to your jewelry collection."

I extend my hand, wiggling my fingers. "I don't know. I don't think you'll ever be able to top what I already have."

He chuckles, gripping my hand. "A diamond would be nice though, right here." He skims the top of my ring finger with the pad of his thumb, and my heart soars at his touch. I smile. "You think you're gonna marry me, Lukas White?"

He shakes his head. "No."

I stop walking, completely stupefied. That's not at all what I was expecting to hear.

Deliberately, he leans down, kissing the tip of my nose before responding, "I *know* I am."

I narrow my eyes when he smiles. "Jerk."

Lukas throws his head back in laughter just as a high-pitched squeal is released in the distance. We both turn to see Sally and Adam grinning, as though they've just planned the entire house's layout.

"You start work tomorrow. How do you like your new place of employment?"

Lukas's eyes crinkle at the sides as he nods slightly, still watching the pair. "I guess it'll do."

"They'd both be happy you're a part of it."

He nods, raking a hand through his hair, a gesture I've come to expect. He misses her. We all do.

I give him his time, looking to Sally and Adam as they approach. "Ready?" I ask them.

"Absolutely," Adam replies.

My hold around Lukas tightens. "Then, let's go."

We all walk together, leisurely making our way across the pasture to where our wildflowers await. It doesn't take long until the familiar patch of white comes into view. Another soft wind blows and I grin happily, watching them dance as we approach. It's not until we're a couple of feet away that every single one of our steps halt, our eyes widening to take in the full expanse of it.

"Is that...?" Adam begins.

Sally gasps.

Lukas stares in complete awe.

And I...well, I choke on a sob.

Together, we crouch to the ground for further inspection.

"It is," I somehow manage to croak.

Timidly, I reach for the single flower, its coloring a very reminiscent shade of hot pink. It bounces happily when I skim the velvety petals with the tips of my fingers and moves with the sea of white surrounding it as the breeze blows by.

She's here.

"I can't believe it," I breathe.

"I can," Lukas says. He shakes his head and laughs softly. "Only her."

Although my eyes are filled with tears, I grin at his correct assessment before looking back at the flower in question.

Sniffles fill the air, and after several moments of watching her joyful movements in silence, we rise to our feet. I grip Lukas's hand in mine then take hold of Sally's. In turn, she reaches to the side to join hers with Adam's. The sun breaks through the clouds, a single ray highlighting where we stand, bringing with it a sense of peace.

I look at the sky again, repeating the words I spoke months ago, now with full understanding.

You are infinite.

Another wave of warmth cascades over me, and I hear a delicate whisper.

And you, my lioness, are the reason.

I smile then glance at Lukas. He meets my gaze with a smile, and that dimple. I turn to see Sally beaming widely through her tears, then to Adam, who mirrors our expressions with his own grin.

We look at our wildflowers and the land where the Genesis House will be built, forever changed by this moment.

Side by side we stand, strength and ferocity uniting us, just as tangible as our joined hands.

Together, we will plant the seeds necessary for change.

We are four.

We are the Wildflowers.

…But guess what?

We aren't the only ones in existence.

We leave our story with you, *for* you, fellow Wildflowers, in hopes that you too will make change.

Take from it what you will, but if nothing else, please hear us when we say this:

You are *never* alone.

THE END

LETTER TO THE READER

Hey, everyone. Chloe here. And as I opened our journey with lessons learned, I'd like to leave you with some as well. I may only be eighteen years old, but I've learned some things over the course of the past year. Here are those I deem most important.

From the mouth of Alexander Pope: "To err is human; to forgive, divine."

Mistakes will be made over the course of your life. You are not, and cannot be, perfect. The key is to take a step back and give an honest look at the wrong decisions made so you can make them right. Be kind and forgive yourself for your screw-ups. They're inherent and come with being human.

Your pain will remain unrecognized until you voice it. Contrary to your belief, the majority of people are not mind readers. Lower your guard when you feel someone understands you, and let them see you for who you truly are. It'll not only work wonders for your confidence, but it will provide you a sense of camaraderie with someone who may need you as much as you need them.

Grieving is a natural process. Allow yourself time, but

don't let it consume you. If you succumb to its vortex, you will lose sight of the very important lives happening around you. Lives that have seemingly moved on, but are incapable of doing so because they're hurting, too.

There are people who will judge you because you don't fit their mold. Don't waste time trying to shape yourself into something they expect you to be. Dig deep and find the courage to accept yourself for exactly who you are, then make your own mold, because you deserve no less. Become infinite.

And for those of you traveling especially darkened paths, there is a light at the end of your tunnel. You may not see it now, but it's there. Hold on. Stay strong. And when you find your light, because you will, hold on to it with everything you can. Allow it to flame and burn within you, then use that fire as motivation for change. You are a catalyst for the future. Believe that, and you will undoubtedly leave the world a better place.

AUTHOR'S NOTE

You are *never* alone. Reach out...so many people are waiting to catch you with open arms.

Crisis Text Line:
https://www.crisistextline.org/
US: Text HOME to 741741
Canada: Text HOME to 686868
UK: Text HOME to 85258

National Suicide Prevention Lifeline:
https://suicidepreventionlifeline.org/
1-800-273-8255

Substance Abuse and Mental Health Services Administration:
https://www.samhsa.gov/
1-800-662-HELP (4357)

Additional Resource:
TWLOHA: To Write Love on Her Arms is a nonprofit movement dedicated to presenting hope and finding help for people struggling with depression, addiction, self-injury, and suicide. TWLOHA exists to encourage, inform, inspire, and invest directly into treatment and recovery.
https://twloha.com/

ACKNOWLEDGMENTS

As always, a huge thank you to my husband and three beautiful girls. I love you all so much and cannot tell you how much your support means to me. Your excitement and enthusiasm for this book is what kept me going over the three *long* years it took to complete this story. I really hope I made you proud.

A special thank you to Sofia. My budding artist. My reading buddy. My middle baby. Thank you so much for drawing the perfect representation of the Wildflowers on the cover. I will never forget us sitting together, figuring out what each flower needed to be in order to represent its character. Also, thank you for helping me rewrite certain sections of this story. Love you, baby.

Marion Fraser. You not only edited this story once, but TWICE. Thank you so much for helping me mold these into relatable characters with so much potential to change lives. You are the kindest, most patient person in the world, and it's been my absolute pleasure to work with you on this book.

Sali Benbow-Powers. Girl. I am so happy you were

available to beta read this book. Your advice and suggestions helped me take this story to a whole new level, the level I had hoped it would be from the very beginning. Thank you for taking your very valuable time to not only read, but to bond with these characters and help with their evolution. You have no idea how much I appreciate you and how much I miss our daily conversations.

Spencer Hill Press. Thank you so much for believing in my work and the messages I aim to share with readers. I am so blessed to work alongside you and am so thankful to you for publishing *We, the Wildflowers*. I can't wait to see our baby on shelves everywhere!

Danielle Sanchez and Wildfire Marketing Solutions. Thank you for all that you do. I know so much of what you do is behind the scenes, and that the majority of it I am completely unaware is happening, but please know how appreciated you are. I say this to you all the time, but I hope you understand how truly blessed I feel to have you in my corner. I adore you.

And of course, a HUGE thank you to all of you awesome readers and bloggers out there. Your excitement is contagious, your support genuine and heartfelt. I love each and every one of you for that. Thank you from the bottom of my heart for not only reading my work, but for helping spread the word about my books and for sharing my stories. It's because of you that I am able to reach those who need to hear my messages, and it's because of you that I continue to write. Thank you.

ABOUT THE AUTHOR

When she's not attending a volleyball tournament, a theater performance, or a cheer competition, L.B. Simmons can be found creating characters that face real life problems. Her goal with each book is to provide fictional friends for those who feel alone or misunderstood so they may help guide readers through the challenges that will mold and shape them. She is also the author of the Chosen Paths series. L.B. lives in Texas with her husband and their three beautiful girls. For her latest news, visit www.lbsimmons.com.